QUEEN of CARRION

DEATH BOUND DUET: BOOK 2

AIDEN PIERCE
R.K. PIERCE

Cover Design: GraphicsbyGeka

Editing: The Fiction Fix

A WORD OF WARNING

Some content within this book may be disturbing or triggering for some readers. Reader discretion is advised.

Subjects include gore, violence, murder, kidnapping, discussions of suicide, breath play/choking, asphyxiation, spitting, praise, primal play, dub-con, non-con/SA (not between MCs), psychological abuse, manipulation, bondage, foreign object insertion, somnophilia and other graphic sexual content.

If you have any questions pertaining to this warning, please don't hesitate to contact the authors, Aiden Pierce and R.K. Pierce.

"Everything I've done, I've done for you.
I move the stars for no one."

David Bowie

PLAYLIST

"Monster" – Hidden Citizens

"A Little Wicked" – Valerie Broussard

"Let the World Burn" – Chris Grey

"Mentally Not Here" – Elita

"Stay" – Ghost feat. Patrick Wilson

CHAPTER ONE

BELIAL

EVERY SECOND I SPENT away from my human treasure was torture, my own personal hell. Images of her, of *us*, replayed in my mind constantly.

While I should have been focused on other things—like tonight's masquerade ball—I kept losing myself in daydreams to find her.

"It hurts being this close to you," Rayven's voice echoed through my skull.

My hands tightened on her hips, claws scoring her perfect, moon-pale flesh.

Her body trembled as I pushed my cock inside her. She told me she hated me, even as she moaned and begged for more. Looking so bleeding perfect in my bed, naked and bent over, with her pretty ass pressed against my pelvis, her pussy stretching to take all of me.

"Do you like the pain?"

Weeping Hells. I'd never forget the way her pulse lunged at the question, how I could feel it down deep inside her, tapping out a frantic beat against my cock.

"Yes…" she whimpered.

"That's what I thought," I hummed, kissing her nape, her throat, her mouth. Savoring her heat, her filthy little noises, her scent, her everything.

The scene slipped away at the sound of a loud cough, the kind meant to get one's attention. Once again, I found myself sitting at the desk in my study.

"My Lord? Did you hear my question?"

I lifted my skull from my palm, blazing eyes boring into the skeletal servant standing before me. I'd forgotten he was there. "What?"

He flinched at my scathing tone. It was obvious I didn't like being pulled from my daydream.

"Forgive me, My Lord. I was asking if you've seen the decorations I selected for the throne room. I hope you approve. We previously discussed an indigo and silver theme. However, I decided to be bold and chose a more royal blue hue to complement…"

The servant's voice faded again as my thoughts drifted back to Rayven. I was supposed to be proceeding with the next part of my plan—the ball where I'd announce my new queen.

But I couldn't get that little grave robber out of my goddamn mind. How could I? Had there ever been a mortal so stubborn and fearless? Where Catherine—my last human pet—had cowered and cried, Rayven fought tooth and nail against me from the moment I dragged her to Hell.

When she'd raided the Petherick family tomb, Catherine's final resting place, she'd been an annoyance. A thief in need of punishment.

Tormenting her had been fun. Poor thing actually thought she'd had a chance at leaving my realm, especially when I'd pretended my lesser form was just a reaper looking to help her escape.

I never intended for things to get this thoroughly twisted. I never intended for her to turn into a full-blown obsession.

My brothers would think this was just Catherine all over again, but no.

Rayven was different. She wanted me. She'd seen past my mask. She'd felt my scars—and she'd fucking *smiled* and pulled me close—when Catherine had only screamed and shoved me away.

How could I not be addicted to the way she looked at me when I'd been starved of that kind of affection for so long?

My desk scraped against the stone floor as I snapped to my feet.

The servant jumped back to avoid being knocked over by the heavy piece of furniture. "M-My Lord?"

I left the skeleton behind without a second glance, storming from my study, cloak lashing angrily behind me with my hurried strides. I couldn't be bothered with boring masquerade drivel when there was one thing so prominently on my mind.

I needed to see her, to feel her closeness, to sate the feral nerves clawing through me.

It didn't take me long to get to my room. I stood there in the doorway, breath frozen in my lungs as I watched Rayven sleep, tucked into the center of my massive bed.

She was mine now, in her entirety. There on the cliff, she'd given me her soul, given me total control over her.

She'd done it because I told her it would give me the ability to save her from the Lord of Bones. I'd lied. I'd lied so I wouldn't lose her.

When she found out I'd tricked her, that *I* was the monster she'd spent the last three days in Hell trying to outrun, she'd hate me.

The dagger of guilt that appeared the moment she passed out in my arms on the cliff sank deeper into my chest.

I wanted nothing more than to crawl into bed with her and hold her against me. I wanted so desperately to take her in this form—she'd be a delicate little doll in my hands, and I'd take pleasure in watching her struggle to take my monster cock.

Too bad the All Hallows' Eve Ball was only a handful of hours away. There was still so much to do, but I couldn't bring myself to focus on any of the details. She was the only thing my mind would entertain.

I should let her rest. I growled to myself as I watched her turn restlessly in her sleep. She already had so many burdens. Soon, she'd wake and discover yet another, that I'd tricked her into becoming my queen.

"Belial..."

Every muscle in my monstrous body clenched when my little human moaned my name in her sleep. *Fuck.*

I was at the side of the bed in a blink, looming over her as she tossed and turned. "Belial, let me see..."

Was she dreaming of our moment on the cliffside, when I'd removed my mask and revealed my marred face?

I shifted from my true form to the lesser shape she'd come to know as her ally and sat on the edge of the bed. Normally, I'd summon my mask with my magic, but I kept my face bare as I reached for her hand and guided it to my cheek.

"Here I am, my treasure," I muttered, directing her fingertips over my scared lips.

"So—beautiful. So fucking..." She sighed, soft and breathy, then fell still as peace found her in her dreams. "Beautiful."

I pulled the covers back to tuck her arm at her side and froze. She was wearing a nightgown and nothing else—a very thin nightgown.

When I'd brought her back from the labyrinth after claiming her soul, I'd had Holga change her for bed. Now, I regretted not doing it myself.

I needed to see her again, needed to feel her soft skin against my calloused hands. I needed to trace her curves, feel her heat, sink myself into her molten warmth.

My hand cupped her breast over her nightgown, the hard metal of her piercing pressing into my palm, the thin linen of her dress barely a barrier at all. It would be so easy to tear. She was under my sleep spell, so she wouldn't wake.

Even if I tore her out of her clothes.

Even if I parted her legs and slipped inside her.

I could unload every drop of cum I'd been saving for her, and she still wouldn't wake. Hell, I could shift and take her in my truest form, the one she hated with every bone in her body.

My cock grew hard at the dark thought, considering it for a moment before dismissing it with a shake of my head. The charms and chains dangling from my antlers clinked together with the motion. "What are you doing to me, little human?"

I cupped her thighs, one in each hand, and slowly slid my grasp up, guiding the hem of her gown over her hips.

No undergarments. Perfect.

Lifting one hand from her thigh, I combed my fingers through the patch of hair between her legs. Then, I spread my fingers out in a V, parting her labia.

"Would you like me to touch you, Rayven?"

She twitched in her sleep, murmuring a garbled yes. Her inner walls flexed, as if in invitation. Unable to resist temptation a moment longer, I pushed a finger inside her.

An involuntary moan dropped from my lips as I slipped in easily. *So hot. So tight.*

Her body seemed to suck me in, wanting more of me, even as her mind was blissfully unaware of the intrusion.

I pulled my finger out and held it up to inspect. Thick beads of her juices dripped down the digit and glistened in the candlelight.

"So wet," I mused with a wicked chuckle. "Even when you're unconscious."

"My Lord?"

I turned to see a skeletal woman hovering in the doorway. She flinched, catching my scathing expression just before my mask appeared on my face in a burst of glimmering blue magic.

"M-my apologies. I should have announced myself," she stammered. If she'd had skin, she would have been covered head to toe in a full-bodied blush.

"Yes, you should have." I smoothed Rayven's gown back down, pulled the covers up to her chest, and stood. "Whatever it is, it better be worth the interruption, Holga."

"I brought the dress for Miss Rayven to wear to the ball tonight." The skeletal remains of the old witch shuffled into my bedchamber, holding out a white ballgown with the puffiest sleeves I'd ever seen.

It was beautiful, exactly the kind of dress I would have liked to see her in, but I shook my head.

"No, not that one. Rayven will hate it."

Holga's gaping eye sockets bore into me. Skeletons couldn't make facial expressions due to the lack of skin and pretty much everything else, but after all these years as the Lord of Bones, I could read them just as well as any living creature. Her confusion was evident, yet she was too afraid to say as much.

I sighed, sweeping a hand impatiently between my antlers, combing through my unkempt hair. "I know I like my maidens in white, but Rayven prefers black. Bring her something darker."

My attention slid back to the sleeping woman, my eyes dropping to the collar around her throat with the skull pendant above the delicate hollow of her throat. Its red eyes shone like drops of blood, tears for the sins that landed her here, in my realm. "Perhaps with a scarlet trim."

Holga nodded in my periphery. "Of course, My Lord."

My head whipped back to pin the skeleton with a pointed look. She could don the sweetest of tones, but it didn't fool me. The disdain bleeding from her was thick enough to choke on. "You disapprove of what I did."

"I don't know what you're talking about, My Lord."

"Don't play stupid, witch." I bared my teeth, and she flinched again. "You know I claimed her soul. She is mine. Pity her all you'd like, but I own her now. There's no changing it. Don't bother trying to help her escape like you did with Catherine. There's no escaping me, not even in death." *Especially* not in death.

Summoning some courage, she squared her bony shoulders and lifted her chin. "She gave you her soul thinking Belial would save her from the Lord of Bones. You'll break her heart when she learns the truth."

"She will be Queen of the Underworld. She doesn't need a heart."

"Says the King of Death who's obsessed with life. You cannot fool me, nor will you fool her for much longer. And when she learns the truth, she'll never let you touch her again."

I stormed toward the servant, morphing into the Lord of Bones. The twin flames in my eye sockets jumped as I sneered down at Holga, who shrank back against my armoire. My jaws snapped, making her jump, and I let out a hollow laugh as deep as the ninth circle. "She won't have a choice."

Leaving Holga to collect herself, I turned my heel and charged toward my chamber door. "She'll wake soon. Tell her nothing. And make sure she loves her dress."

CHAPTER TWO

RAYVEN

BLURRY IMAGES SWIRLED THROUGH my groggy mind as I reached for consciousness, none of them clear enough to grasp. I couldn't remember falling asleep, but I did remember Belial taking off his mask to show me his face. He was more handsome than I'd imagined—with his sharp jawline, aquiline nose, and deep scars stretching down to the bone.

Then, he kissed me, a kiss so hot and possessive, it was like he was branding my soul with his lips.

Belial.

With a sharp gasp, my eyes flew open. Blinking frantically, I expected to find myself on the cliff's edge, the black ocean crashing against the jagged rocks below. Instead, I found myself in Belial's four-poster bed, staring up at the familiar canopy, the dusty smell of the castle assaulting my senses. The worst part? Belial was nowhere in sight.

My heart lurched into my throat, and I frantically looked at my wrist. There were two marks—*only two.*

I already knew I wasn't getting out of here, but my third and final day wasn't up yet. That meant there was still time before the Lord of Bones came for me—before he came for *us.*

I had no clue what Belial's plan was to deal with his Lord. There was no way the King of Limbo was just going to give me to his ferryman, right? Chaining me to his bed my first night here was one thing, but he wouldn't accept our permanent bond.

The Lord of Bones would never let me go. I knew it deep down, despite Belial's flippant confidence.

Judging by the murky daylight filtering in through the heavy curtains over the window, there were a couple of hours left before sundown.

Why had he brought me back to the castle? Right under the Lord's nose...

I had to trust Belial. He'd helped me through the labyrinth. He'd protected me. When he brought me back to his room to rest and bathe, he'd shown me the book where my father's soul rested and shared pieces of his life I'd known nothing about.

He'd even removed his mask to show me his face.

All it had cost me was my soul.

I'd do it again.

After everything we'd been through, after everything he'd done for me, I'd give him my soul all over again and probably more.

Fucking hell. Where was he? If he insisted on taking me back to his bedroom, he could have at least done me the courtesy of being in his bed when I woke.

My dreams of him had been...vivid. Like he was really touching me.

I sat up and whipped my head around, searching for the ferryman. Movement caught my eye near the wardrobe, and my heart jumped with a whisper of hope, but when the figure came into clear view, my stomach sank.

It was Holga.

She was no longer wearing her tattered dress, but a floor-length, plum-colored gown that clung tightly to her ribcage and spilled in a wave around her feet. Her silver hair was pulled back neatly into a bun, and for the first time, I could almost imagine how she was in life: poised, regal, serious. She looked good—well, as good as a skeleton could look.

Panic slammed back into me a second later.

"Where is he, Holga?" I asked, throwing back the blanket. Someone had removed my boots, dressed me, and tucked me in. My feet hit the floor before I could stop them, and I was marching toward the middle of the room. "Where is Belial?"

The witch shifted, her bony fingers clicking as she wrung her fleshless hands together. "He's not here, child."

I stilled, fear zipping up my spine, and a painful weight sank in my chest. "What happened?"

She didn't answer. Somehow, she didn't need skin for me to read her face. How could bone be so expressive?

"Holga! Tell me!" I snapped, losing my patience. "Where is he? Did the Lord of Bones take him?"

Holga heaved a sigh and tilted her head to the side. If she'd had eyes, I imagined they'd be full of pity, but as it was, the empty sockets stared at me lifelessly, making my hair stand on end. What did she know that I didn't? "I...I don't know. I'm sorry."

She was lying. I just knew it.

The Lord of Bones probably commanded her not to say anything.

"Tell me, please." I grabbed her hands, pleading with her. "Nothing can happen to him."

"That man doesn't deserve your concern, Lady Rayven..."

My chest tightened at the thought of the Lord of Bones punishing his ferryman. My ferryman. My *mate.* "Can you at least tell me he's safe?"

"We must get you ready," the witch insisted, shaking my hands free as she dodged yet another question.

My brows knitted together. "Ready? For what?"

"The masquerade ball."

With a sweep of her bony hand, she gestured to the wardrobe, and that was when I finally noticed a billowing red and black gown hanging from the front of it. It was a goth girl's dream dress, with blood-red fabric that shimmered beneath a layer of intricate black lace. The corset top was flecked with tiny black crystals that glinted subtly in the dim light, and it had short, off-the-shoulder bubble sleeves.

It was the most stunning thing I'd ever seen.

Too bad I didn't plan on wearing it.

I gave an adamant shake of my head. "Yeah, I'm gonna pass. Not really a party person. I'm supposed to be in the labyrinth anyway, not here. My time isn't up. If you can find Belial for me..."

Crouching, I scanned the floor for my boots and found them tucked neatly under the side of the bed.

Next, I needed to find Belial's dagger earring. All I had to do was spill a drop of my blood to summon him. Together, we could hash out a plan on what to do about the Lord of Bones.

Maybe we could escape back to the human realm and lie low together.

Or take his ferry and travel the Styx for a while.

I marched to the bathroom in search of the earring. It was the last place I'd had it, when I'd stabbed him for nearly drowning me. Getting on my hands and knees, I probed under the claw-foot tub. When my fingers found the tiny blade, I pulled it out with a triumphant grin.

Holga filled the doorway and flew into the room when I put the blade to my wrist. "Lady Catherine, no! Not again!"

The terror in her tone made me freeze, the dagger's tip piecing my flesh enough for a fat bead of ruby liquid to slip down my skin and fall on the floor. Hearing Catherine's name was like a splash of icy water, slicing through my frantic thoughts. She too had tried to escape the Lord of Bones' castle...by whatever means necessary. But she'd been unsuccessful.

I refused to follow in her footsteps.

However, seeing me like this had clearly given Holga a bad flashback. "Forgive me, I..."

"You don't have to apologize. I'm sorry. I'm not trying to hurt myself." I held up the tiny blade for her to see. "This dagger is Belial's. Spilling my blood with its blade summons him."

Holga grabbed a hand towel that sat folded on a table beside the wash basin and pressed it to my arm with a disapproving hiss. "That's dark demon magic, and you'd do well not to invoke it."

I blinked. "Belial won't hurt me. I know you don't like the Lord of Bones, and I don't blame you, but Belial isn't like him."

"Love blinds you, mistress." Holga shook her head as she applied pressure to my cut.

My stomach lurched. Were my feelings for Belial that obvious?

I stilled at the thought of him, fear seeping down my spine like venom. Something was wrong. Belial wasn't coming. Usually, he'd appear before my blood could hit the ground.

"Holga..." My voice trailed off as I struggled to string everything together. She knew something she wasn't telling me, and now, Belial wasn't showing up when I called for him. "Why isn't he coming?"

The witch's teeth clacked. "Best guard your heart, girl. Now, let's get you ready for the ball."

What the hell was I supposed to do? Wait around in my ivory tower for my prince-not-so-charming to show up and rescue me?

Fuck that.

"The guests will begin arriving soon, and we shouldn't keep the Lord waiting," Holga said, breaking my train of thought. "He'll come searching for you before long."

"The Lord of Bones can kiss my ass," I bit out, anger flaring. How dare he rob me of the last few hours I had to escape? That door had been too far away for three days to ever be enough time. He was a filthy cheater for not upholding his end of the bargain.

He knew I was doomed from the start, but he let me think I could escape to watch me struggle.

What a sick, sadistic fuck.

"No. I'm leaving." I started to charge out of the bathroom, but before I could clear the door, my legs froze, one foot suspended in midair. My limbs were locked in place, refusing to move no matter how much I tried.

"What the hell?" I managed, even though my jaw was stiff. It was like every muscle in my body had suddenly gone rigid, holding me in place. I managed to shift my eyes in Holga's direction.

She approached slowly, her footfalls getting closer until she stopped at my side. With a wave of her hand, I was able to stand up straight and glare at her.

"What are you doing?" I asked in disbelief. I tried to move forward, to reach out and grab her bony arm, but my body didn't obey. I was at the mercy of Holga and her magic.

"I'm sorry, Lady Rayven," she said, her voice soft and sad. "The Lord has requested that I get you ready for the evening, so that is what I must do. There is no escaping him. The best you can do is temper your heart. Don't give into any more of his tricks."

"Holga, please," I begged, the corners of my eyes stinging as the weight in my chest returned, threatening to drag me to the stone floor. "You don't understand. The Lord of Bones can't claim me anymore. Belial owns my soul now."

"Oh... No. Please, child. Tell me you didn't..."

"I did."

She shook her head slowly, her empty sockets falling to the space of floor between us. "Then there is no escape for you now."

My heart crystallized. What was she talking about?

I opened my mouth to speak, but she cut me off before I could utter a sound.

"Come, let's bathe you first." Holga stooped over the claw-foot tub to draw a bath. My feet moved of their own accord now, allowing me to climb in after I pulled off my clothes.

The skeleton witch bathed me, twisted my hair into the most elegant updo to show off the collar around my neck, and helped me into the ball gown.

She offered me a pair of beautiful black heels, but I waved them away and pulled on my Doc Martens, which she allowed. If the old boots were the only bit of comfort I had for the night, I was wearing them.

Once I was fully dressed, Holga produced a pair of breathtaking, red teardrop earrings, which she let me put in myself. All the while, I fought back tears.

This was bullshit. Total fucking bullshit.

Why had Belial left me?

What was Holga not telling me?

Had he betrayed me?

Giving him my soul had been stupid; he'd even said as much. I didn't care. Giving it to him still felt right, even if everything else felt oh so wrong.

I had all the pieces to the puzzle, but the foreboding sensation hooking in my belly told me not to put them together, that I didn't want to know the truth.

My mind whirled as Holga applied a dusting of makeup to my face—charcoal to darken my eyelashes and a stain of red to my lips. I barely registered when she'd finished, my mind consumed with thoughts of Belial.

I felt sick, and when I stood in front of the full-length mirror, I barely recognized myself. Staring back at me was a gothic beauty. I looked regal, powerful, the opposite of everything I currently felt.

Acid burned up my throat at my next thought.

I looked like a queen.

I hated how easily I could imagine myself standing next to an ominous throne made of bones—or in it, perched on the Lord of Bones' lap, like in that dream the plum had brought on.

"Show me all that I own..."

A shiver worked through me, one that turned hotter the deeper it sank through my core, but I shoved the sensation away, locking it up tight.

There was only one man I wanted to see, only one demon I wanted, and he was certainly *not* the demented specter of death who'd dragged me here and made me believe I had a chance to escape when I'd really been a prisoner all along.

I would *never* forgive the Lord of Bones for what he did to me.

CHAPTER THREE

RAYVEN

"Come, Lady Rayven," Holga urged, turning to head for the door. "We mustn't keep the Lord waiting."

"Wait. *Now?*" I froze, my throat tightening. "But I have a few more hours before my time runs out."

I rubbed my wrist where the King of Limbo had carved two marks into my flesh, soon to be three.

I wanted to rebel. I wanted to lock myself in Belial's room and refuse to come out until the Lord of Bones showed up to drag me downstairs himself, but with a snap of Holga's fingers, my feet moved of their own accord again. "The ball starts now."

Falling into step beside her, I followed the witch's lead down a long corridor, my heart sinking lower with every step. "Didn't you say this was a masquerade? Don't I need a mask?"

"The Lord doesn't want your face covered."

Of course. Why wouldn't the Lord of Assholes take the opportunity to make me stand out like a sore thumb?

I needed to find Belial. I had to do something. Run, fight, flee. Anything.

But all I could do was follow Holga in silence as our footsteps echoed off the stone walls around us, my mind careening out of control as my heartbeat gradually picked up speed with every turn we made.

We rounded another corner—I'd lost track of the hallways several turns back—and a sound nearly stopped me in my tracks. Or it would have, if I had control over my own feet.

The sound was soft, the ghost of a melody drifting lazily through the castle halls, prickling along my skin and inviting me closer.

The clearer the haunted tune became, the more it invaded my senses, wrapping its cold fingers around my heart. On the surface, it might have been beautiful, something worth dancing to, but underneath the guise of beauty was the unnerving truth of what it represented.

The tune was a death march, and I was moments away from being face-to-face with death himself.

We stopped in front of a set of double doors, gray and imposing like the rest of the castle, guarded by two suits of armor. The haunting music seeped through the sealed entrance, tugging at my insides. It was as if the tune was singing to my very bones.

As much as I didn't want to be here, I couldn't deny the curiosity burning through me.

I wanted to see what a masquerade ball worthy of the Prince of Hell was like, if only for a moment.

If I could get away from Holga, maybe I could make a break for it, and then… I had no idea what I was going to do, but I had to try to escape.

There was still time left.

I didn't belong to the Lord of Bones *yet*.

After a beat of hesitation, the suits of armor sprang to life with a chorus of creaks and squeaks. The heavy doors groaned open, and I craned my neck to get my first glimpse of the ball. My chest constricted, and I fought the urge to be impressed.

It was the most incredible thing I'd ever seen.

The hall itself was enormous. Bone chandeliers hung from above, ornate pillars running up the walls to meet the high ceiling. At least a hundred bodies swirled around the room, all swaying to the hypnotic music coming from a live band of skeletons in the corner. Haunted suits of armor, skeletons, and demons were all dressed to the nines, swathed in glittering fabrics. There were ball gowns and waistcoats and a sea of black, white, and silver masks.

I watched in awe as a couple, a tall skeleton woman and a headless demon, twirled by before disappearing into the crowd. No one batted an eye in our direction as Holga and I stepped into the room, nor when the heavy doors closed ominously behind us, sealing us inside.

"I don't want to dance," I said, shooting Holga a nervous look. It wasn't that I didn't know how—I'd watched enough movies to have a good idea—but I didn't want anything to do with the festivities, not if all these people were here to watch the Lord of Bones gloat over winning our little bet.

They could all get fucked.

There was only one person I wanted to dance with anyway, and I had no idea where he was, or if he would even attend the ball. *If he was even still alive.*

"Why can't I just go to my room?" I asked, unable to keep my eyes from wandering through the hall. "If the Lord wants me here so badly, he can fetch me when he's ready. I don't want to be here."

I wanted to sulk alone. I wanted to cry.

"You have no choice, my dear," Holga tutted. "None of us do in the Lord of Bones' realm. You could at least try to have a good time."

Under different circumstances, I couldn't think of anything I'd enjoy more than a horrifyingly glamorous goth ball, but this was the last place I wanted to be.

Holga seemed genuinely sorry she couldn't help me. Her fear of returning to one of the lower levels of Hell outweighed her compassion. I couldn't say I blamed her, but I wished someone in this fucking castle would help me slip past the Lord of Bones' watchful eye.

My thoughts turned to Belial, and my heart pitched toward the floor. He'd done so much to help me, and then he'd disappeared. It didn't sit right with me. He wouldn't just leave, not after I'd given him everything. He wouldn't just take my soul and leave me behind…

Would he?

Either he was dead or he'd betrayed me, and I didn't think I could live with either one.

"Go on," Holga nudged me forward by digging her sharp elbow into my ribs. "You might even find what you're looking for."

My head snapped in her direction, but she wasn't looking at me. Her empty sockets were glued resolutely to the waltzing couples around the hall.

"Holga," I said, my voice just loud enough to be heard over the eerie melody. "Is Belial here?"

She didn't answer, but her magic gripped my muscles and forced my feet forward, carrying me across the dance floor against my will. Despite my efforts to turn back, the invisible force dragged me farther away from the witch until I was good and lost in the swirl of twirling dancers.

Then, the hold over me ebbed, and I continued forward on my own.

Now that I was here, I might as well look for Belial. If I couldn't find him, at least I could try to slip through the throng of people and shake Holga from my tail.

The music floating in the air, coupled with the constant movement of dancers around me, made my thoughts fuzzy. It was ethereal, something straight out of a movie—one I didn't remember auditioning for. If it wasn't for the painful throb in my chest, I might have chalked all of this up to another plum dream.

I made my way through the sea of masked faces, eventually catching a glimpse of Holga and Cecil—the Lord's personal librarian—waltzing together around the perimeter of the room. Angry as I was, the sight put a smile on my face. Now it made sense why she'd been so nervous when she and Cecil came to Belial's room. I would have guessed that the two didn't like each other. Maybe I'd misread the tension, and the frustrations were more intimate in nature.

Which was understandably frustrating, since only one of them had skin—if the aged leather stretching Cecil's frame could even be called skin.

When I broke through the crowd at the other end of the hall, my stomach dropped through my ass to the ground. Elevated on a stone dais was a throne made of bones, the same one I'd seen in my dream, looming menacingly before me. It was an omen, a stark reminder of what would come shortly. In front of it, splitting the marble floor in half, was a crimson river drifting along somberly. *The River Styx.*

My insides twisted, visions from the dream flooding my mind once again.

"Show your Lord all he owns," the Lord of Bones had rumbled in that voice that touched me all over, as palpable as a lover's caress.

Heat thrummed through me as the image of me bending over and spreading myself open for him surfaced. He'd made me touch myself in front of all those souls.

Fuck. That damn dream. I couldn't get it out of my head.

A flood of arousal pooled between my legs and slicked down my thighs. I pressed my dress down, trying to soak up the fluid with the fabric.

Of all the layers Holga had provided me with, underwear wasn't one of them. Something told me that had been yet another instruction from the perverted Lord.

"Fucking prick," I mumbled, quickly turning on the spot to watch the dancers once more.

At least there was no sign of the Lord of Bones. Yet.

I probably didn't have long, minutes at most, before he made his appearance. Before he came to claim me.

In front of all these people.

I took a shaky breath, searching for an exit.

Aside from the doors where we'd entered, which were still sealed shut, there was no other way into the hall. There was no escape.

As I tried to hash out an escape plan, a flash of antlers had my blood freezing in my veins. My blood went molten hot on the next breath when I registered the jewelry decorating them, silver charms and chains I'd recognize anywhere.

Then, a mask I knew well appeared through the crowd. It was gone again on the next beat of the music.

My heart slammed to a painful stop, and time seemed to slow.

"Belial?" I whispered, maneuvering and trying to catch sight of the mask again. The silver on his antlers caught the light. That had to be him. *Was he dancing?*

My stomach pitched toward the floor, and I hurried forward, nearly getting trampled by a waltzing pair of demons. I muttered an apology and pressed on, weaving through the crowd while the haunting music swallowed me.

I frantically searched for the demon who possessed my soul, probably looking ridiculous as I spun around without a dance partner, but I didn't care. No one seemed to be paying me any attention, lost to the music.

"Rayven," a voice said behind me, and I stilled. With a sharp inhale, the scent of sweet strawberries pierced my hazy thoughts and lit up every nerve in my body.

I pivoted. Belial stood there, storm gray eyes practically glowing behind his mask as he looked me over. My skin prickled with unease, and suddenly, my mouth was bone dry.

He looked incredible. His black slacks and fitted silver shirt hugged his muscular frame like they were made for him—they probably were—and a black cape with intricate silver details was tied around his shoulders. He looked elegant and sinister, every bit the conniving henchman who'd set his eyes on the villain's prisoner, determined to make her fall for him.

He was temptation incarnate, and I was helpless against his influence.

I could only stare as he stepped closer, eliminating the space between us without breaking eye contact. Relief like I'd never known washed over me in a crashing wave, but mixed emotions quickly surfaced right after.

I wanted answers, and I wanted them now.

"What have you done?" I asked, my voice threatening to crack. "I'm supposed to be in the labyrinth. I didn't ask to come back to the castle."

"I know," he said gently, offering me his hand. "Everything will make sense soon."

"Soon?" I asked, staring down at his outstretched fingers. My skin was burning to touch him, even just his gloved hand, but I couldn't move. I couldn't do anything until I knew he hadn't betrayed me. "I want the truth *now*, Belial. Why are you doing this? The Lord of Bones is going to show up any minute. We need to go. If he catches us..."

Belial grabbed my chin gently between his fingers, successfully silencing me. I stared up into his eyes for a long moment, caught in their web of sincerity.

"As many times as I've saved your life, you should have more faith in me," he said shortly. He leaned forward, and the scent of ripe berries made my head light again.

"Faith," I muttered, thoughts swimming. "You're a demon."

"And yet..." He traced a finger along my jawline. Goosebumps exploded over my skin, despite the heat sinking through me. "You gave your soul to me. I'd say that requires a fair bit of faith, don't you?"

Shit. He had me there.

"But the Lord—"

"Dance with me, Rayven," he interrupted. His gaze dropped to his outstretched hand, silently urging me to take it. "Please, give me this."

CHAPTER FOUR

RAYVEN

PART OF ME WANTED to deny Belial's request—now was not the time for dancing. But for the short time I'd known him, I hadn't been any good at resisting him, especially when he had that dark gleam in his eye.

So, I took his hand, and he pulled me against him hard enough to knock the air from my lungs.

I caught my breath, staring up into his stunning gray eyes as he began to lead us in a slow waltz. "Belial, please," I said, keeping my voice low as he spun me around. "We have to run. There's still time for us to get away."

"I can't do that." He shook his head, and his hand on my back dipped lower to grab my waist.

"Why not?"

He didn't answer at first, leading me around the dance floor with all the poise of a king until we were good and lost among the crowd. I could feel eyes swinging in our direction, but they were a blur, barely a second thought as Belial's gaze bore into me from the holes of his mask, demanding every shred of my attention.

Part of me never wanted this moment to end, to dance with Belial forever and forget about everything else, but another part of me knew we needed to get the fuck out of here.

"Running will do no good, little treasure," he said, dipping his head to whisper in my ear. "Even if you found your way back to the exit, you couldn't leave. You gave me your soul. This is where you belong. Here, with me."

The music changed to a slightly faster, more ominous pace, but I hardly noticed. Belial and I continued to dance slowly as couples whirled past at a dizzying speed.

I clung to his words, ignoring the ache that formed in my chest as he spoke. I wanted to believe everything he said, but I couldn't shake the feeling deep in my marrow that something was incredibly off. My fear of the King of Limbo loomed in the back of my mind, casting a shadow over my excitement for the future.

My future as Belial's mate.

The Lord of Bones would surely kill the ferryman when he arrived and learned I'd given my soul to Belial.

Would he kill me too? Or torture me in front of these spectators for a laugh?

Belial seemed confident in his ability to sway the lord's decision. I wasn't so sure. I needed to make the most of however much time we had left together.

Tentatively, I reached up with my free hand and slipped my fingers beneath the edge of Belial's mask. He froze instantly, his hand flying to grab my wrist, but he didn't pull my hand away from his face.

"What do you think you're doing?" he said, his voice low and ice cold.

I scowled, pressing my lips together as my eyes narrowed. "You'd think after I gave you every fucking part of me, you'd trust me more."

His grip on me loosened—only just—and with a scoff, he allowed me to lift his mask enough to expose his mouth. I rose on my tiptoes as he leaned down to kiss me, a swell of heat ripping through me at the contact.

For a beat, everything else melted away—the music, the ball guests. It all disappeared, and for the briefest moment, it was just us. Nothing else existed, and a ripple of mixed emotions flooded my system. Belial was everything I never knew I wanted and everything I shouldn't have.

When he pulled away and snapped his mask back into place, there was a curious glint in his eyes that hadn't been there moments ago.

"You kiss me as if you're saying goodbye."

The lump in my throat swelled, growing by the second. "I—"

Fuck. How was I supposed to tell him I was scared shitless by the very real possibility that the Lord of Bones would destroy him once he found out Belial claimed my soul?

Before I knew it, we were dancing again. Round and round we went, the haunting music and the chatter of the busy ballroom meshing into a white noise that had my skull spinning.

My hand clutched Belial's shoulder, holding on for dear life. I was terrified he'd let me go, and I'd go plunging into the crowd, down, down, like I had in the oubliette, with nothing but the cold hands of the dead to catch me.

Belial brought us to a stop and pulled me close to his chest, smoothing a gloved hand over my hair in comfort. "Hey, *shhh*. It's alright. You're here, safe with me."

I lifted my face, fat tears running down my burning cheeks. "Safe? For how long? Until the Lord of Bones kills you for claiming my soul before he could?"

Those shocking orbs of gray swam with so much emotion, like there were a million and one things he wanted to say but couldn't figure out how to voice them.

"I..." He sighed and thrust his fingers into his hair, smoothing his dark locks behind his antlers. "You just have to trust me on this, Rayven. The Lord of Bones isn't going to kill me. He isn't going to do anything to me. He *can't*."

I blinked at him. "W-what do you mean?"

"I know the Lord of Bones won't kill me because—" He paused. The words froze in his throat. Before, I didn't think a demon like Belial could feel fear. Now, I knew that wasn't true. Even with the mask, I could see he was terrified.

"What is it?" The sinking ball of dread in my stomach grew spikes. "What are you not telling me?"

His pronounced Adam's apple twitched as he swallowed. "How about I show you what I mean?"

Right here? In front of everyone?

My stomach cartwheeled.

No one was paying attention to us, other than the occasional glance over a shoulder. I didn't know what he was going to show me, but I got the feeling it was something I wouldn't want an audience for.

I didn't want to stay at this party for a minute longer anyway. I hadn't even wanted to come in the first place.

"Whatever you need to show me, it can wait." I moved to grab his sleeve so I could tug him off the dance floor to somewhere more private, away from prying eyes. "Let's get out of here first."

The demon snatched my wrist again before I could grasp onto him, his firm touch—lacking the warmth it had before—doing nothing for my anxiety.

"It can't wait anymore, little human." His voice grew darker, more guttural. "*I* can't wait one more bleeding second. I'm done with the trickery."

Visceral dread hooked in my gut, sharp and painful. "What trickery? What are you talking about?"

Belial dropped his hold on me and took a few steps back. His demeanor darkened as powerful magic began to whirl around him in a shimmering swirl of blue and white. Sensing the oncoming spectacle, every guest cleared off the dance floor.

My curiosity morphed into shock and horror as Belial's form grew, his muscles swelling. His skin turned deathly pale, with that familiar blueish tinge. The flesh on his skull melted, and the bone elongated into something monstrous. His antlers shifted and cracked, morphing into horns that stretched out and up toward the ceiling.

Blue flames leapt to life in his eyes as he stretched to his full, terrifying height.

Murmurs rippled through the throne room—clearly, I wasn't the only one who didn't know the Lord of Bones had two forms.

As realization set in, the guests all bowed to their host and master.

"This is why the Lord of Bones won't kill Belial. I am one and the same." He held his huge, claw-tipped hands out to his sides. "Do you understand now?"

My heartbeat roared in my ears, drowning out the music, the murmurs of the crowd, the Lord of Bones calling my name.

The Lord of Bones... *Belial.*

This whole time, they were the same fucking person.

I should have known it was nothing but a twisted joke. Of course, this magical ferryman didn't just happen across me in the maze, looking to help out a poor random soul in exchange for a fuck.

What actual servant would disobey his lord and king?

It was the Lord of Bones, using himself as a decoy, a distraction to throw me off the trail so I wouldn't find the exit, literally fucking the hours away until I became his.

And I'd fallen for it.

He made me think he'd fallen in love with me. He'd tricked me into giving him my soul, and for what? At the end of the three days, I would have been his anyway. That was the deal.

He probably thought it was funny, getting me to willingly give him pieces of myself.

My soul, my body…my heart.

"You manipulated me." I hated how heartbroken I sounded, surrounded by these elegantly dressed demons and departed souls, all of whom had stopped their dancing to watch.

Even the music had paused.

The Lord of Bones' eye sockets flickered with twin blue flames. He was so close, I should have felt their warmth, but they were cool. It was his hot and heavy breath that flushed my skin. "I did what I had to."

"Are you fucking kidding me?"

Murmurs broke over our audience. They were probably wondering who the hell I thought I was, speaking to the Lord like this.

I was the bitter bitch who wasn't going to get screwed over into spending eternity with a monster who got off on my suffering.

"You didn't have to do any of this!" My voice cracked, but I didn't care. The initial shock had worn off, and rage was setting in. "This is all just one sick fucking game to you, isn't it? Everything was a lie."

"Not everything," he corrected, grabbing me by the arm again.

"I don't believe a single thing that comes out of that maw of yours. You're a snake. A sadistic, perverted-as-fuck *snake*. You made me do things, you made me give you parts of myself, all for your help through a maze I was never going to find my way out of in the first place."

The Lord of Bones straightened to his full height, teeth gnashing with his growl. Everyone in the room watched us like we were putting on a goddamn play. He didn't seem to care who watched.

His attention was manacled to me alone.

"Everything you gave me, you did so willingly, little human."

"I…" I could barely squeeze any sound past the fist in my throat. "You made me believe this—this thing I've felt between us—was real. But it was just a game to you."

"It's not a game. I did this to make you mine in every way I can. I won't apologize for that."

I tried to yank my arm from his bruising grip, but it was hopeless. In this form, his hand swallowed my whole arm. "I don't want to be yours."

"You're lying. Even if you weren't, it wouldn't matter. You don't have a choice."

"Just like Catherine didn't have a choice?" My every syllable oozed venom.

"Catherine was different," he snarled, flames flickering in his sockets. "Catherine was a fleeting obsession. You... I want to possess you for all eternity."

"Your slave queen," I said in a threadbare whisper, repeating the Lord of Bones' own words.

His grip on my arm turned sharp as his claws bit into my forearm. He jerked me close and lurched over me so his set of deadly teeth were precious millimeters from my nose. "You're only a slave if you try to leave me."

The silence punctuating his words suddenly had me uncomfortably aware of the guests. They were watching me through the holes of their eloquent yet somehow equally hellish masquerade masks.

The Lord dropped his cruel grip on me and offered me a hand. The music started again, and everyone gaped, waiting expectantly for me to take his hand in this next dance.

Like the obedient little pet I was.

Everyone expected me to obey. Why wouldn't I? Belial was the God of this realm, and I was nothing but a toy for him to amuse himself with.

None of these people knew how much I loved breaking the rules, that the reason I was here in the first place was because I refused to acknowledge the laws of man. Why would the laws of a god be any different?

I made my own rules, my own decisions. I wasn't about to stand here and be ordered around in front of his court. Especially not by this fucking backstabbing asshole.

So, I turned and ran, pushing my way through the crowd of onlookers.

There was a great crackling sound, and the room flashed blue as Belial cast his magic. The guests parted with a gasp, and something whipped through the air behind me.

I flung a backward glance over my shoulder in time to see a chain made of blue light snapping through the air toward me. It wrapped around my ankle as the Lord of Bones wound his end of the chain around his hand.

He jerked on it, viciously yanking me off my feet. With a squeak, I crashed to the ground hard enough to knock the air out of me. Hooves, skeleton feet, and rotting flesh all dressed in fancy shoes went in and out of focus as my vision blurred.

The chain slithered up my body, over my dress, and between my breasts before the end found my collar and latched on.

A blink later, massive black boots came into focus. I lifted my eyes to see the horned devil to whom I willingly sold my soul marching past me, toward his throne. He took a seat, and from across the room—the crowd had parted and spread to the perimeter—he beckoned me with the crook of a meaty finger.

"Come here, little human. My brothers will arrive any minute, and I'd like something pretty on my lap while I greet them."

CHAPTER FIVE

BELIAL

For just a moment after Rayven kissed me, I thought she might forgive me. Her lips against mine... The touch felt so final. I knew, in her mind, she was saying goodbye.

I hadn't exactly planned on revealing myself like this, but I couldn't wait a second longer. She had to know this wasn't goodbye.

We'd be together forever.

When I revealed myself, I'd expected her to be angry at first. I'd anticipated the tantrum.

What I didn't expect was just how scathing her reaction would be.

Whatever flickering flame of hope I had that she'd sweep her hatred for the Lord of Bones under the rug was devoured by something darker, something possessive.

How dare she try to flee from me again?

I'd prove to her and everyone else just how *mine* she was.

I jerked on the chain connecting her to me, and she stumbled forward, quickly catching her balance. The hot fury in her gaze burned into my fleshless skull from across the hall, but I didn't care. She would be my queen, and she'd wear my crown. It was up to her whether I'd have to force it on her.

Wrapping the chain around my forearm, I dragged her closer to where I sat on my throne. She fought me with every inch I pulled her closer, tugging on the magical links.

It was hopeless, even without the chain. If only she knew the power she'd given me by selling her soul…

"F—fuck—off!" she seethed, and the crowd whispered their shock at the way she spoke to their Lord.

I chuckled beneath my breath. They had no idea how much I loved this wild little human, how hard I got when I watched her fight me.

She wandered dangerously close to the Styx, the river that carried souls from this realm to my brothers'. Before I claimed her, the souls of the dead would have lurched from the Styx's bloody depths and dragged her along to the second circle of Hell, but now, she belonged to me. The Styx's dark magic would have no effect on her.

She was still fighting, thrashing and pulling at the chain connected to her collar, begging for me to set her free. As much as I loved hearing her beg, her pleas fell on deaf ears. She'd rejected me in front of my subjects. My pride was wounded, and she needed to be taught a lesson.

Rayven—and everyone else—needed to understand exactly who she belonged to.

"Stop, please." She grabbed onto the chain. "Some-one—Help me!"

My teeth gnashed with a displeased growl. Who was she asking for help? No one would help her. No one, soul, demon, or otherwise, would dare oppose me.

"I said *come*, Rayven." This time, I yanked the chain so hard, she stumbled forward, crashing into the shallow, blood-filled river. Corpses and bits of carrion drifted by slowly, and she shrieked when a head without eyes floated past.

Crimson droplets beaded her exposed flesh as she fought to stand in the steady current. She looked up at me, eyes full of hate.

"Fuck you," she spat, her gaze falling to her soaked gown. It was darker now, drenched in blood, and as I dragged her up onto the dais with another wrench of the chain, rivets of dark liquid poured off her.

Weeping Hells. She was a vision in red, like Lilith herself, looking so fucking gorgeous wrapped in gore and fury and lace.

"That can be arranged." I pulled her onto my lap, my eyes falling to the vibrant red welts the collar around her throat created. A distinct heat sank straight to my cock. I lowered my voice. "Would you like to give our guests a show? Or maybe after the ball, I can fuck you right here, on my throne. You'd like that, wouldn't you, pet?"

"I hate you," she gritted out, but I knew it wasn't entirely true. She could lie all she wanted, but I sensed the way her pulse picked up at my salacious suggestion, the way her pussy dripped with arousal when I punished her, desperate to feel me. She might have hated me, but her body didn't.

"I don't think you do," I countered, and she attempted to shove me away. I gripped her chain tighter with a dark chuckle. "Don't look so vexed, little mortal. Everyone's here to see you, and you look stunning when you're soaked in blood." If my fleshless skull had lips, I would have been smirking. "Pity it's not my blood. You look the best when you're dripping with me, blood or otherwise."

"We can arrange that." She scoffed, pinning her eyes firmly on the spectators below us. "Give me a knife, and I'll gladly stab you again."

She refused to look at me.

"Dance."

I snapped my fingers, and just like that, the music started, and our guests began dancing, with only the occasional curious glance tossed in the throne's direction.

"You're going to learn to obey me, Rayven." I attached the end of her chain to my throne, just below one of the armrests. With my newly freed hand, I traced a finger over her shoulder, admiring its curve. "Love me. Fear me. Obey me. That is all I ask of you."

Her piercing glare landed on me. "No wonder Catherine killed herself to get away from you."

I moved fast, my hand snatching the back of her neck and wrenching her up so her face was an inch from mine. "Stuff that bratty mouth of yours, or I'll do it for you. I'm sure you can imagine what I'd use as the gag."

Before she could open her mouth and fire off another rebuttal, there was a collective gasp from my subjects.

Cutting a harsh path through the crowd was the Lord of Lechery himself, Asmodeus, darkness pouring off the three-headed beast in tangible waves. He wore a gold mask on each of his faces and was dressed so scantily, I had to do a double take to make sure he wasn't naked. A few straps of gold-studded leather crossed his broad chest, and just enough of a loincloth shielded his cock from the partygoers.

One of my skeletal servants was leading him to us, an anxious air about him as he tried to keep his distance from the demon lord.

"My L-Lord," the servant squeaked, stopping just before the River Styx that separated us. He bowed his head to show respect before snapping upright. "Lord Asmodeus has arri   "

"Out of my way." His words cut off abruptly when Asmodeus' fist slammed into the back of his skull, punching straight out the front of his face. Rayven tensed on my lap with a tiny gasp, shrinking back against me. The servant's body clattered to the floor and slipped into the Styx, joining the slow procession of body parts sweeping out of the hall.

If I'd had eyes in this form, I would have rolled them. The fucker had always been one for theatrics.

"Belial." He nodded his three heads in unison. The bull head on the left huffed a cloud of smoke as he spoke.

"Brother." I tipped my horns. "Did you really have to dispose of my servant?"

Asmodeus' cloven hoof scraped the floor with his huff. "Oh, fuck off, Bel. You have enough servants as it is. By Baal's dick, you have countless souls dribbling from every nook, cranny, and corner of this festering hell hole..."

The three-headed demon's tirade trailed off when his attention found my pet.

"What a tasty-looking mortal toy you have there." All six of his hungry eyes landed on Rayven, and a jealous fire tore through me. They lingered too long, and I couldn't help but imagine myself ripping off every one of his heads, starting with the smallest one between his legs. "Is she the dinner I was promised on the invitation?"

He started for the throne. "What's everyone else gonna eat?"

If he'd taken a step closer, the Styx would have turned bloodier. A growl rumbled from my chest, stopping him in his tracks.

"Come on, Bel," the middle head snickered.

"Aren't brothers supposed to share?" the head on the right finished.

"Not on your fucking life, you three-headed creep," Rayven said, voice cracking through the air like a whip.

My cock hardened at the sass in her voice. Leave it to my little mortal to talk back to one of the most powerful demons in the nine circles of Hell. I had to hand it to her; she had one fuck of a backbone.

The energy spilling off Asmodeus darkened, a wave of pure cruelty and violence radiating from him.

"You're going to let her speak to me that way?" His flaxen-haired middle head cocked to the side.

I lifted a shoulder. "Can't take what you dish out, brother?"

His jaw fell slack, his eyes narrowing. "You always had a thing for fragile mortal females, Belial. It'd be a shame if this one ended up...broken."

My fists clenched around the armrests of my throne, claws scraping divots into the bone.

A threat, and not even a thinly-veiled one. Another growl rolled up my throat, my patience waning. "This one's not fragile. Now, eyes off unless you intend to lose all six of them, Lord Asmodeus. I'll make my guests count as I pluck them out one by one."

"No need for bedroom talk. I get the picture." His tone was laced with disdain. With three smirks, he turned and marched away, his furry ass cheeks on full display as he went.

Instinctively, I grabbed Rayven by the waist and pulled her closer to me. She resisted slightly before giving in, my throbbing erection pressing up against her ass through the layers of fabric separating us.

I wanted her, nearly enough to say fuck the ball and tear her clothes off right here, but I didn't want anyone looking too long at her naked body. *Especially* Asmodeus. I'd kill them all. Her delicious, perfect form was for my eyes alone.

"You should probably watch your tone when addressing the lords of Hell," I muttered in her ear, my forked tongue dancing out of my maw to lick the crusted blood on her shoulder. She shivered and tried to lean away, but my hold on the collar kept her in place.

"Why? Are you worried they'll hurt me?" she asked, her eyes finally finding mine.

I laughed in earnest, the sound echoing over the music. "I'd gouge out their eyes for looking at you the wrong way. If they laid a finger on you, I'd butcher them all."

Next to approach the throne was Leviathan, his angular cheekbones peeking out from beneath a vibrant green mask. He was dressed in all black, with copper accents that glinted in the candlelight. He bowed, his serpentine eyes bouncing between Rayven and me.

"What a lovely party," he admired, gesturing to the dancing crowd behind him. Unlike most of my brothers, Leviathan was often cordial, damn near tolerable. Of all my brothers, I liked him most, though *like* was a strong word.

"And what a lovely..." the demon lord hesitated, finding the right word, "pet."

"Thank you, Lord Leviathan." I tipped my horns to him as I struggled with what else to say. I'd say it was good to see him, but that would be a lie.

I hadn't seen my brothers in person in centuries, and I liked it that way.

All I wanted was to proudly show off my soon-to-be queen.

A terse grin curled his thin lips. "I hope the reason you gathered us here tonight has something to do with you resuming your Judgement duties. The lower layers of Hell are a bit sparse on souls these days. I thought you had done away with the distractions..."

His slitted gaze slithered back to the woman in my lap. She was so small compared to this form, and she easily balanced on one knee.

"But now you've gone and gotten yourself a new female pet... Interesting."

Before I could retort, he slithered back into the crowd, blending in much better than Asmodeus.

"Being a dickhead obviously runs in the family." Rayven crossed her arms over her chest. Crimson liquid oozed from her dress, blood cascading like tears over her skin, but she didn't seem to care.

"Would you expect anything less from the lords of Hell?"

"No." Her heated gaze snapped in my direction. "Not when you're King Dickhead, ruler of the evil and remorseless."

"Oh, but you love how dark and demented I am, don't you, little treasure?" I reached for her chin, but she flinched away from me.

Before I could say anything else, a pair of figures appeared in the corner of my eye. A quick glance almost made me chuckle, but I swallowed it down. Standing before the throne were Mammon, the Lord of Greed, and my shapeshifting brother, Belphegor, who'd shown up in his preferred female form.

With the way he draped himself on Mammon's arm, Asmodeus wasn't the only one he'd set his sights on.

The difference was, Asmodeus had slept with his brother not knowing who it was. It seemed Belphegor had decided to recycle the same joke, this time with the Lord of Greed as his victim.

This female form had a new face, but I could see beneath the magic disguising him.

"You have no shame," I addressed the female Belphegor.

Mammon's brows crinkled with confusion before he smirked. "Shame's a funny thing to bring up, considering the human toy you're proudly displaying at a royal affair. At least my date is a demon."

Mammon wore a smoke gray suit and cape with too many embellishments and too many iron rings on his fingers. A black mask hid most of his wide face, and a spill of oily black hair fell just over his shoulders.

Belphegor was his polar opposite, with voluptuous curves in all the right places. Flowing white hair fell around his narrow shoulders, and red eyes peeked out from behind a delicate filigree mask. If he moved too suddenly, his breasts were going to pop out of his little black dress.

I could sense Rayven's curious gaze lingering on him, wondering who this stunning woman was. "Who is that?" she whispered beneath her breath.

The flames of my eyes flickered at the lack of hatred in her tone. My brothers were providing a decent distraction from her anger. At least they were good for something.

"Remember the story I told you about Belphegor taking on the form of a woman to trick Asmodeus into fucking him?" I whispered to her.

Her eyes widened and, for a moment, there was the trace of a smile at the corner of her mouth. "Your family has baggage."

"Oh, little human, you have no idea."

Rayven stifled a laugh that my brothers seemed to miss before they disappeared into the crowd. She watched them go, her eyes glued to the dancing crowd waltzing effortlessly to the melody playing from the live band.

"Admiring your subjects?" I asked, hooking a claw beneath her chin and turning her face toward me. Her eyes glimmered with hatred.

"*Your* subjects," she spat. "I am not your queen."

I chuckled, amused by her stubbornness. "You *are* my slave queen, and once I make the announcement, everyone will know it."

Grabbing her wrist, I trailed a finger over the two marks above her wrist. *My* marks.

"Soon, my pet. You don't have much time left."

Her eyes narrowed, and she snatched her arm away.

"Fuck you. I'm not your queen, and I never will be."

She jumped off my lap, and I watched her go, laughing as she hopped off the dais straight into the river Styx. Her fear from earlier had been replaced by rage that rippled through me in waves of ecstasy. Oh, how I yearned to fuck that attitude out of her.

Struggling against the current, she climbed out on the other side, once again soaked to the bone in blood. As she dashed into the crowd, she left a smear of crimson in her wake.

She gathered a bundle of the chain in her arms to make running easier, but the end of it remained attached to my throne. It would grow as she fled, adding links until she tired.

I leaned back, debating my next move.

I'd let her run...or at least, I'd give her a head start before tracking her down. I adored how she still thought she stood a chance at escaping.

Her time might not have technically been up, but if she wasn't tired of this game of cat and mouse yet, I'd let her play.

I'd let her run.

Because there wasn't anything I loved more than chasing her...aside from the part where I fucked her after.

The day was nearly out. When I caught her, her time would be up.

I stood and slowly started to follow the chain trail she'd left me, counting down the seconds until I cut the third mark into her arm.

The only question was, would I do it before or after I fucked her?

CHAPTER SIX

RAYVEN

BITTER TEARS STUNG MY cheeks like acid as I fled the throne room. I hoisted a bundle of my tether against my chest as I ran, the magical chain surprisingly light in my arms. My heart thundered in my throat as I braced for the Lord of Bones to yank on the leash again and drag me back to his side while his audience laughed.

The asshole probably got off on humiliating me in front of his subjects, especially with his cruel brothers watching. That was probably why he'd invited them in the first place. They all came to watch the human get her heart broken in front of the entire realm then be chained up to the lord's throne.

Like a fucking dog.

Belial was a bit of a sadistic fuck, I knew that, so I wouldn't put it past him to drag me back, kicking and screaming, to give his guests a good show. Heck, my public humiliation was probably printed on the invitations beforehand.

I could see it now.

The Lord of Bones cordially invites you to the All Hollow's Eve Masquerade Ball.

There will be a formal dinner service, dancing to follow, and the complete and utter ass-blasting of my pathetic little fuck slut.

However, a tug on the chain never came. It only seemed to lengthen as I kept running down the winding hallways, taking every random turn and zipping my way around, desperately looking for an exit.

There was still time... He hadn't given me the third cut on my arm marking the third and final day of our bet. There was still time. *I could still win.* Assuming he'd honor our agreement to let me go if I could find the exit.

That was a big if. He'd taken me to a door on the cliff, showing me the exit right before I stupidly sold my soul.

The door hadn't even been inside his labyrinthian garden—if a desolate wasteland filled with rotting corpses and hellish monsters could even be called a garden. Chances were damn slim that I'd make it out in time.

Still, my feet pushed forward. What other choice did I have? Sit and cry while my time ticked down?

Fuck. That.

Various knick-knacks, framed paintings, and furniture—all inhabited with lost souls seeking refuge while they awaited Judgement from the Lord—called out as I passed, but I ignored them. I'd learned my lesson the last time an object tried to guide me through the twisting hallways and countless rooms, nearly jumping to my death at its instruction.

When I finally found a window, I stopped running and dropped the bundled chain to the floor. There were bars over it to keep the Lord's last mortal pet from escaping—one of the ways Catherine's memory still clung to these halls. Even without the bars, it would be too high up to climb out.

I wiped a clean patch in the murky glass with the lace of my dress and peered outside. My heart sank when I saw how far off the garden wall was, the cliffside far beyond that. Even if time didn't run out before I could reach it, the chain would only stretch so far.

"You'll never reach it in time."

Belial's voice came out of nowhere, like a phantom bleeding from the walls. My flouncy skirts twirled dramatically as I whipped around to face the demon lord.

The Lord had now appeared in his lesser form—the one I'd stupidly fallen in love with. Coming to me in this form was probably strategic on his part, yet another way to manipulate me.

"Get away from me," I spat, my back hitting the hall.

Ignoring me, he prowled forward slowly, every step meant to torture me.

"Even if by some dark miracle you did manage to escape," he drawled in that deep, honied baritone, "aren't you forgetting something? I own your soul. You're mine forever, little treasure."

"Stop calling me that! I'm not your treasure. I'm your fucking prisoner."

"You said you wanted to be with me. I gave you the opportunity to leave, remember? On the cliff, I showed you the door. You had an out, and you chose me."

"That was before I knew you were just the Lord of Assholes in disguise."

"I wasn't in disguise. This—" He gestured to his human-like form. "This is me too, how I looked before I became the Lord of this realm. Minus the antlers."

I shook my head silently, unable to respond for fear I'd start crying. I wouldn't give him the satisfaction. "I never should have trusted you. It was just one big fat lie."

"How many times do I have to tell you?" He took another step, then another, until there was no space left between us. The chains draping from his antlers jingled as he canted his head. "Almost everything I said was true—how I want you to be mine, how I think you're stubborn and brilliant and addictively brazen...." He stroked the back of his index finger down the edge of my jaw.

His touch was electric. I wanted to shy away from it and pull him closer all at the same time.

His eyes dropped to my lips then darted up to lock with mine. "How I will protect you, just like I promised I would."

"How do I know what's real and what's not?"

"You're a living, breathing person in the realm of the dead. It's like being caught between dreams and real life, not knowing bottom from up. Does it matter if you allow yourself to enjoy the ride?" The mouth of his mask brushed against the shell of my ear, and he dropped his voice to whisper, "Isn't that what you want? To *enjoy* me?"

I swallowed down the rebuttal burning the tip of my tongue, resisting the urge to spit it in his face.

I could deny my attraction to him all day long. He'd still know I was lying. He'd betrayed me, but with the way I grew wetter, hotter, my pulse accelerating as he stalked closer, my stupid, traitorous vagina didn't give two shits.

"What I want is for you to unchain me," I snapped.

He paused, contemplation banking in his eyes as he seemed to consider my request. After a beat, he waved his hand, and the magical chain keeping me anchored to his throne flickered and disappeared.

My fingers ghosted over the metal choker around my neck, though it was more accurate to call it what it was—a collar. Yet another mark of his ownership. "Can't you remove this too?"

"Sorry, little treasure. That's never coming off." His drawl was laced with something I couldn't parse. He closed the last bit of distance between us, forcing me against the wall.

I was trapped, even without the collar. I'd sold my soul to the devil. There was no running from that.

"What does it mean, now that you own my soul? And before you say you own me for the millionth time, I want an actual answer."

His cold eyes glimmered with amusement. "It means I control you, Rayven. Down to your bone."

Likely sensing another question on the tip of my tongue, he took a step back. "Allow me to demonstrate?"

"Allow?" I snorted. "Do I have a choice?"

Another tense stretch of silence passed before he answered with a clipped, "No."

He raised a gloved hand, pointing with his index finger and giving it a whirl in the air.

A small cry was wrenched from my lips as my body jerked toward him, as if pulled by invisible strings.

My ball gown fanned out in all directions as I whirled around and around, my head spinning just as fast. *What the hell was happening?*

A second later, I stopped abruptly and danced toward Belial, my limbs moving of their own accord—no, of *his* accord—taking his offered hand and gripping his shoulder.

We danced in the hallway to silence, our rhythmic footsteps echoing off the marble around us, before a simple tune began to play a few moments later. My eyes landed on a music box with some poor lost soul trapped inside, playing from a nearby table.

We weren't alone after all.

"Perfect form, My Lord," a suit of armor said, the soul's voice echoing from the suit's dusty helmet.

"What a beautiful couple," a candelabra added.

Other various knick-knacks and furniture all muttered in agreement.

"I couldn't agree more." There was no missing the smile in Belial's voice as he beamed with admiration, as if he wasn't forcing me to dance with him.

"You're a bastard," I gnashed out as we twirled down the hallway to the music box's melody.

"Yet, you still crave my touch. Even now, while you're under my influence." He canted his head, his gaze darkening. "By the scent bleeding from your cunt, I'd say *especially* under my influence."

Fuck. I hated how acute this demon's senses were. It made hiding my arousal a near-impossible task. "You're fucking delusional."

"Oh, sweet little human. What have I told you about lying to me?"

Using his magic, he pushed all the objects off the nearest table, sending the music box clattering to the ground. The melody abruptly came to a stop. Belial banded his arms around my middle and lifted me onto the table, my legs dangling over the side.

Another flick of his hand, and my thighs parted with a jerk. His hands swept under the hem of my dress, bunching the fabric over my hips.

He tore the glove of his right hand off with his teeth and gave his fingers a wave, as if to silently tease me, since we both knew exactly what he intended on doing with them.

"Wait—"

With his other hand, he tore off his mask and tossed it onto the table next to me.

Only yesterday, I would have given everything to see the man behind the mask. I *had* given everything.

The thing that hurt the most? I'd probably do it all over again. Because under all the heartbreak, all the betrayal, all the pain and resentment, I still wanted him.

"Look me in the eye and tell me you don't want me to fuck away the ache between your legs, Rayven."

He reached up to tuck a rogue piece of my hair behind my ear, his touch suddenly gentle, a juxtaposition to the magical restraints forcing my body open for him. "Don't you want me to make you feel something other than pain?"

CHAPTER SEVEN

RAYVEN

I COULDN'T FIGHT HIM off even if I wanted to. His magic was too powerful.

Even if I hadn't sold my soul to the devil, it was damn near impossible to resist Belial when he was like this, feral and dominant—completely devoted to my suffering.

The bastard knew just how to tease and tweak me, manipulating me into enjoying his brand of torture. No, enjoying wasn't the right word. I craved it, and somehow, for some stupid reason, I still wanted him.

Belial was like a dangerously addictive amphetamine.

And his body? *Jesus Christ.* His pants were looser than the ones he'd worn in the labyrinth, but the bulge in the front was still just as noticeable.

Without his mask, he was achingly handsome. Despite what I said to hurt him, I would never understand how Catherine hated that face enough to kill herself to get away from it. He had scars, sure, but those only seemed to add to his wicked allure.

I hated the Lord of Bones with every fiber of my being, and I loved Belial with just as much intensity. Now that I knew they were one and the same, my mind and my body were at war.

I wiggled against the invisible bonds that held me in place on the table. Belial watched me, and with the heated look on his face, you'd think I was purposefully putting on a show for him.

"Look at you. I've lived for so damn long, seen so much. Yet nothing has been quite so beautiful as watching you squirm for me." His hands skated up my thighs, dangerously close to my exposed center.

Goosebumps exploded over my skin in the wake of his touch, and he hummed lowly, his hands sliding back down over the bumps. "Weeping Hells, you're so responsive to me."

I opened my mouth to fire off some obscenity or other, but only a moan slithered out as he stroked his index finger through my folds.

He held his finger up, rubbing it with his thumb to demonstrate the thickness of my arousal. Then, he popped the digit into his mouth, sucking it clean.

"You taste fucking delicious." He surged forward, a dark glint in his eye.

His bare hand gripped my throat over my collar as his mouth came down on mine in a savage kiss.

He gagged my cry of surprise with his tongue, thrusting into my mouth and sweeping possessively over my teeth, the roof of my mouth, twirling with mine.

The scent of strawberries and pine leached down my throat and sat heavy in my lungs, making the simple act of breathing an impossible task.

One hand gripped my thigh tight enough to leave bruises while his other curved around my nape, tilting my head back, allowing him deeper access to my throat.

There was no space left between us now, his torso smashed against mine and the bulge in his pants rubbing against my open center.

I was drowning in him, and the worst thing about it all was how much I still wanted this...

My teeth bit down on his tongue hard, and blood bloomed instantly over my tastebuds.

He reeled back with a growl, blood dripping from the corner of his mouth, making him look more feral than before. He angrily wiped his mouth on the back of his hand, which only smeared the blood across his face.

A slow, manic smile spread his bloodied lips. "You know that docsn't count as 'stop', right? Your safe word is black widow. Or have you forgotten?"

I hadn't forgotten. It just hadn't occurred to me to use it. Would he listen if I did?

I opened my mouth to say it. No words came out.

Fucking hell, I was seriously messed up for not wanting this to end. "You don't deserve me."

"I never said I did."

He stepped forward again, and I spat at him, gobs of blood and saliva flecking his face. His smirk widened. "Don't give me that, little human. You're acting like you don't want me, but you haven't used your safe word yet."

"I want the person you pretended to be. The person I thought I was giving my soul to."

"I *am* that person."

"Fuck you, Belial."

I squirmed harder against his bonds, and he shook his head, tutting. "Admit it. A part of you is enjoying this."

His eyes dropped to the small puddle that had already formed between my legs.

"I'm naturally wet, asshole. You know how many panties I have to go through on a regular basis back home? Trust me, it wasn't because Mark was some stud."

At the mention of my ex, Belial's gaze turned sharp.

What I said was true, but usually, I wasn't *this* wet. He was right; I did like being tied up. I found that out the night he'd manacled me and fucked me with the wine bottle.

"You want to touch me? You want me to *enjoy* it?" I bit out. "Then get on your knees and beg for my forgiveness."

"Beg?" He looked like every bit a king would when told to beg for anything.

"Yes, beg! Because a simple apology isn't enough. You broke my heart, you son of a bitch!" My voice cracked, and bitter tears filled my eyes. "You need to do something for the pain you've caused, and you can't do it with your dick, Belial."

I wouldn't have believed the demon lord was capable of regret—not for his own actions, anyway—if it wasn't for the fact that it was carved plain as day into his marred features.

"Even if you accepted my apology, it would be yet another lie." He shook his head, the chains dangling from his antlers jingling with the motion. "Because I'm not sorry for making you mine, just for the way I was forced to go about it."

"You could have told me—"

"Oh, bullshit, Rayven," he cut me off with a humorless laugh. "If I had revealed I was the Lord of Bones, you would have never trusted me to help you through the labyrinth."

"And for good reason, you snake!"

He took a step back, his eyes full of thoughts. "What can I do to earn your forgiveness?"

"Remember that cliff where you tricked me into giving you my soul? Go jump off it."

He blinked. "You want me to…"

"Take a flying leap, yeah."

A slow grin spread his ruined lips. "I'll do you one better."

He unbuttoned his cloak, letting it fall to the ground, and ripped his shirt off, along with his other glove a beat later, adding to the pile at his feet.

He was left in only his pants and boots, his scarred torso on full display.

In a glimmer of blue magic, he produced a dagger seemingly from thin air. I recognized it immediately as the one he'd taken from me, the one I'd used to escape my room my first night in the castle.

He fell to his knees and held out the knife to me, presented on the flat of his palm.

The restraints holding me were gone in the same instant, allowing me to hop off the table and smooth down my skirts.

I eyed the dagger for a moment before taking it carefully in my hand. The last time I'd held this thing, the soul trapped inside had spoken to me and tried to get me to leap to my death—that was the only way she knew of to escape the Lord of Bones.

"Kill me, Rayven."

I gaped down at the demon, who lifted his head to peer at me through the curtain of his unkempt locks. "Bury the blade in my heart."

I shook my head slowly, unable to fully process what he was telling me. This had to be another trick. The god of death couldn't die... Could he?

"What will happen?"

"You will get your revenge."

"But will you die?"

"Is that what you want?"

What I wanted was the version of him I thought I was getting when I gave him my soul. According to him, that was also him. What if it was just another lie?

"Do it…"

The voice hadn't come from me, or any of the household items watching the scene unfold. It hadn't come from Belial either.

"Strike him in the heart," the soft, feminine voice said again. It was coming from the dagger.

Belial seemed surprised for exactly a second, and then his smile locked into place. "Pierce me in the heart, and two women will get their revenge. What's that human phrase? Two birds, one stone?"

"Two women?" I paused, my blood turning frigid. My gaze bounced between him and the blade. "Who else would want…"

"Catherine." Belial's voice was emotionless. "Her soul clung to the blade in your hands the last time she died."

My throat tightened at the truth, and I fought to swallow my unease.

"Kill him now, before it's too late," Catherine's faded soul whispered.

"Shut up!" I snapped, my fingers clenching tighter around the dagger as my hand began to shake. "I'm trying to think."

"She's right, Rayven." Belial's smile was unwavering, even though I was sure it was just another mask. "I gave you the opportunity to run on the cliffside when I showed you the door back to your realm. This is your second and final chance to leave me."

"You will die, won't you?"

"That doesn't matter. Stab me, and you'll wake up in the Patherick tomb as if nothing happened." The demon's lips peeled back to reveal unnaturally pointed canines. "Well, except for your pathetic little boyfriend. He'll still be dead."

I looked down at the face I loved and loathed in equal measure. What in the actual fuck was I supposed to do? This decision would change the course of my life forever. I did believe this would be my last chance to leave Limbo.

If I stabbed him in the heart, I'd wake up back home, and I could go on with my old life—not that I really had a life to begin with. In the human world, I had to constantly hustle to get by. Now that Mark was dead, I'd have no one. Plus, what had happened to his body? Belial had taken his spine to make into a crown, but he had to have left the rest of the body there in the cemetery.

There'd be questions if I returned out of the blue with my boyfriend dead.

When Belial first showed me the exit on the cliff, I'd made my decision. I wanted to stay with him.

But things were different now.

I'd never forgive him for what he'd done... But could I still be his queen?

"If you don't stab that dagger into my heart right now, you'll have made your decision," Belial warned in a low rasp, seeing the conflict in my eyes. "And you'll never escape me again."

As much as I resented him for tricking me, I'd made my choice. I'd given him my soul, and something told me I'd prefer the pain of a future as the Queen of Bones, or corpses or whatever my title would be, than the pain of returning to my meaningless human life.

My grip on the dagger loosened, and after what felt like an eternity, I released the breath I'd been holding and lowered the blade.

Belial got to his feet and reached to cup my cheek. "That's my good girl. I knew you'd—"

I slapped him so hard across the face, the crack of flesh striking flesh echoed down the hall, nearly drowning out the collective gasp from the onlooking furniture and knick-knacks.

"I'm not your *good girl*, you asshole."

Belial slowly slid his deadly glare back to me, his cheek bright red. A vein in his jaw ticked, but he said nothing as I continued my tirade.

"If I'm going to stay here, you better treat me like the goddamn queen I'm to be, Lord of Bones. Otherwise, this castle won't be my prison. It will be yours."

Raising the dagger, I placed the point at the hollow of his throat and donned his signature smirk. "Now, get back on your knees. I told you to beg for my forgiveness. If you don't satisfy me, maybe I'll stab you after all."

CHAPTER EIGHT

BELIAL

I HADN'T OFFICIALLY CROWNED Rayven yet, but here she was, already spouting demands like the queen she'd soon be. How could I not obey?

Keeping my eyes glued to my little human, I lowered myself to kneel at her feet.

I'd never submitted to anyone or anything, but here I was, giving over control to this not-so-delicate mortal female. That was one of the things I'd come to love about her. She breathed life into my cold and lonely existence.

She peered down at me with a thunderstruck look in her eye, as if she hadn't expected me to obey. I couldn't blame her. I almost didn't.

But Rayven was right—she deserved some sort of retribution for what I'd done to her.

"You look good on your knees." Her tone was hard, but her words were sheathed in velvet.

She looked at me like I was going to be her next meal. Bleeding *fucking* Hells, no one ever looked at me like that. Not this face, not with these scars.

Pleasure burned through me as she licked her lips, her tongue swiping up the final traces of my blood. "Maybe I should make you crawl, like you did with me our first night together."

The memory had me smirking, but it fell away with my hiss as she suddenly pressed the dagger's point under my chin, forcing my head back as far as it would go. "But first, I'd like to hear you beg for my forgiveness."

Her eyes stretched to the size of dinner plates as I leaned into the dagger, pushing the weapon's tip into my skin enough to draw blood.

I could feel the warm liquid dribble down my chest.

Rayven's dark eyes rounded as they trailed the wet beads descending my torso, soaking into the waist of my pants. By the rosy tint of her cheeks and the feminine scent filling my nose, she liked watching me bleed.

Twisted little thing. She really was perfect for me. "I'll do more than beg, my treasure. I'll *bleed* for you."

I flattened my hands on the floor and slowly snaked them under the hem of her dress, grinning up at her as my fingers curved over her ankles. "I'll tear down kingdoms for you. I'll drape you in silver."

My hands traveled up her legs, and my cock throbbed at the tears of arousal rolling down her inner thighs. "I'll bring the heads of your enemies on pikes and build you a throne of their bones."

I ached to grip my dick, to stroke myself at the sight of her towering over me, shadows in her eyes that were as violent as they were lustful. But I resisted, keeping my hands anchored to her. She was asking for my devotion, and oh, gods help her, I was about to give her every ounce of my ravenous attention.

"I'll lavish you in riches of the dead, and I'll fuck you like only a demon king can."

Her thighs quivered beneath my hands, and her breathing picked up with the rhythm of her pulse. I shoved the hem of her dress up with a growl and felt the fabric catch on my antlers. My hands slid higher to part her labia.

She inhaled sharply as I brought my face close enough for her to feel my breath sweep over her exposed core. A chuckle dropped from my lips at her frustrated huff as I turned my head to paint a lick up her thigh instead. "I'll tongue fuck you until you're teetering on the edge of ecstasy and unconsciousness. I'll milk you of every drop of cum I can wring from your pretty little cunt. All you have to do is forgive me..."

"I didn't say bargain. I said beg."

My mouth curved against her, teeth scraping flesh. *"Please."*

Her breathing turned to panting. "Please, what?"

"Forgive me." My voice was barely more than a rasp, made rough with hunger and lack of patience. I needed her now. I wanted her begging for *me*. But I'd give her what she wanted. I'd make her scream either way. "Forgive me, and I'll feast on the flesh between your legs like a starving wolf."

She grabbed one of my antlers—an offense that would have been a death sentence for anyone else—and wrenched my head back from under her skirt to hit me with a look fitting an evil queen. "There the demon goes again, making more deals. You can't help yourself, can you?"

I licked my lips. "My self-control is almost non-existent when I'm around you. Your taste, your smell, your everything. It makes me feel like every bit the monster I am."

"How about you feast on me anyway?" She dragged the dagger's point up the column of my throat, over my jaw, and traced the scars on my lips. "Make your queen come with your mouth, or I'll add to the pretty little collection of scars you have. Maybe I'll just do it anyway. They're so fucking sexy on you."

My new mate was enjoying the feeling of being in control for the first time in days, probably even longer. She was stepping into a dominant role like a fish taking to water. She'd make such a perfect queen.

I dove back under her skirts and picked up her leg, throwing it over my shoulder for a better angle.

"Hold onto my antlers," I instructed her. Before the last word had left my mouth, my tongue stoked through her folds. Her taste had my balls tightening, but the best part of pleasuring her like this was always the feeling of her heart pounding against my tongue. I pushed my head lower and speared her with the hot muscle. Her body jerked, the heel of her boot stabbing into my back.

"Belial..."

"Shh," I breathed against her, my voice coming out muffled and contorted.

One of the things about being a demon was having a tongue that was longer than an average human's. This form had nothing on my more formidable one, but it still filled her up enough to have her moaning as she held onto my antlers for dear life.

Her walls clamped tight around my tongue before fluttering and spasming with her climax.

I licked her cum from my lips. "Forgive me?"

"N–no."

I set to making her come again. This time, my tongue circled her clit while I fucked her with my finger. After a few thrusts, I pushed a second digit inside her heat. "You take me so well, my queen. I can't wait to bend you over and watch you take your lord's cock."

She let out a shaky breath, her walls quivering with the motion. I pumped faster, harder, her cute little cries full of the raging inferno of lust growing inside me.

My ministrations grew rougher, more fervent. She grew wetter, her moans getting louder to the point where the guests downstairs might hear. Good. Let them hear. I wanted them to know how well I could pleasure my woman.

She came again. Her insides turned molten hot, and another wash of fluid coated my fingers—she was so wet now, there was an obscene sound every time I thrust into her.

"Forgive me." It wasn't a question anymore. Now, it was an order.

"N–no." She could barely articulate.

I kept finger fucking her through her climax, picking up speed. If it wasn't for the fact that I was holding her up, she'd collapse. "I can go on like this all week, baby. You have to give in some time."

It was with her third orgasm that she forced out a fragmented "N–e–ver."

Pulling out of her with a snarl, I emerged from her skirts and shot to my feet. She raised the dagger, but I seized her wrist this time, gripping it hard enough to make her drop it.

Our eyes locked, the few inches between us buzzing with electricity.

The heart in my chest, the one I thought was dead and gone for the longest time, beat hard enough for me to know it was there.

That's what this little human did to me. She had melted the ice around my heart, made me something I thought death could never be. She made me feel alive.

I spun her around and bent her over the table, her stomach flush with the flat surface.

"Lift your dress."

I half expected her to rebel, but she rushed to obey, reaching back to gather the black and burgundy fabric and bundling it around her waist.

"All I have to do is make you come a few times, and you turn right back into my good, obedient little queen."

She cast a glance over her shoulder, shooting me a heated look. Her brows crunched with frustration. "If you're going to fuck me, just do it already, before I die of old age."

"Perhaps I spoke too soon." I grinned and slapped her ass. "Spread your legs."

Swallowing, she positioned her legs wide.

"Now, reach around and spread your ass for me. Show me what's mine."

She reached around to spread the round globes of her ass, giving me an unobstructed view of her tight asshole and dripping pussy.

I leaned back to take in the sight of her with the script flipped, her now submitting to me, and committing the image to memory.

"So fucking beautiful," I crooned as I quickly worked to undo the buttons on my pants.

Rayven's thick lashes fluttered as she watched me pull myself out. I spit in my palm and rubbed it over my shaft, making sure the silver cuff, the hoop decorating my head, and the silver chain connecting them were properly lubricated for her.

Of all the filthy things I wanted to say to her, a simple "thank you, little human," was what left my tongue. "You have given me the world."

She may not have fully forgiven me. Knowing her, she probably never would. But I had earned a shred of her trust back, or, if not that, her desire. It was a start. I'd spend the rest of eternity earning every shred of her devotion I could possess.

"Brace your hands on the table."

She did as she was told, and when her hands lifted from her ass, mine replaced them. I palmed her supple flesh before giving a few smacks to the left cheek, then to the right. I mumbled a curse as I watched a bright red imprint of my hands appear on her flesh.

I'd never get tired of that color on her.

There was a mirror mounted over the table, a small one framed in silver. I pulled the pin holding her updo in place and gathered her hair in my hand, gripping it at the base of her neck. Pulling up, I forced her up to look in the mirror.

"I want you to watch me enter you. Keep your eyes on me. I want you to see what you do to me."

She sucked her bottom lip between her teeth and gave a nod.

I held her eyes as I kept one hand on her ass while my other encircled my base, guiding my cock to her pussy. My hips canted forward, slipping into her at an agonizing pace. As I stretched her, my mouth dropped open with a strangled moan, my scarred face twisting with pleasure.

She bit tighter on her lip to swallow back her cry. I gave an angry shake of my head, the chains and charms tangling with my antlers at the motion. "I want to hear your sweet and slutty sounds, baby. Let everyone know I can make you feel more than pain."

I sank another couple of inches into her with a harder jab of my hips. This time, she unleashed an animalistic groan that had my cock twitching inside her. Just as quickly as I'd fed it to her, I pulled it out and pushed it in again, letting her get used to my size.

One day, she'd take my full form, but not today. It would be a while before she'd be ready for that. It was possible she'd never want me to take her in my true form. She associated the bone-headed beast with nothing but pain and suffering.

Her whole body shook as I pushed more of me into her, the entirety down to the silver cuff now inside her.

"Goddamn, the chain... I feel it, r-rubbing i–inside."

"And you take it like a fucking goddess," I praised her with another purr. "Now, push yourself back on me, my sweet human."

She leaned back, moving slowly. I finally ripped my eyes from hers to watch the rest of my shaft disappear inside her. "Good girl. You swallow all of me so beautifully. A perfect fit."

"I feel so full."

"That's because you have nine inches of demon cock buried inside this little hole."

"Oh God," she whimpered.

My head snapped up, eyes flashing dangerously in the mirror. "What did I tell you about crying out that name when you're with me?"

"That...that God has no place here."

"Yes, and?"

She swallowed again, her eyes glazing as she stretched back to my words that first night I'd chained her to my bed. "There's no god here. Only darkness and the screams of the damned."

"That's right." I pulled out and slammed back into her, hard enough to make her hands slap against the table. A heated scream tore from her throat, making me thrust in and out of her body at a rapid pace that had her eyes rolling into her head.

I wanted to ride her like this for the rest of the day, ball be damned. But—*blood and darkness*—I couldn't hold back any longer.

My balls drew tight against my body, my cock throbbed inside her, and with a series of frantic, shallow thrusts, I poured myself into her with a broken groan.

She cried, coming for a fourth time seconds after my own climax.

Caught up in the euphoria of it all, my mind was a haze. If I'd been thinking clearly, maybe I wouldn't have gone through with what I was about to do next, but all I could think about was how I needed more of her. Forever. For always. Now that she'd turned down her last chance at freedom, she needed to know she'd be mine for eternity.

There'd be no escape now.

I reached around and grabbed her wrist, twisting it behind her back.

She winced at the awkward angle. "Ow, what are you—"

Her words melted into something between a scream and a moan—an unholy sound that had me hardening again inside her as I sliced into her wrist with my claw.

I made the third cut on her arm, marking that her time was up.

Leaning over her, my chest crushed her against the table. I kissed the shell of her ear, whispering, "You're all mine, little thief, until eternity's end…"

She shivered at the words I'd used when we'd first struck our deal.

I pulled out of her, and she immediately flung herself away from me, cheeks red and eyes full of tears. She stooped and grabbed Catherine's dagger without a word, darting down the hall and away from me.

The thought of chasing after her sprung to mind, but I dismissed it with a dark grin as I stuffed myself back into my pants.

I'd give her space—for now.

It wouldn't be long until I found her again.

CHAPTER NINE

RAYVEN

My feet were moving before I realized I'd decided to run. Without the chain attached to my collar, I was faster than before, whipping around corners and tearing down long, deserted hallways.

I clutched the dagger so hard, my fingers went numb. I wasn't even sure why I grabbed it—I didn't need a weapon—but it felt wrong to leave it behind now that I knew it was Catherine's soul inside.

It's not like I owed anything to the woman who'd died decades ago, but it still felt wrong leaving her with Belial. In any case, he'd offered it to me. It felt like mine now. Plus, Belial had told me to stab him with it. If he did anything shitty to me again, I'd take him up on his offer.

Darting past a suit of armor, I barely registered when it groaned at me to slow down. I was too consumed by the swell of emotions knotting my insides to focus on anything other than the rhythmic beat of my footsteps and my determination to get away. If the weight of reality didn't crush me, my warring thoughts would surely tear me apart.

I needed space. I needed to *breathe.*

Everything was too much and not enough at the same time.

I'd been so sure of myself, so in control for a moment, with Belial on his knees before me.

I forgot his betrayal and lies.

I forgot the manipulation.

I'd gotten so lost in him, in how fucking *good* he felt inside me, that I'd forgotten everything horrible he'd done to me...until he sliced the third cut into my wrist, and all the ugly truths came rushing back.

At least now, all the fucked up facts about this whole situation didn't outweigh the good parts. There was a large part of me—a stupidly smitten, twisted part—that loved Belial *more* than I hated the Lord of Bones.

After what happened just now, I couldn't deny it anymore. I was intensely infatuated with the demon who owned my soul, to the point where I'd been given a second chance to leave and I'd turned it down.

I kept running, knowing if I slowed down or stopped, I'd fall apart. I'd succumb to the wave of emotions chasing me and probably end up sobbing in the middle of the corridor while

Belial's haunted possessions watched—though what was there to be embarrassed about now that they'd seen their lord dick me down over a table?

A violent shiver rattled down my spine at the fresh memory—one so fresh, I could still feel his fingers on my skin, his breath on my nape, and his cum inside me, leaking down my thigh.

Belial kept his word and made me feel something other than pain, but I never imagined I'd feel this *much*.

A catch in my side eventually forced me to slow, and I headed down a flight of stairs. I was lost in the never-ending maze of corridors, with the shifting hallways and useless directions of talking furniture.

I had no clue where I'd been or where I was going. My dress wasn't even trailing blood anymore, so I couldn't retrace my steps.

Though I guess I wasn't trying to find a way out anymore.

Belial would come for me soon and drag me back to the ball. Or his bed.

I fought off the heavy thoughts weighing on me for as long as I could, but once the adrenaline began to ebb, they took over. Belial on the cliff. Seeing his face for the first time, handsome underneath all those scars. Dancing with him in the throne room. The moment he revealed his true self. How I swore I felt my heart breaking when I realized I'd been played. Being dragged through the Styx to sit on his lap like some kind of dog on a fucking leash. Belial on his knees in the hall, begging for my forgiveness. Fucking me senseless in my dreams, in his bed, in the labyrinth.

It all felt like a fever dream, but over the last few days, my wildest fantasies and darkest nightmares had been my reality. I was covered in enough blood and bruises to prove it.

My gaze dropped to the three marks on my wrist, and the corners of my eyes burned. I blinked furiously, but the tears fell anyway, sliding slowly down my cheeks. The truth I'd been avoiding slammed into me with full force, a sob racking my chest.

I leaned my back against the wall and sank to the floor, my blood-stained dress ballooning up around me. I twirled Catherine's dagger between my fingers, watching the candlelight dance over the blade, cursing every decision that led me here. From grave robber to bone queen. Oh, how the tables had turned.

My fate was sealed. There was no running from it now.

I made my choice.

I officially belonged to the devil.

More than that, I was in *love* with the devil.

Approaching footsteps made my chest tight with anxiety. I'd hoped Belial would've waited a few more minutes before he chased after me. I enjoyed our cat-and-mouse game more than I liked to admit, but damn. A girl needed a breather after getting bent over and railed by the Lord of Death while his creepy haunted furniture watched.

Even if he didn't want to have sex again, which seemed doubtful, I wasn't ready to go back to the ball yet either. I wasn't ready for him to announce me as his queen or to wear the spine of my ex-boyfriend as a crown.

I wasn't ready for any of it. Right now, all I wanted was a decent meal and a week-long nap. I picked myself up and smoothed down my dress. Maybe I could bargain with Belial for a burger—if such a thing existed in Limbo—and a bed before he expected an encore of the filthy little show we'd put on earlier.

A dark figure rounded the corner at the end of the hall, and all the blood in my face drained when I wasn't met with Belial's familiar black mask. Even his towering, skull-headed form would have been a welcome sight over the three-headed demon casually strolling in my direction, all six of his devilish eyes pinned on me.

The ridiculous harness and loincloth number would have been comical if it wasn't for the look all three heads were giving me as he approached. I didn't know much about the demon, but it didn't take a genius to know this one was bad news.

What was he doing this far away from the ball? He sure as shit wasn't out for a casual stroll, and with the castle's shifting walls and countless corridors and doorways, chances were low he'd just happened upon me.

This fucker was looking for me.

"What a surprise," the middle head said in a tone that didn't sound surprised in the slightest. "My brother let his new bitch off the chain after all. Guess that means he doesn't care if I have a turn with the pretty mortal cunt you have hidden under that dress now that he's had his fun."

The demon's words were so cruel and heated, I had to choke down my gasp as I hurried to my feet. "I—No. Belial let me off my leash because he realizes I'm not some animal. I'm going to be his queen, and he's going to treat me like one, you creepy fuck."

All three of the demon lord's heads chuckled or laughed, as if I'd told a joke. "Belial might be the softest of us all toward mortals, but he still sees you as a lesser being. Know why?"

He prowled forward, the clomping of his hooves making my skin crawl.

"Because you *are* lesser, you little bitch. Mortals exist in the Nine Hells to serve the demon lords, living or dead."

I shook my head frantically, backing up as he approached. "No. Fuck that. I belong to Belial."

The demon wagged his meaty finger at me. "The Lord of Bones thinks he can horde all the souls passing through his realm, but he can't. Think of this as his lesson on sharing."

"He'll slit your throat and watch you bleed out with a smile if you so much as touch a hair on my head," I threatened, hiding Catherine's dagger in the folds of my skirt. An icy wave clawed up my back as the distance between us shrank. "You'll be lucky if that's all he does."

The threat wasn't working, not with how my voice splintered with fear.

Whatever fucked up plan this demon had for me, he had every intention of going through with it.

His ram head let loose an evil chuckle, and the bull blew a plume of smoke through its nostrils. "If you come quietly, I promise to keep your blood inside your body... Well, some of it."

He held up his hand and wiggled his fingers, showing off his deadly claws. "When I'm bored with your three holes, I'm going to make new ones to fuck."

"Get away from me!" I screamed before whirling around and sprinting down the hall.

The time spent catching my breath had alleviated the pain in my side, but I was still tired from all the running and fucking. If I could just keep my distance for a few minutes, Belial would find me. He was probably already hunting me through the halls, chasing me down like prey.

It wouldn't be long now. He'd catch up, and everything would be okay—

I turned a corner and slammed into something large, tripping over the skirt of my dress and falling back on my ass. My eyes climbed the form, ignoring most of the gaudy gray outfit, and landed on a masked face wearing a wicked smile.

"Where do you think you're going?" Mammon cracked his ring-laden knuckles and took a step toward me. With a gasp, I crawled backward, kicking hastily to put space between us while still clutching the dagger in my hand.

"I can smell my brother dripping from your cunt, girl." He inhaled deeply, letting his chest swell before releasing a throaty groan. "You must really have Belial's dusty cock wrapped tight around your fingers to earn the Lord of Bone's obsession. He doesn't give two fucks about anything these days, not after his last human pet."

"What do you want?" I snapped.

I had a weapon, but I didn't know how much good it would do. These dangerous males were demon kings—hell, they were practically gods. It's not like I was dealing with human thugs you'd find on the streets.

Even if I managed to stab one of them, I was outnumbered and outmatched.

"I think we both know the answer to that, mortal," Mammon huffed in that grating tone of his.

Unable to tear my gaze away from him, I kept scooting back across the threadbare rug, my attention on those beady, bottomless eyes. "We want Belial to resume his duties of ushering souls to the lower levels of hell, but he's too...distracted." He stepped on the hem of my dress to pin me in place. "If we remove the distraction, perhaps things will return to how they were. How they should be."

"Fuck you," I gritted out. I pulled at the dress, but it didn't budge.

"Is that an offer?" Asmodeus' voice came from behind me, making my stomach churn. I'd almost forgotten he was there. "I've never had pussy with a pulse before."

With a cry, I pulled on the fabric again, and it tore, freeing me from Mammon's giant boot. I staggered to my feet and ran, diving past the three-headed demon, and sprinted away while their laughter rattled down the hall after me.

"What a flighty little bird," Mammon laughed, but I could barely hear the words over the heartbeat thundering in my ears. "It'll be much harder to fly with her wings clipped, don't you think, As?"

"She doesn't have any wings, idiot," the three-headed demon snarled. Clearly, he wasn't the brightest of the brothers. "Let's keep this simple and break her legs."

CHAPTER TEN

RAYVEN

Asmodeus' words were terrifying, but what scared me most was Mammon's laugh.

"You're disturbed, As," he chastised, but it sounded more like praise than anything else.

I rounded a corner so fast, I skidded on the rug and nearly crashed into the wall.

"Oooh, careful lovey," a voice said with the sound of clinking porcelain in every word. I looked down to see the frog-shaped teapot sitting on a small table next to a flameless candlestick. I'd run into them my first day in the castle.

My heart lurched into my mouth as I launched into a full sprint down the hallway.

I'd been in this section of the castle before, and it was almost familiar. If I wasn't mistaken, this was the floor with Belial's study. Maybe he'd be there.

When I sped past Catherine's portrait, I remembered the dagger still clutched in my hand. I held it up, hissing, "Any help would be appreciated. You know this place better than me. How can I get away from them?"

When the dagger didn't respond, I shook it and held it to my ear. "Hello? Anyone home?"

I would have felt ridiculous if it wasn't for the fact that I was being chased down by demon lords in a magical castle with shifting walls and sentient furniture.

"Let them catch you," Catherine's voice finally whispered, faint and almost impossible to hear over my labored breathing. It wasn't nearly as clear as the first time she'd spoken. "It's your chance to escape this place."

Okay, so Catherine wasn't going to be any help.

She didn't know shit if she thought Belial's brothers were the lesser evil...

I didn't know if any of them would actually hurt me. I'd gotten the impression that Belial was their ruler—or at least, he had been. Maybe there had been a time when they'd listened to him and obeyed. But if he'd been depriving the other lords of souls, hoarding them here in his realm, would any of them fear him enough not to kill me?

Maybe they'd do it just to prove a point. I wouldn't put it past them if it meant Belial resuming his duties and restoring order in hell.

I swallowed hard and turned down another hall, unsure of how closely the brothers were following me. Were Leviathan and Belphegor involved? Were they hunting me now, as I tried to lose the other demon lords in the labyrinth of corridors?

A figure slid into view at the end of the hall, and I stumbled to a stop. He was dressed all in black, snakelike eyes gleaming behind a horned emerald mask with scale-like spikes. The parts of his skin that I could see were green and scaly. Seeing him was the most surprising of all; I thought of all Belial's brothers, he'd gotten along with Leviathan the most. Now, it seemed he was a snake too.

"Don't be afraid," he said. "I won't hurt you—much."

"Kiss my ass, you creepy motherfucker." I turned to dart back down the hall, but Asmodeus was already making his way toward us.

Fuck, fuck, fuck.

I needed help. As much as I hated to admit it, I needed Belial.

My fingers instinctively went for the dagger that would summon him, but my hopes were dashed in an instant as I remembered I didn't have it on me.

"Belial!" I screamed just as the wall next to me opened up. I dove into the new hallway and screamed his name again, finding relief in the way it echoed off the walls.

Surely, he'd hear me.

I ran, getting even more lost in the maze of halls before checking over my shoulder for my pursuers. To my surprise, they'd disappeared, but I knew better than to assume they were gone. They were probably regrouping, working out a plan to corner me. I couldn't outrun them forever.

Hiding was probably my best bet at losing them. Belial would be able to find me whether I hid or not, but his brothers? Maybe they'd give up and fuck off.

The first door I came to was unlocked. After checking the hall again, I slipped inside and gently closed it behind me. Light from the crimson moon crept in through a window on the opposite wall, illuminating the room in a bloody glow, just enough to see the layout. It looked like an old study that hadn't been used in centuries, everything sprinkled with cobwebs. Bookcases and a small desk were covered in a thick layer of dust.

There weren't any places to hide except beneath the desk, so it would have to do. I couldn't risk going back out into the hall again.

I crawled under the desk, tucking the huge bell of my skirts around me, and tried to slow my frantic breaths.

Belial will save me. The words played in my head like a litany, over and over again, until I really believed them. *Belial will save me.*

He had to. I belonged to him.

For the first time, that didn't seem like such a bad thing.

I'd take the crown made of Mark's bones over this shit. Over running scared. Over being hunted by awful, deplorable demon lords who wanted to do who knew what with me.

Something shifted outside the door. I held my breath, even though my chest hurt.

Had they found me so quickly? Had Belial finally caught up?

The doorknob clicked, and the door swung inward with a groan.

"You can't hide from us so easily, human," a soft, delicate voice danced through the air, making my blood seize. "You reek of mortality. Your blood calls to us demons like a beacon in the night."

Fuck. I was stuck with no way out.

I clutched the dagger for dear life, my fingers aching. If I couldn't run or hide, I'd have to fight. What else could I do?

Fear left me frozen, perfectly still as the footsteps grew louder.

Maybe they'd change their mind. Maybe they'd go away.

Maybe Belial... *Maybe he'll come for me in time.*

"Come out, come out, little human." A demonic hand tipped with vicious claws reached beneath the desk, locking around my wrist, and dragged me out of my hiding space kicking and screaming. I fought before I even made out the white-blonde hair and little black dress, swinging Catherine's dagger at Belphegor's exposed skin. I managed a cut across his chest, which instantly bloomed crimson, but he hardly seemed fazed.

"You're a feisty little bitch," he snarled, grabbing my other wrist with impossible strength. He squeezed until the dagger clattered to the floor. He might have looked dainty in his female form, but his strength was obvious as he snatched my arms behind my back and bent me over the dusty desk. "I'm gonna have fun breaking you."

He pressed close behind me, and everything in me froze as I prayed to whatever god was listening that he didn't shift and...

"Fuck off, Belphegor," Asmodeus said, stepping into the room. "I called first dibs. Wait your turn."

He stepped up, coming to stand on the other side of the desk, a smug smile on his middle face as he dragged a claw down my jawline and over my collarbone. I cringed, fighting the urge to gag. I didn't want his filthy hands anywhere near me.

"Fuck you, you ugly bastard."

"I can see now why Belial likes you so much," Belphegor snickered in my ear. "I wonder what else that filthy mouth can do."

The thought of my mouth near any of these demented fucks turned my stomach, and bile burned the back of my throat.

"I'd rather die," I huffed, fighting in vain against Belphegor's hold.

"That can be arranged." Mammon appeared in the doorway, a dark smile on his face.

"I can arrange to cut your dick off. How about that?" I spat.

In a blink, Asmodeus grabbed the front of my collar, wrenching me up onto my tiptoes. A nauseating grin broke across all three of his faces as he laughed. "I'm going to enjoy every second of you, little slut."

"Belial will slaughter you all." My nose flared at the threat. I could already see the Lord of Bones kicking in the door and ripping them apart with his bare hands.

"If my brother wants you back in one piece, he'll do his fucking job. And if not..." His fingers wrapped around my throat, squeezing until I whimpered against the pain. "...he won't get you back at all."

I opened my mouth to fire off another retort, but something heavy bashed into the back of my skull, and everything went black.

CHAPTER ELEVEN

BELIAL

I DESERVED A DAMN medal for resisting the urge to chase after Rayven and bend her over again, maybe this time in front of my suits of armor in the west wing. I was possessive over my little human, but fucking her in front of the souls languishing around my castle was oddly satisfying. Turned out, I liked showing off my most precious possession.

Maybe one day, I'd take her in front of the mirror I used to communicate with my brothers and let Leviathan watch. It wouldn't help convince my brothers this wasn't the same kind of infatuation I had with Catherine, that what I had with Rayven was different. Still, it might just be worth it to see the Lord of Envy's scales turn an even deeper shade of green.

I leaned against the table I'd just bent her over, one hand flat against the veneered surface while I popped my index and middle fingers past my lips. I watched myself in the mirror as I licked the last traces of my mate clean from my flesh.

Just days ago, I couldn't stand to look at the bare face of my lesser form, not without my mask.

Now, it seemed odd I'd been so ashamed of it for so long. What was there to be ashamed of when a woman like Rayven looked at me like she had?

Catherine had been wrong.

I wasn't hideous. And even if I was, was it such a horrible thing when Rayven found my ancient scars attractive?

Holding eye contact with my reflection, I dropped my hand and slipped it into my pants. My digits curled around my base, and my lips curved when I found the outer metal of my cuff still wet with her.

Smearing her cream down my shaft, I stroked myself, using her as lubricant.

I was aware that the souls seeking refuge in the various pieces of furniture, paintings, and knick-knacks were watching me with bated breath, and frankly, I reveled in the attention. I wanted every soul in my realm to know what she did to me.

Everything about Rayven held me captive—her scent, her taste, her bratty little mouth, those eyes and the way they silently begged me for all the things she didn't dare say out loud. Her smooth flesh with its moon-pale color and the way it stained red beneath my rough hands.

And I hadn't even explored every part of her yet. I still needed to fuck that tight ass.

I wouldn't be surprised if I'd be her first lover there. That pathetic mate of hers from before didn't seem like the type to enjoy her in such a manner. I wasn't sure how many others she'd been with, but I doubted she'd let them venture there.

The thought had my fingers tightening, choking my shaft as my pace turned frantic. My brows twisted, my jaw tightening as the expression on my face took on something wolfish, hunger etching every crease, every scar.

"You're fucking mine, Rayven. You sold yourself to Death, and now, I'll own all of you. Every inch of you. Your soul. Your heart. Your pussy. Your everything. It's all mine. Mine! Down to your very marrow."

My words came out in short, harsh breaths as I chased my release like a rabid dog in heat.

The corridor, despite it being filled with dozens, if not hundreds, of lost souls, was quiet, filled only with my own mutterings and labored breathing...

Until a voice from nearby—the mirror on the wall where I'd forced Rayven to watch herself be taken from behind—spoke. "My L–Lord. Please..."

The ornate mirror sounded so eager, it must have been torture keeping quiet while I had my way with my little queen-to-be. It seemed its patience had run dry. "I've been waiting so long for Judgement. So long. I–I don't even remember my own name, My Lord. I must find peace. Rest, wherever that might be."

I gritted my teeth, anger flaring at the interruption. Keeping my grip anchored to my cock, I swiped at the mirror, knocking it off its hook with my free hand.

"How dare you interrupt me, soul?"

It bounced off the table, shattering the glass and sending shards everywhere before it clattered to the ground. The soul slithered from the ruined object in a wisp of smoke, dissipating to find refuge in something else.

The images of Rayven's naked body, her face contorted with pleasure, the sound of her moans soft in my ear—it all shattered along with the mirror at my feet.

I laced myself back into my pants with a growl and trudged down the hall in search of Rayven. I'd had a feeling pleasuring myself wouldn't sate the fire roaring in my core anyway.

I only felt at rest when I was inside her. It was for that reason, aside from her beauty and her addicting mouth, that I couldn't get enough of her.

My addiction to the mortal female was worsening by the hour. In three days' time, my anger had turned to curiosity, and curiosity had morphed into ball-obliterating obsession.

I needed her, now and always.

I'd chain her to my bed—hells, I'd chain her to my fucking cock for the rest of eternity if it meant abating this gnawing need to have her body wrapped around mine.

Luckily, finding her wouldn't be much of an issue, even in the never-ending halls of my labyrinthian castle. The collar around her neck, or rather, the gem affixed to it that had once belonged to Catherine, was a tracking spell.

I'd released her from the chain tethering her to my throne, but she was still very much on a leash. She always would be.

It was not only for her protection, but for my own sanity.

This way, I'd always know where my little human was.

I followed the tracking spell, its magic calling to me through the twisting hallways, venturing further and further away from the throne room.

Why had she fled this deep into the castle? Maybe she'd gotten lost. She'd learn her way around eventually, and as the castle grew more comfortable with her, it would help her get where she meant to go.

"I know you're close, Rayven..." I drawled as I entered an old study that hadn't been used in decades. The tracking amulet was so close, its magic had the air buzzing. "Why are you in here? Are we playing a game of hide and seek? Because I *will* find you. And when I do..."

I wrenched open the door to a large wooden storage cabinet, expecting to find her hiding inside.

Pure, unholy fury strangled me in its unforgiving grip as I took in the collar lying at the bottom of the cabinet. The metal had been snapped in half—it was sealed with magic, so she wouldn't have been able to break it on her own.

I spun around, searching the room for clues as to what had happened to her.

That was when I smelled them. *My brothers.* The stench of Asmodeus' bull breath and the metallic tang of Mammon's iron still clung to the air. There was a whiff of something else too.

I stepped closer to the old desk in the middle of the study. The dust had been disturbed by a smeared impression of Rayven's breasts.

Rage ignited in my veins as I took in the scene, putting the pieces together on what had happened here.

Someone had bent her over this desk, and she'd struggled.

A few droplets of dark liquid staining the desk's veneer caught my eye. I swept a finger through it and popped it in my mouth. Belphegor's blood.

My teeth ground together as sinful rancor spread through me, turning my insides to ash.

They took her.

My brothers had kidnapped my precious treasure right from under my nose.

* * *

The oversized doors to the throne room slammed open as I burst inside, sending suits of armor flying, their pieces scattering across the floor. The music halted, the dancing guests coming to an abrupt stop as they whirled to face me.

I'd entered as the Lord of Bones, the form that demanded the respect and fear of every soul unfortunate enough to be present.

My rage was palpable. Every being here could taste it, radiating from me and lacing the air like poison.

I stormed through the crowd, and it parted for me, no one daring to stand in my way.

The fire of my eyes leapt in my eye sockets as I searched the throne room for my brothers.

"Where is she?" My voice thundered through the silent hall. "Where is Rayven?"

The guests turned to look around, muttering to one another with confusion in their eyes. They didn't know who Rayven was. I hadn't properly introduced her. I hadn't crowned her.

I should have when I had the chance. Maybe then, they'd give a damn.

My fists balled at my sides. I'd make them give a damn, whether she wore my crown or not.

"Find her! Find the demon lords, and you'll find her!"

Everyone stood still, staring blankly like the helpless sheep they were. Useless, every last one of them.

I roared my anguish, my arm swiping angrily at my side and knocking down a demon with a half dozen horns sticking from his skull. He crashed to the ground, hard enough for everyone in the room to hear, for everyone to take a step back in fear.

Good. They should be scared. They should be *terrified*. That was what they got for not caring that the only thing I'd ever loved was gone. Ripped away from me, right from under my nose.

"What are you all standing around for? Find my queen!" My demand came out so raw and guttural, the castle itself responded. The walls quaked and my bone chandeliers swayed, raining down dust like ash after a volcanic eruption. The Styx splashed up, crimson water washing over the marble floors.

Women screamed, lifting their skirts as the magical fluid containing lost souls soaked into their shoes, panic erupting through the room that had been filled with merriment and music minutes ago. The souls who were unlucky enough to be sprayed with crimson were tangled in the river's blood magic and dragged into the river while they desperately kicked and clawed and fought to escape.

They could all be dragged down to the ninth layer for all I cared.

From the chaos, a skeleton hurried forward. "Lord Belial! You're scaring the guests!"

My attention snapped to the woman, the purest anger snaking through my veins. "You. You were supposed to watch her! That was the entire reason I rescued you from Asmodeus' clutches in the first place!"

I reached for Holga, but instead, I snatched the collar of my librarian who'd darted in front of her, using his skeletal body as a thin shield. "My Lord, please! We thought she was with you!"

Training my flaming gaze on Cecil and his toothy eye sockets, I released my hold on him. I nodded, my hatred turning inward. He was right. I was supposed to be watching her.

It was my job to keep her safe, my job to protect her from anything that could do her harm aside from me, and I'd failed.

"W-we can find the other demon lords, My Lord," Holga stammered from over Cecil's shoulder.

"No…" It was useless. I knew they weren't here. They weren't anywhere in my realm. They'd kidnapped her, and I was the fool who'd left her alone long enough for them to do it.

"Tell the guests to get out. The party is over," I said as I slowly backed up toward the entrance. "I…I have to go."

Cecil looked puzzled, his head tilted to the side. "Go where, my Lord?"

"Down." I turned my back on both him and Holga, unholy fury once again bubbling in my veins. "I'm going to bring my queen back and make these thieves pay for what they've done."

CHAPTER TWELVE

RAYVEN

My senses bled back into focus as I slowly regained consciousness. I'd blacked out once Belial's brothers had caught up to me, but I had no idea how long I'd been out of it. It could have been minutes. It could have been hours.

An unnatural cold prickled over my skin, slowly leeching down to my bones and making my marrow ache. I forced my eyes open with a groan, and as my vision focused, an unsettling feeling pulled under my gut.

I didn't recognize the sharp stalactites stretching down from the dark ceiling. They looked like weapons threatening to fall and skewer me.

The dank smell of dust and decay shoved its way into my lungs, the cold air making my chest seize. I blinked a few times, listening for any movement in the nerve-rattling silence, not keen to let anyone know I was awake.

I swallowed hard. My throat was dry.

Where the fuck am I?

The question repeated over and over in my head, even though I was afraid I already knew the answer. The jagged, unfinished walls didn't belong to Belial's castle. Neither did the icy air, nor the putrid stink of decay.

This must have been a lower level of Hell.

A numbness spread through my insides as the demon lords' plot came slamming back into my mind. They wanted to kidnap me and hold me prisoner until Belial resumed his duties. Did they really expect that he'd just get back to work when he discovered I was missing?

By kidnapping me, they weren't removing a distraction. They were provoking a monster.

Belial... At the thought of my demon lover, an invisible fist squeezed my heart, making my whole chest ache. He was probably still searching, tearing his castle apart to find me.

My hand flew to my throat, a tiny gasp escaping my lips when I found it bare. His collar was gone, and while I'd always imagined the relief of its absence, I felt naked without it. My physical tether to him, the constant reminder of his ownership, was gone.

What would he do when he discovered I was missing?

He definitely wasn't going to go along with his brothers' plan of making him judge every soul in Limbo before giving me back. That would take forever.

I sprang up onto my elbows, head swimming a little, and instantly regretted it.

The bed I was in looked like something straight out of a murder scene, with crimson stains smeared over the ratty old sheets.

It was fucking disgusting, having so much blood everywhere, but whoever called this bed theirs was into it, if the white substance crusting the blood stains was anything to go by. My stomach heaved, and I quickly scrambled off the mattress to the floor before I could add a vomit-colored puddle to the mix.

More blood continued on the floor, on the walls—*fuck*, there was even some on the ceiling. Dismembered torsos—and their various appendages—were tucked into corners and mounted on the walls.

It was a serial killer's wet dream.

I would have thrown up again if my stomach wasn't empty.

There weren't words to describe the terror that flooded my system as I scanned the rest of the room.

Whoever called this place home was truly evil.

Aside from the bed, there were other pieces of furniture, or what I thought was furniture at first glance. A few steps closer instantly had me backpedaling when I realized they were all torture devices, blood-stained and well-worn.

A shiver danced up my spine.

On the opposite wall, a shredded piece of black fabric was tossed over what looked like a standing mirror, and next to it was a closed door. A flicker of relief pierced the dread flooding my system, and I ran for it before I could work out anything resembling a real escape plan. I just had to get out of this filthy, sin-soaked room.

Then, I'd figure out a way to get back to Belial.

I might have been a prisoner in Limbo, but it was nothing compared to the utter despair of this place. Hell, it had almost started to feel like home.

I ripped open the door, ready to run, and found my path blocked by a towering figure.

A scream froze in my throat when I found myself pinned under the glare of six narrowed eyes. My attention flitted between all of them before settling on the pair in the middle, dark and gleaming with malice.

"Going somewhere?" Asmodeus chuckled, and I backpedaled, tripping over the skirt of my dress and landing on my ass. I cried out as my tailbone smacked the stone floor.

I didn't miss the way the bulge tenting his loincloth twitched at my scream.

"You can't leave yet. The fun hasn't even started." The demon entered the room, closing the door behind him. The click of the handle latching shut had a lump swelling in my throat.

I guess this really was Hell, because I couldn't think of a worse fate than being locked in this place with a creature like Asmodeus. It seemed his type of lust extended from mere physical attraction and sex to full-on bloodlust.

"I'm leaving," I said, sounding much braver than I felt as I staggered back to my feet. "Get out of my way."

He laughed again, this time louder, the noise echoing off the barren walls. "I thought you would have gotten the picture by now, you pathetic bitch. You're meant to serve the demon lords, and for the time being, I'm your new Lord and Master."

He took a step toward me as he undid the leather strap of his loincloth and tossed it to the side, leaving him completely naked.

If the three mismatched heads and the creepy, goat-like legs tipped with hooves weren't enough to put me off, the thick, wrinkly dick hanging between his meaty thighs sure was.

"Like what you see?" He smirked at me like he was proud.

I wrinkled my nose. "Not really. Your brother's is, like, twice as big."

This wasn't the time or place to run my mouth, but I couldn't help it. There was no "switch" to turn off my bratty attitude, which was exactly what had gotten me into trouble with Belial in the first place. Well, beyond the whole robbing his ex-pet's grave thing.

Even though I knew I was tits-deep in shit with Asmodeus, I couldn't help firing off the first smart-ass retort that came to mind.

The demon moved so fast, there was no time to react before he back-handed me across the face, hard enough to send me flying onto the bed.

Skull ringing and my cheek stinging, I blinked away the stars dancing across my field of vision in time to see the demon lord charging at me.

I tried to scramble away, but his huge, sausage-like fingers caught my ankle and dragged me back across the soiled linens. "Get back here, you bitch."

Using every iota of strength, I thrashed as hard as I could, but it was no use. He was three times my size, easily. It was like a fly trying to take out a gorilla.

He crawled on top of me, his guttural laugh scraping over my skin like sandpaper and his noxious breath filling my nostrils, making my head swim.

"Get the fuck off me!" I screeched, nails slashing at his eyes—any of them. He kept laughing as he gripped my wrists in one hand and pinned them over my head while his other reached for the hem of my dress.

No. No. *No.*

This couldn't be happening.

Another scream tore from my throat. Asmodeus wasn't laughing anymore. His eyes flashed with anger, and his bull head breathed a cloud of smoke in my face while the middle head growled at me to shut up.

"Stay still, or I'll move you from the bed to The Rack."

I wasn't sure what "The Rack" was, but I ventured a guess that it was one of the grisly torture benches decorating Asmodeus' bedroom.

When his hand brushed my upper thigh, I bucked, and my knee came up—slamming right into his balls.

He stiffened, and his grip on my wrists loosened just enough to pry a hand free and bury my fingernails into the eyes of his center head.

The howl of pain he released pierced my ears, the pain of it dulling the second smack he gave to my other cheek.

"Asmodeus." The voice that echoed through the room shattered through my senses and rattled me down to my bones. I had no idea where it came from, but it was there, clear as day. That deep baritone haunted my dreams and soothed me in my darkest nightmares. "Do you know what you've done? What you've stolen from me?"

From the dread knotting my insides rose a glimmer of hope as Belial's voice filled Asmodeus' room. How was he speaking to the Lord of Lechery all the way from Limbo?

"Belial! Help—" Asmodeus clamped his clammy palm over my mouth, silencing me. He glared at the mirror. *The mirror!*

I craned my head as far as the demon's grip on me would allow, and my attention landed on the mirror next to the door covered by the sheet.

Maybe it was some kind of communication system the lords of the nine realms used to communicate with one another.

"I know exactly what I've stolen from you, brother. I've re-homed your mortal pet. I'd like to see for myself how good her warm pussy must be to distract you from duties for three fucking centuries."

"It's my *queen* you've kidnapped, you three-headed fuck smear. I'm going to take immense pleasure in tearing off your pus-filled heads one by one and sticking them on a pike. It will make a pretty little scepter for my new queen."

Belial's threat seemed to make Asmodeus falter for a moment, but he recovered a beat later, throwing his heads back with a mirthless laugh. "If there's anything of your *queen* left once I've had my fun with her."

A gust of wind carried through the room, coming from the mirror and blowing the sheet covering the glass to the ground.

The Lord of Bones' reflection filled up the reflective surface. He looked imposing in his heavy cloak that revealed his muscular chest heaving with every breath he took. The fire filling his eye sockets leapt high, like gas being poured over an open flame, as he clutched my broken collar in his fist, holding it tight to his heart. "Rayven, if you can hear me—"

With a roar, my captor reached for a severed hand on the nightstand and hurled it across the room. It slammed into the mirror hard enough to shatter the glass, and Belial's reflection flickered. I screamed against Asmodeus' sweaty hand as the image faded, replaced by a fractured image of his bedroom.

My view of the mirror blurred as fat tears filled my eyes, but I refused to let them fall. Crying would only heighten the sickening satisfaction Asmodeus was getting out of this.

"On your fucking knees, bitch. Kneel before your new lord."

His hand left my mouth, only to knot in my hair. He wrenched me off the bed and shoved me to the floor. My knees scraped against the rough stone, sprinkled with shards of bone and other pieces of god knew what. Keeping one hand rooted in my hair, he took his other and fisted his cock, giving it a pump before pushing it toward my face. "Open that whore mouth. Bite me, and I'll slit your throat."

There was no time for me to scream. It wouldn't have done any good anyway. I needed a plan...

Belial knew I was here, but I didn't know how long it would take for him to come and get me.

I couldn't just sit around like a damsel in distress, waiting for her knight. Not when I was stuck in a castle with the knight's rape-y brother.

Asmodeus filled my mouth with a thrust of his hips.

In my periphery, all three of his heads fell back on his broad shoulders, groaning his delight, "Fuck me. If your other holes feel half as good as your mouth, no wonder Belial has his dick in a knot over you. You make for one hell of a cock sleeve."

Disgust wound through my body, and if I had anything left in my stomach, I probably would have vomited on his cock. Too bad—the fucker deserved it.

Though, knowing him, he might enjoy knowing how sickening I found all this. Because that's all this was; A fucked up kind of torture, which, by the look of things, was the Lord of Lust's specialty.

His fingers curled tighter into my hair, claws scraping my scalp as he jerked me against him, sinking his member deep into my throat.

One of his heads snickered at the way I gagged, barely able to breathe around the invasion.

"Look at me," he demanded.

My eyes lifted to meet his. His lips bowed at the hateful shadows roiling behind them. "Suck me, *little queen.*"

The mocking in his voice had liquid fire tearing through my veins.

He tasted like rancid flesh, and if I lived through this, I was scared I'd never be able to wash his taste from my mouth.

He'd warned me not to bite him...but if I died, what would become of my soul? It would probably still be here, trapped with him until Belial came. And Belial *would* come for me, whether I was dead or not.

So, what was there to lose?

Before I could talk myself out of it, I bit down on the appendage—hard.

Asmodeus let out a roar loud enough to shake the nine realms, but I didn't let up. I bit down again and again. Thick, viscous blood bloomed over my taste buds, washing away the taste of old cum and sweaty flesh.

He tried to scramble away from me, but it was too late. The final bite severed his flesh completely, and I felt it come loose in my mouth.

I spit out the chunk of severed meat along with a mouthful of blood. It streamed down my chin, dripping down my chest and peppering the floor at my knees.

My wide eyes pinged up to see the demon lord stumbling, falling backward onto his bed, pure shock etched into each of his sheet-white faces. He clutched the jagged bits of skin between his legs where his cock had been a second ago.

And just like that, I felt my power return. Even now, on my knees, covered in blood with a shriveled dick before me. Hell, especially now.

I rose to my feet, my lips slowly stretching into a manic grin. "And when Belial gets here, he's going to remove your other heads. Isn't it cute, the way we coordinate like that?"

CHAPTER THIRTEEN

Rayven

"You...fucking...bitch," he bit out between whimpers of pain.

"Serves you right, you nasty fuck."

I spit out another mouthful of blood at his feet then turned and ran for the door. I barreled into the hallway as I heard Asmodeus struggle to his feet behind me. I only had a few seconds to get a head start before he caught up.

I had to find a way out—*now*.

There was more carnage in the corridor. Blood and bones and soft blobs that looked a lot like rotting flesh were strewn all over the floor. If there were servants, they were nowhere to be seen.

There was only the eerie sensation that I was being watched, probably by the poor souls who were sentenced to spend the rest of their eternities here.

No wonder Belial didn't like sending souls down the Styx to his brothers. Fading away inside a teapot didn't seem like such a bad fate compared to this hellscape.

Asmodeus' entire castle looked like something straight out of an old-school swords and sorcery movie, an old underground fortress that had been built into an ancient cavern. Spikes rose from the ground, one decorated with a male torso that had long since had its limbs removed. Another had a full skeleton, entrails wrapped around its neck like a scarf.

Okay. Fuck. This would all just have to go in the little box in the back of my mind, the same place I'd stuffed my run-in with the flesh-eating tree that nearly had me for lunch back in Belial's labyrinth. This was no time to let the human emotions out.

Exit. That's all I could afford to think about right now. Find a way out before Asmodeus could put his hands back on me.

Feet moving as quickly as they could carry me, I searched for an exit. I was exhausted from all the fucking running, but Asmodeus' heavy footsteps behind me pushed me forward. Now that he couldn't rape me, his punishments would probably get more creative. I was sure it would involve his macabre collection of medieval torture instruments.

The floors were uneven, and the halls were unnaturally tight in some places, feeling more like an elaborate cave system than an actual home.

It was strange and immediately disorienting, even more so than Belial's castle. I made a right and hurried down a flight of steps carved into the stone, thankful for the torches burning along the corridors to light the way. There were no windows, no other lights.

Such a dim, lifeless miserable pit of a place. No wonder Holga was desperate to stay in Belial's good graces; an eternity of servitude in Limbo was better than any amount of time here.

A left turn led me into a huge cavern that looked to be the throne room, and I stumbled to a stop to catch my breath. It was a wide space, with a high ceiling, more giant stalactites, and a horde of mangled body parts tucked into every corner. Interesting patterns of stone stretched their way up the walls like pillars, but my eyes were drawn to the middle of the room. What I thought was a red carpet at first was actually a coagulated layer of blood gleaming on the stone floor in the torchlight.

So. Much. Blood.

"Jesus—" I said, but a rumble beneath my feet cut me off.

The stone was vibrating like it was suddenly alive, and I squeaked. A distant roar sounded behind me, coming from deep within the maze of hallways, and I took off across the throne room.

Past the giant spill of blood, which was tacky beneath my boots, sat a large, twisted throne. I assumed it was carved from wood, given that the rest of Asmodeus' castle looked hand-chiseled, but as I got closer, the sickening truth of the royal chair had me gagging.

Bodies, all beautiful—or at least, they once had been—nude women, were curved and contorted to create the Lord of Lechery's disturbing throne. Their lifeless faces were now hollowed and blood-stained like the rest of their flesh.

I wanted to scream, but the sound stuck in my throat.

Those poor women, all forced to serve that sick, demented bastard even after their souls were long gone.

I was even more glad I'd bitten off his dick. It was hardly retribution for all the horrors he'd caused, but it was a start.

Prying my eyes away, I darted deeper into the room. I could hear Asmodeus' curses and snarls growing louder, the tremors in the stone growing stronger as he approached.

Just like in Belial's castle, the walls, the floors, and even the furniture seemed to submit to their lord and master.

I searched for another exit, but there was none.

Ahead, drifting lazily by, was the familiar River Styx, just as it had in Belial's throne room.

Slow, somber, unperturbed. Bits of carrion bobbed in the bright red water, which drifted in through a small, shallow opening in one wall and disappeared out the one opposite.

A wild idea sparked, but I wasn't sure if it would work. The last time I was in the Styx, I hadn't been whisked away magically or anything but...could it get me out of here?

I shifted on the spot, knowing my seconds were running out before Asmodeus came barreling into the throne room, but I was unsure. It was my only option right now, but if it didn't work, if Asmodeus caught me and drowned me in the river of blood...

"I'll make you pay, you fucking bitch!" I spun around to see Asmodeus stumbling into the room, his hand still clutching the bloody stump between his legs.

With the way he staggered with every step, maybe he wouldn't be able to catch up to me.

Another quake shook the cavern, dust raining down from the ceiling. My hand launched out, grasping for something to steady myself. "Oh, fucking nasty," I cried out when my fingers plunged into the rotting chest cavity of a one-armed torso speared onto one of the spikes.

I yanked my hand back and screamed when the torso's arm snatched for me, its bony fingers—with bits of flesh still clinging to the joints—capturing my wrist.

My pulse lurched as the human remains strewn around the giant cavern started to twitch and shift to life. Skeletons rattled to their feet, severed lumps slithered across the floor, leaving slimy trails of gore in their wake. The bodies impaled onto the stalagmite spikes shivered and gurgled, reaching for me with whatever rotten appendages remained.

An invisible hand raked down my back, ice branching down my spine and freezing my system over. This was like when I'd fallen down the oubliette with all those hands reaching for me, touching me. *Hurting* me.

Only, Belial wasn't here to pull me to safety.

With a scream, I slammed my free hand down on the joint of the skeletal arm holding me, karate-chop style. The dusty joint broke, and I shook myself free, the bone clattering to the ground.

"Don't let her get away!" the demon lord snarled at the carrion as he limped toward me.

I hopped over a hand dragging itself in my direction, trying not to look too hard at the tattered flesh from where the arm had been severed at the elbow. Another hand pulled at my dress, and a skeleton pierced to a wall with a rusted spear snatched at my hair.

Tamping down on my fraying nerves, I plucked myself free and whirled around, making a break for the Styx.

"Oh my..." My whisper came out hoarse, terror and pure shock winding tight as I took in the most gruesome, horrifying sight I'd ever laid eyes on.

Standing in my direct path to the Styx was the Lord of Lechery's throne of rotten flesh.

It had come to life.

Writhing flesh began to ripple and shift, like water under a foam-choked pond. Then, the limbs and hunks of meat started to discorporate from each other, and I could make out the female bodies as they rose, reaching out for me.

Their skin was a mottled gray, with bits of bone peeking out from the holes in their ripped and mutilated flesh. They sloshed and creaked as they moved toward me, and I couldn't tell if it was bones and bodies breaking or reknitting themselves together. Dozens of dead and gaping eye sockets honed in on me, and I could see a deeper presence behind them.

Almost like parts of their souls remained.

"You fucking monster," I cried out to Asmodeus, anguish and fury making my voice shake. "How could you do this to poor, innocent women?"

"Innocent? They are anything but," the demon retorted, his voice demonic and booming as it filled the whole room. "Or they wouldn't have been sent to me."

"No one deserves this. No wonder Belial doesn't send you souls anymore. You don't deserve to govern rocks, let alone mortal souls."

When I'd first learned of the souls languishing around Belial's realm, I'd felt sorry for them. But languishing around in what was Hell's waiting room for all eternity was paradise compared to here.

Belial hadn't stopped sending souls down the Styx because he was lazy, or even because he was distracted. It was because he was merciful.

If he had the time and the help, I was sure he'd place almost every soul in his library where they could rest in some version of peace.

"As the future queen of Limbo, I'm going to make sure this place never sees so much as another soul." My words came out sure, sounding every bit the vow it was.

The throne's pieces faltered, and they collapsed on the ground, one by one. It took me several intense seconds to realize they were kneeling.

Holy. Fuck.

These bodies were submitting to me.

As if I was their lord and master, instead of Asmodeus.

Like some kind of queen of carrion.

Asmodeus roared another command to his army of undead, but they weren't listening.

Using the distraction, I made my way to the edge of the River Styx, steeling my nerves before jumping feet first into the bloody current.

My skirts billowed up on the surface like a makeshift life jacket. At some point, this thing would be so crusted over, it would stand up on its own.

I waited, but nothing happened, my flicker of hope dimming.

"Fuck, why isn't it working?" I muttered, turning around to see Asmodeus storming through his throne, kicking the women aside.

All six of his eyes were lit with deadly hatred.

Shit. Shit. Shit!

If this sick bastard got his hands on me, there wouldn't be any pieces of me left for Belial to put back together.

I turned and hurried with the current toward the wall with the small opening where the Styx trickled out, hoping that some magic current would come along and sweep me to the next realm. Whatever lay further down the river, it had to be better than here. I banged on the stone wall, pain lancing up my arms, but to no avail.

"Please, please, please."

"Please. Please. Please," Asmodeus mocked as he stepped closer to the edge of the Styx. His goat head brayed as his other two laughed cruelly. "Don't you see? There's no escape for you. You'll never get back to Limbo. You'll never be queen. The closest you'll ever come to demon royalty is when I sew you into my throne. What a pretty new addition your corpse will make."

My eyes burned with acid tears, visceral hatred snaking through my veins. "Whatever Belial does to you, I hope you fucking suffer. "

With a sharp inhale, I plunged into the water, completely submerging myself. It was a feeble attempt to buy a few more seconds, though I was sure it was pointless. After all, since Belial owned my soul, the Styx didn't affect me. I'd known that, but still, I'd hoped...

I want to get away. Please, take me away.

Something grabbed my foot, and I fought the urge to scream—drowning in blood and who knew what else wasn't how I wanted to go out. The thought of Asmodeus ripping me out of the Styx was instantly torn away when I started to move, dragged along with the current. The tug intensified, and my thoughts turned to white noise.

The current grew stronger, carrying me down river and away from Asmodeus' throne room to the next unknown layer of Hell.

CHAPTER FOURTEEN

RAYVEN

My lungs burned as the current rushed me along, but I couldn't move or swim to the surface. I was trapped, my limbs pinned to my sides as I slowly suffocated.

I couldn't die like this.

I hadn't survived Asmodeus' sexual torture just to accidentally drown.

When there was no air left in my lungs and unconsciousness began to leach from the corners of my mind, something grabbed me by the arm and wrenched me upward.

Before I concerned myself with who or what had hold of me, I gasped and swallowed as much air as I could get into my lungs the second I breached the river's surface.

I sputtered and coughed, wiping the blood from my face with equally blood-soaked hands.

I was drenched and dripping with death, half-starved and out of my mind, but I was alive.

A few blinks cleared my vision, and I stared up at my savior, who was perched on the river's bank, looming over me with a curious gleam in his eyes.

Without his masquerade mask, Leviathan's face looked much more serpentine. Pronounced cheekbones curved down to his pointed chin, and his slitted eyes locked on me with unbridled curiosity. His skin was green and snake-like, his scales glimmering like wet stones in the dim lighting.

I immediately snatched my arm from his grip.

"I'm surprised you got away from my brother in one piece," Leviathan chuckled, reaching down to offer me a hand. "Asmodeus must be losing his touch."

I shrank away, crossing to the other side of the river. "He definitely lost more than his touch," I snapped, voice dripping with poison.

My eyes darted past the serpentine demon to observe this new area.

It was another cavern, built straight into some cliff face or another, but this cave had a totally different feel from Asmodeus'. Streams of water dripped down the dark walls like an oil spill, and the steady crash of water in the distance hit my ears. It was exactly the kind of place a snake like Leviathan would call home, but at least it wasn't covered in blood and littered with body parts. Not to mention, the temperature here was normal, and it smelled vaguely of salt, seaweed, and something entirely unique to this realm, exotic and smokey.

My attention slipped further down the Styx, noting how it stretched into the distance and dissolved into darkness. I couldn't make out anything that far into the cavern, but I was tempted to keep following the bloody river. Granted, it was taking me farther away from Belial, but the thought of lingering in any of these other realms was enough motivation to keep running.

"You won't find what you're looking for down there," he said, jerking his head in the direction I'd been staring. His snake-like tongue uncurled from his mouth, licking his thin lips before darting back in again. "Come. I can help you."

"And why the fuck would I believe you, asshole?" I stared at his hand like it might grow fangs and bite me. "How do I know you won't try to rape or kill me?"

A thin smile split across his face, making him look even more serpent-like. "You don't. But as the Lord of Lust, it's kind of Asmodeus' thing to rape and pillage. The rest of us aren't such..." He clicked his tongue as he seemed to search for the word. "Brutes."

I barked a hollow laugh. "Brute? Fuck off. The guy is the straight up devil."

"We all are," Leviathan mused. "The Demon Lords of Hell all have their unique ways of showing it. Asmodeus' is just the least creative."

My head was spinning as I scrambled to come up with a plan. At first, I thought it was because I was overwhelmed, but then, the cavern began to spin too. I stumbled, my eyes fluttering. After everything I'd done to get here, I was going to pass out and drown in the damn Styx. Leviathan only cocked his head, bemused.

"I..." No words would form. It was too late. I was going down.

I slumped, trying and failing to catch myself on the slick stone wall behind me.

Then, just as Leviathan stepped into the Styx with darkened eyes, everything went black.

I was swaying, rocking slowly back and forth, clutched tightly in the strange safety of Belial's embrace. He'd removed his mask, his handsome features and scars on full display as he carried me across his bedroom.

"Belial," I tried to say, but my voice didn't come.

He laid me on his bed, the familiar ceiling stretched overhead, and smiled down at me. One of his hands danced over my arm, teasing my breasts, dipping lower. I gasped, surprised by the coldness of his touch.

The image dissolved, and I blinked my eyes open, expecting to find myself nestled in Belial's bed. Instead, I found myself staring up at more than a dozen curved copper bars that met at a point above me.

Everything came rushing back like a maelstrom. I wasn't in Belial's castle anymore.

No, I was in the care of his brother Leviathan, the scaley motherfucker who'd been the most aloof of the demon brothers who'd attended the masquerade.

I rose up on my knees, feeling too light-headed to stand. I was in a giant cage, one that didn't appear to have a door of any kind—likely sealed with magic.

But the lack of a door was the least of my problems.

I was completely fucking naked.

My arms flew up to wrap around my exposed body. I frantically searched the cage for my dress, but I knew it was gone. He'd taken it and my boots.

My boots. Fuck!

I'd already lost them once, but something told me they were gone for good this time. I definitely wasn't doing any sexual favors to get them back like I had in Belial's hedge maze.

Panic clawed up my throat, and my heart pounded so hard in my chest, I thought it might explode.

There was only one thing I trusted about Leviathan, and that was for him to be no worse than Asmodeus. Maybe that was giving him too much credit.

Frantically, I grabbed two bars and tried to pry them apart, but they wouldn't budge.

"Don't hurt yourself, pet," a voice said, making me jump. I turned to see Leviathan sprawled out on a bed next to the cage, his scaly head propped up on one hand. He was smoking a hookah, smoke ringlets puffing out of his slitted nostrils periodically as he ogled me like I was his most prized possession.

"I'm not your fucking pet." I did my best to cover my chest, though it didn't matter. He'd already seen all of me if he got me out of my dress. Still, I felt gross with his eyes on me.

He hissed a laugh, the noise snaking through the cavern. "I've got you trapped in a cage. I'd say that makes you my pet, don't you?"

I scowled, hot anger flashing through me. "Where's my dress?"

"I burned it." He took another drag from the hookah's mouthpiece before exhaling a cloud of winding smoke. "I'm surprised Belial kept you clothed at all. Pets don't wear clothes, especially considering what he used you for."

A chill worked through me at the way the snake demon eyed me. "I'm surprised he didn't keep a prize like you naked and chained to his bed around the clock. But then again, he's always been reckless with the things he didn't deserve."

Understanding suddenly clicked into place. "You're the Lord of Envy, aren't you?"

If he was surprised by my guess, he didn't show it. "Clever girl. I suppose I'm not surprised the Lord of Bones likes showing you off."

With another puff on his hookah, he blew an enormous cloud of smoke. It morphed into the shape of a snake, twisting and coiling through my cage bars. After a few seconds, it dissipated, and he sent me a sly smile. "Entertain whatever delusions you have in that pretty head of yours, but you've only just met Belial. I've known him for centuries..."

"So?" I hissed, my hands gripping the bars of the cage.

"*So,* he tires of his toys and moves on quickly." He chuckled dryly, shaking his head. "Once he resumes his duties, I'm sure he'll forget all about you."

I knew he was lying—there was no way Belial wasn't coming for me after what he'd seen in the mirror—but the words still stung. It was true; I'd only known the Lord of Limbo for a short amount of time, but he owned my soul. He *loved* me.

Wherever he was right now, I knew he was looking for me. The feeling sank all the way to my bones, making them ache.

He would come for me, and he'd punish every one of the demon lords who had anything to do with kidnapping me. He'd turn the nine realms inside out—anything to get me back.

I had trust issues with the King of Limbo, but if I trusted him to do anything, it was that.

"You *think* you know Belial," I countered, turning my back to him. The cavern Leviathan used for a bedroom opened to reveal a cloudy sky over a jet-black ocean. White crests rolled onto a beach, and in the lulls of conversation, I could hear the water crashing. "How long has it been since any of you gave a fuck about him? People change, even demons."

Another smoke snake slithered in through the bars of the cage, wrapping around me. Its mouth nipped at my exposed nipples before I swatted a hand through it, diffusing the smoke.

"You've seen so much for a human yet know so little."

Leviathan slithered off the bed, his bare feet padding over to the side of my cage, where he squatted to be eye level with me.

The cage was so small, there wasn't much room to put distance between us—it was only a few feet wide in length. I didn't like how close we were—enough to feel his breath through the bars, dancing over my naked skin.

His slitted eyes roamed over my body with unguarded desire as a fork-tipped tongue flicked out to lick his thin lips. Ugh. He was a total creep.

"How will you feel when he doesn't come for you? When he leaves you here to rot in my realm?" He stuck his hand through the bars, which were barely wide enough to accommodate his arm, and trailed his fingers along my cheek.

I jerked back from his touch and forced a disturbed smile across my lips. "Careful—I bite. Just ask Asmodeus."

"Yes..." the demon mused, a thoughtful look pulling at his scaly features. "What did you do to the Lord of Lust?"

"Let's just say he's going to need a new title. What, with not having a dick anymore."

Surprise lifted Leviathan's hairless brows. "Really?"

"Really," I snapped, my fiery gaze locked on his. "So keep your hands to yourself, or I'll chop your dick off too."

Leviathan tsked his tongue. "That's no way for a delicious pet to behave, especially if she wants to be fed."

My ears perked up at the mention of food.

He produced a half-shell oyster out of thin air, holding it up between his fingers for me to see. I scrunched my nose at it; I'd never been a big seafood fan, but oysters were probably the bottom of the barrel as far as my least favorite foods went.

Despite that, my stomach rumbled loudly as he shoved the shell through the bars.

"I'm not eating that."

"You can always starve." Leviathan shrugged a shoulder and started to withdraw his hand. "It makes no difference to me."

The hunger pains cramping my stomach had me rethinking my decision. "Wait."

He froze while I struggled to cling to the last shred of willpower I possessed. I was starving. How long had it been since I'd eaten anything? Twenty-four hours, at least? I couldn't afford to be picky.

"What did you do to it?" I asked, eyeing the nasty, booger-colored blob nestled in the Lord of Envy's palm.

The last time I took food from a stranger, I had magical pervy dreams. Not that I regretted my sex dream with the Lord of Bones, but I had a feeling Leviathan's oyster wouldn't be anything like Belial's plum.

"If I wanted to kill you, I've had ample opportunities so far," he said without moving. "I'm not going to hurt you."

I scoffed, rolling my eyes. "Oh, so you only want to hurt me in front of your brothers? Now you want to, what? Keep me safe? I'm not buying it."

This close, I could make out his sharp, serrated teeth when he grinned, and they made my stomach drop. Leviathan might have seemed docile compared to his brothers, but there was something dark lurking beneath his charming façade. He might be playing nice for now—aside from the whole stripping me naked and shoving me in a cage thing—but I knew he could be vicious, deadly if I pushed his buttons.

"Keep you, yes. Safe? I suppose that depends on how good of a pet you are," he said, wiggling the oyster in front of my face. My stomach churned at the way it jiggled in its shell. "You'll find I can be rather...persuasive when it comes to getting what I want."

I wasn't sure what exactly he wanted, but it had to be more sinister than me eating an oyster.

We sat there, eyes locked in a stalemate, before my hunger won out over my willpower. I reached for the shell in his hand, licking my lips at the thought of sustenance, but he snatched it back out of my reach.

"Open," he urged, shoving the shell in my face.

Gross—he wanted to feed me.

"Get fucked, asshole," I growled, clamping my lips shut. I was already trapped in a cage; I didn't want to eat out of his hand like a goddamn animal. I was also tired of men shoving things in my mouth without my permission.

"Come now, pet," he urged, wiggling the oyster back and forth. "Be good and eat for me. You have to be hungry after your ordeal."

My stomach growled painfully again, and my resolve crumbled. As I opened my mouth and allowed him to tip the oyster against my lips, I decided I hated Leviathan just as much as the rest of Belial's brothers. I hated them all, but if it meant I'd get to eat, I'd behave—for now.

What the fuck else could I do?

As soon as I got the chance, I wouldn't hesitate to chop off one of his body parts. I hoped I got the opportunity.

I nearly gagged as the oyster slid down my throat, swallowing extra hard to choke it down. It was just as awful as I'd expected, but at least it was nourishment.

Leviathan stood and tossed the shell aside, sending it skittering across the damp floor.

"You're quite pretty when you do as you're told," he admired, but his voice wasn't full of lust the way Belial's was when he said it. He almost sounded impressed, like I was an oddity he wanted to observe and study. Something he wanted to admire until he got bored and eventually destroyed me.

As uncomfortable as I was, I could still safely say I'd rather be here than fucked to death by Asmodeus. It was the tiniest of silver linings.

"You said you'd give me more food," I said, expecting him to produce some bread or fruit—or hell, even another oyster—but he didn't.

"Yes, but I didn't say *now.*"

The serpentine demon lounged back onto the bed, snatching up the hookah and taking a long drag. We sat like that, staring at one another through his constant cloud of slithering smoke, for what felt like hours.

"You're probably tired," he said, finally breaking the silence. His eyes roamed over me, that gleam of curiosity never leaving his gaze no matter how long he stared. "You should rest while

I watch over you. Let me hear all the delicious noises you make while you dream."

"You want to watch me sleep?"

"I want to watch you breathe, sleep, *be*." He blew a fat smoke ring into the air above him. "Living creatures don't exist in the land of the dead. You're the most exciting thing to happen in this realm in the last five hundred years. Why wouldn't I be fascinated?"

"You're a fucking creep." I rolled my eyes and laid down on the bottom of the cage, facing him and curling in on myself so he couldn't jack off to the site of my tits while I slept.

It's not like I could do anything else in my prison, and I did need to rest. My body was weak with exhaustion, and my eyelids were heavy. If I got the chance to escape, I needed my energy.

I had a feeling I'd be fighting off more demon lords before everything was over.

CHAPTER FIFTEEN

BELIAL

"THIS IS YOUR LAST chance to get off the ferry, both of you," I grumbled down to Cecil and Holga from the back of the gondola. "Don't say I didn't warn you."

Soon, we'd be entering Asmodeus' realm. The moment we passed the barrier, there'd be no turning back—not until I had Rayven. I'd chase her down to the frozen lake if that's what it took.

"We're not leaving you alone, Sire." Cecil sat beside Holga on the bench at my feet, his boney arm wrapped tightly around her shivering form.

I couldn't blame her for being terrified. Her soul had resided in the second layer, in Asmodeus' care, for hundreds of years. Knowing that brutal fuck, he'd done unspeakable things to her.

Something akin to guilt stabbed at my chest. I'd been the one to send her off to him. Back then, it felt like a just punishment for trying to help Catherine escape.

Maybe I was just as cruel and heartless as my brothers. All she'd done was what I'd asked of her: protect my mortal treasure from all dangers. The witch took her job seriously, so of course that meant protecting her from the greatest danger of all. *Me.*

Now, here she was, insisting she accompany me to the second circle so she could help protect and care for Rayven, even if it meant returning to the horrible place she'd been trapped in for years.

Poor Cecil was terrified too. As my librarian, he'd never been to the other eight realms of Hell. He was used to the quiet of my library and nothing else. But when Holga had insisted on accompanying me, he'd refused to stay behind.

"You're fools then," I muttered as I pushed the oar made of bone and tipped with a blue-flamed lantern, guiding the vessel deeper down into my realm. It had been so long since I'd ferried one of my own gondolas. Hells, it had been forever since any of my psychopomps had gone to the lower realms.

There weren't enough souls passing Judgement through limbo to warrant the ferries anymore. There was only the occasional soul, in which case I'd simply toss them into the Styx. Any of the souls I could stomach sending to my brothers these days didn't deserve the fanfare of an official ferryman.

"My Lord, if I may..." Cecil turned in his seat to look up at me with his tooth-filled eye sockets. "Perhaps we should summon one of your ferrymen to escort us? You are the king. You shouldn't have to—"

"I may be the king of Limbo, but I am still a psychopomp. If I am going to send a ferry to rescue Rayven, it's going to be with me at the helm."

Not to mention the added fact that I possessed Rayven's soul. No other demon deserved to ferry my queen over the Styx but me.

It had been so long since I'd traveled the Styx downstream. It was beautiful, at least in my realm. My castle was long and winding, with marble pillars draped with laurels and bones standing tall on either bank. A grand farewell to any soul passing through.

Eventually, we passed beneath the stone arch that funneled us outside. It was nighttime, and the blood moon dipped low in the sky, nearly kissing the Styx. The river of souls ran under my hedge maze, the roots spilling into the crimson water, drinking from the nutrient-rich liquid.

The brush was thick, but it peeled back, roots shuffling and disembodied heads grumbling their irritation as the vines shuffled them along with the rest of the shrubs for the gondola to pass.

"My Lord!" Cecil's voice shot up an octave with his panic as he spotted a sharp drop ahead. "Waterfall!"

I said nothing and continued to push the ferry along. The teeth in the librarian's eye sockets practically chattered together with nerves. Holga soothed him, quietly explaining how the ferry magic worked since she'd taken this journey before.

Cecil gripped the gondola's silver-gilded edge, yellowed knuckles turning white from the pressure.

His exhale of relief was audible, even over the rushing water. While the crimson liquid, carrying various chunks of human remains, had a sudden drop of several dozen feet, the gondola drifted down slowly at an angle, floating along as if it had never left the water.

When the gondola rejoined the Styx, we were underground in an elaborate cave system colder than death.

"The second circle…" Holga whispered, her tone rife with apprehension.

"It's alright. We're safe with Lord Belial," Cecil reassured her, squeezing an arm around her. "There's no deceased soul safer than those in his care."

The skeletal witch stiffened. If she was going to respond, she likely thought better of it.

I knew what she was thinking. All souls were safe with me—so long as they didn't anger me.

As the Lord of Limbo, I could shatter souls in my realm as if they'd never existed. And if I wanted them to suffer, I'd sentence them to a worse fate by ushering them down the Styx to become wards of my brothers' realms.

"I won't ever send you back, Holga," I told the witch, breaking the silence after a few quiet minutes of drifting down the river. "You have my word."

I pulled the gondola up to the dock in front of a large flight of steps carved into the stone. When the boat glided to a stop, flames leapt to life in the gilded braziers flanking the steps.

"I can't promise I can keep your souls safe if you leave this boat."

I stepped onto the dock, and by the time I turned around to level Cecil and Holga with a firm stare, I was in my true form. My cloak settled over my shoulders, complete with silver-plated pauldrons I'd fashioned from ribcages and a crown of bone between my horns.

I only wore a crown on special occasions, and today, the day of Asmodeus' death, was a special occasion.

"Neither of you are permitted to move from that bench. Is that understood?"

When I got a nod from both of them, I turned with a swirl of my cape and ascended the steps to the Lord of Lechery's palace—if it could be called that. The place wasn't much more than a glorified pit in what was otherwise a miserable shithole of a realm.

I climbed the steep stone staircase toward the main entrance, using my oar as a walking staff, my lantern lighting the way. Its blue flame was small, but the light was powerful, illuminating the vast cavern and all the carnage that decorated it.

The only similarity I shared with Asmodeus was a love of decorating our dwellings with the remains of our subjects. My preference was bone, of course, and his was flesh—*rotting* flesh.

The place stunk like a disease-ravaged mass grave. Ultimate paradise for the flies and maggots and total Hell for everything else.

Asmodeus sat slouched on his throne of brutalized women, all three of his heads bowed as if in some unholy prayer. He didn't bother looking up as I approached him.

"She isn't here anymore." His growl bounced off the stone walls, making him sound every bit the monstrous demon lord he was. "You're too late, Lord of Bones."

My chest tightened, and it took everything within me to keep my wrath caged just long enough to get answers. I was capable of beating it out of him, but I'd get to Rayven sooner if Asmodeus cooperated.

"Too bad for you. I might have spared your life if she was still here."

"*Liar,*" the bull's head huffed, the first of the three to look at me.

The flaxen-haired head was the next to meet my heated glare. "You need to muzzle that rabid bitch of yours."

I'd always hated the voice of the human-looking head the most. It was an obnoxious fucking sound, even more irritating than its punchable face.

"Even if you hadn't kidnapped her, I'd put you down like a dog for talking about my queen that way." I stormed toward him, terrifying purpose in my heavy stride and murder in my flaming eyes. "Right after I make you eat your words by choking you with every tongue I cut from your heads."

Asmodeus' spine straightened as he sat up, lifting the shadows covering his lower half and stopping me in my tracks.

Copious amounts of blood streaked his thighs and ran down his goat legs, matting in their wiry fur. His six eyes were stark with the foulest loathing, and it was enough to make me laugh. If this form had skin on its skull, I'd even crack a smile.

"By blood and darkness," I snickered. "Did she do that?"

My eyes dropped to the gaping wound between his thighs. Nothing but shredded skin hung over his uncomfortably large ballsack.

The look on his faces confirmed my suspicions. "My mate took your fucking cock."

My gorgeous, brilliant, unholy terror of a mate had robbed a lust demon of what the humans would call his "money-maker." The thought of Rayven's face, lips, and chin wet with Asmodeus' blood, thick beads of red streaking down her throat and peppering her perfect tits while the Lord of Lust screamed, holding the tattered vestiges of his manhood...

It made my cock hard, and it swelled enough for Asmodeus to notice.

"And they say I'm the fucking sadist," the bull rumbled as the goat brayed.

It dawned on me then that the Lord of Lust would have had to do something truly fucked to push Rayven to that point. My maw snapped, saliva sprawling as I loomed over Asmodeus' throne and unleashed a roar. "Where is she? What the fuck have you done to her. If you touched her, I'll—"

"You'll what?" the demon challenged. "You already plan on killing me. At least I had a little fun first."

Rage built in my core until I couldn't contain myself for another breath. My hand snapped out, taking him by his middle throat with one hand and shoving my oar between his legs. The screech of agony would have burst my eardrums had I any in this form.

"Tell me where she is," I hissed into his face as he screamed into mine. No more threats. I'd let his imagination fill in the blanks, all the ways I could make him suffer for kidnapping my most precious treasure.

"She...she jumped into the Styx before I could catch her. She's probably with Vine or Leviathan now..."

Vine. The name had me seething. The Lord of Pride was a complete bastard, but he usually kept to himself. He didn't like to acknowledge the existence of the other demon lords and was more reclusive than even me.

No soul passed through a realm without the master knowing of it. Would he have helped her? Doubtful. With any luck, she would be safe with Leviathan. Of my brothers, he was the only one I'd call a friend. He'd keep her safe for me until I came to collect her.

I continued to shove the oar into Asmodeus' groin. His scream reached a whole new octave I didn't know a growly demon like him could even hit as I rammed it inside him and stretched out the hole Rayven had made.

"Aw, what's the problem, As? Don't you love fucked up shit like this?" I drawled, my voice hard steel wrapped in silk. "Or are you just too chicken-shit to take what you dish out?"

The oar was speared deep enough inside him that it would have killed any other creature. All three of his mouths opened, gurgling blood and strangled whimpers of pain as his organs and flesh stretched around the invading object.

I laughed, taking pleasure in watching him suffer. "You know, I've always hated you. I've fantasized about killing you, but you've never given me a reason until now."

"You—You're a demon lord," he sputtered. I didn't flinch at the blood he spat onto the bleached bone of my skull. "The god of bones, of death. You have no business taking a mortal queen."

"You forget, brother..." Using all my strength, I rammed the oar as deep as I could into him. The sound of skin tearing from the inside could be heard even above his screams. The lantern fell to the floor, blue fire catching on my cloak and engulfing me. "As the god of death, life is also mine to play with. *All* life...."

I was immune to my own flames, but Asmodeus was not. He writhed and thrashed as the flames consumed his entire body while the end of the oar made a grisly exit from the mouth of his center head. It was a horrific death, yet all I could do was laugh at the disturbing scene.

"Including yours."

CHAPTER SIXTEEN

RAYVEN

A RUSTLE OUTSIDE THE cage made my eyes snap open. It was probably just Leviathan, back to ogle me while I slept. That or possibly hand-feed me more oysters, but I needed a few more hours of unconsciousness to mentally prepare for whatever he had planned for me.

I promptly closed my eyes and remained still, pretending to be asleep, but then, a familiar voice sent a bolt of adrenaline through my veins.

"Rayven..."

That voice, that rumbling baritone as deep as Hell and as sweet as arsenic.

My eyes shot open to see a hooded figure with antlers decorated in silver chains approaching. He pulled back his hood, and the shadows receded, revealing Belial's familiar masked face. He crouched beside the cage, and his black mask vanished in a spark of blue magic.

Reaching through the copper bars, his knuckle tenderly stroked my cheek.

"My treasure..." His voice softened. "I'm so fucking sorry I let them take you."

"Belial..." I could barely believe my eyes.

He'd come for me. He was here to take me back to Limbo.

"What are you— How did you—" My sharp whisper was cut off by the screech of metal as he took the cage bars in his hands and bent them with ease.

"Wait!" I whispered sharply, worried Leviathan would come running if he heard the commotion.

The creaking and groaning of metal being contorted tore through the cavern, and my head swiveled, searching for any sign of the serpent demon. There was none. His bed lay empty, the cavern eerily still.

Had Belial killed him while I slept? Or had he ventured off, confident I wouldn't be able to break out of my prison?

"I'll always be able to find you, my little treasure," Belial answered me, the volume of his voice indicating he wasn't worried about being heard. When he'd bent the bars wide enough for my body to slip through, he reached inside and offered me a hand. "There's nowhere in the nine realms that could keep you out of my reach."

I took his hand and stepped out of the cage, all the while gaping at his beautiful, marred face. My mouth hung open as I drank him in, relief flooding me as the shock of seeing him here eased.

"I don't understand," I muttered, blinking up at him. He was wearing his favorite white shirt with lantern sleeves and black pants that left nothing to the imagination when it came to the bulge in the front.

I wanted to laugh, to cry. After everything I'd been through, seeing him was pure ecstasy.

His arms banded around my waist, and I collapsed against his hard chest. The sweet smell of ripe strawberries invaded my senses, soothing my nerves and quieting my frantic thoughts.

"You're here. You're really here." I closed my eyes and clung to him, his subtle warmth seeping through his clothing, heating my naked body. As much as I wanted to get the fuck out of this place and never look back, I wanted to enjoy this moment. The pain and heartache of everything that had happened bled away, leaving nothing but relief and gratitude in their wake.

"I'm so sorry," he said again, stroking my hair. The touch was surprisingly tender. Careful, like I might break. "I shouldn't have left you alone. I was stupid, so stupid to let you run off..."

"It's okay," I assured him. How could he have known his brothers would betray him, kidnap me from under his nose, and drag me to the bowels of Hell? I was the one who ran off. If I would have stayed with him, if I had just gone back to the ball instead of having a meltdown, none of this would have happened.

I'd still be in Limbo, in his castle.

I'd still be home.

"It's okay," I repeated, pulling back to look up at him. I'd never seen so much sadness in his eyes. His cocky, aggressive demeanor had diminished, revealing something that had my stomach tingling with butterflies. "What's wrong, Belial?"

"It hurts to be this close to you but not be able to save you," he said, so low I nearly missed it.

I cocked a brow, wrapping my arms tightly around him. "I...I don't understand. You're here with me. You did save me. Let's go."

I took him by the wrist and tried to guide him back to the Styx, but when he wouldn't budge, I spun around with a confused expression. "What are we waiting for?"

"Rayven," he said, the sound of utter despair making his voice crack. "None of this is real."

I blinked. "What do you mean?"

"I mean, you're dreaming."

Dread sank through me like a stone, settling in the pit of my stomach. It threatened to bring me to my knees. Tearing my gaze away from Belial's, I studied the details of the cave, searching for anything out of place, anything to prove this wasn't real.

The ocean waves crashed against the shore. The stone walls of the cavern glistened, illuminated by the pale green moonlight spilling in from outside and a single torch hanging in the corner. Nothing looked amiss, and Belial... He felt so real.

"How can I be dreaming?" I asked, running my hands down his arms, over his chest. I stroked my fingers over his scarred lips, reveling in the shudder that followed.

"Do you remember the dream you had after you ate the plum? The one where you bent over in my throne room and showed me every part of you?" His eyes turned darker, lust replacing the sadness that had been there moments ago. "When I told you to show me all that I own?"

Heat scorched my cheeks. How could I not remember? That image had been burned into my memory, branded on my soul ever since. I nodded.

"It was magic that allowed me to visit you in your dreams," he explained. "To come to you now." One of his hands dipped to cup my bare ass cheek. He squeezed, and even through his glove, I could feel the warmth of his palm. I wanted his rough, calloused hands all over me. "This is a dream."

"But I haven't eaten another plum."

"You don't have to. One was enough. The spell never fades."

"I..." I didn't want to believe it. He was here, right in front of me. All I wanted was for him to take me far away from this place. I didn't want to sink deeper into Hell and out of his reach.

My stomach flipped like the ground had suddenly disappeared from beneath me. I felt like I was falling, even though his arms kept me upright.

"Don't worry." His fingers came up to lift my chin, his storm-colored eyes grounding me. "I'm coming for you. I'll destroy the nine realms if I must. I'll cut down anyone who stands in my way to get to you."

With that, he closed the last bit of distance between us and pressed his lips to mine, immediately sweeping his tongue into my mouth. It was slow, powerful, unlike how he normally devoured me any chance he got. When he pulled away, there were tears in my eyes.

"Belial, I'm...scared," I admitted. Being this vulnerable with him was new, but then again, so was being trapped in a cage in the pits of hell, waiting for the god of death to rescue me. I didn't want to seem weak, but in this moment, alone with him in my dreams, I knew I could be vulnerable. "What if... What if you don't get to me in time?"

His voice turned sharp like a knife. "That won't happen." Then, it softened just as fast. "I will find you. I'm already on my way, Rayven. You just have to be brave for a little longer. Can you do that?"

I nodded.

He slowly let me go and turned to walk away. The air caught in my lungs and I thought my heart might shatter. Was he really leaving me alone? Just like that?

"Wait!" I ran after him, stopping short when he paused next to the bed. "Don't leave me. Not yet."

Rather than disappearing, he moved to grab something off the floor. It had been tucked away, just out of sight beyond Leviathan's bed, and when he lifted it, a gasp tore from my lips.

It was an enormous femur bone that had probably once belonged to some hellish monster. At least eight feet long, one end looked to have been fashioned into an oar. The other end was jagged and bloody, a makeshift pike where he'd stabbed three severed heads, stacked one on top of the other. Shriveled and blackened, they were burnt to a crisp, but I could still make them out: one bull, one goat, and one human head with clumps of flaxen hair.

"Are those...real?" I didn't know what else to say as disbelief turned my insides.

He nodded, watching me carefully with a hooded expression. "They're real, alright. It's the least the bastard deserves."

My throat swelled with emotion. "So he's gone for good? His soul...?"

"Demons don't have souls. So, yes. He's gone for good."

My sigh of relief had Belial's brows furrowing, and the shadows behind his eyes were stark with a peculiar cocktail of violence and concern. "He touched you, didn't he? Rayven, if he—"

"He shoved his cock in my mouth. That's as far as it got, and I made sure he regretted it the second he did it."

"Are you alright?"

How was I supposed to answer that? I wasn't hurt, but it felt like my nerves had been thrown into a blender and pureed. "I will be so long as you get me. Soon."

"Soon," he agreed.

He moved to prop the oar up against the cage I'd escaped from, making sure the eyes were facing Leviathan's empty bed, before grabbing my hand and dragging me into him again.

"Do you have to go now?" I asked, fighting to keep my voice level. I didn't want him to leave, not yet, but the way he clung to me made it feel like he was getting ready to say goodbye.

"Not yet." He led me backward to the bed, laying me down on the mountain of silk sheets Leviathan slept on. He made a show of crawling on top of me, his hungry eyes trained on me. "First, I have to show you exactly what you've done to me..."

I stared up at him, blinking. "What do you mean?"

"When I found out you bit off the Lord of Lust's cock...it took everything in me to keep myself from coming at the thought of it."

The demon settled between my thighs, his bulge pressing against my dripping center. My arousal soaked the front of his pants, which made his cock twitch.

He kissed his way around my throat, his tongue dancing over my skin. He didn't care that I was filthy, covered in blood and sweat and who knew what else. I expected him to sink lower, for his mouth to dip to my breasts to tease my nipples with his teeth, but he pulled back, his eyes meeting mine.

"I need you, Rayven. Gods below, do I fucking need you," he said, his voice low and soft. The unguarded reverence in his eyes surprised me, scared me.

He'd given me glimpses of what lurked beneath the various masks he wore, but I was much more used to the cocky, arrogant

Belial who teased me into knots and left me begging, desperate for more. The softer side he tried so desperately to cover up had me just as wrapped around his fingers.

"Fuck me," I said, my voice husky and rife with need. I wiggled my hips beneath him, lips parting as the rock-hard erection rubbed over my center through his pants—leaving me desperate for more friction.

He didn't move. Instead, he bent down, his antler charms softly clinking as he pressed his lips carefully to the corner of my mouth.

I sighed against his gentle warmth, reveling in how real this felt.

"I'm going to fuck you...but that's not exactly what I mean when I say I need you."

"What do you mean?"

"I need you. I need you more than I've ever needed anything before, more than I ever thought I was capable of. I told you before, caring is new for me, but this..." His voice trailed off as his eyes locked with mine again, his hand coming up to cup my cheek. "Understand when I tell you that you're the goddamn air in my lungs. When you're not with me, I can't breathe. I can't think. In three days, you have gone from the little thief I found rooting around in Catherine's tomb to the entire reason for my existence. I want you to know, down to your marrow, that I am coming for you. Because if I don't have you close, if we're not together, I don't know how I'll go on."

I swallowed thickly, my chest tight and my heart thrumming so hard, I could feel it in my mouth. "I understand."

"Good." He kissed me on one eyelid, then the other. They were two of the gentlest kisses I'd ever received, packed with the kind of love I didn't think this man was capable of three days ago.

This moment was not unlike the first plum dream I'd shared with the Lord of Bones, in that it was intense and I'd never forget it. At the same time, it was completely different. This time, it was a sweet and tender moment we shared.

But it changed as he pulled back, his quiet smile morphing into something dark and hungry in an instant. "Now that you know that, I need you to know you make me fucking feral. You're so sexy, so terrifyingly stubborn, and so bloody cutthroat when you're cornered."

He dropped his mouth to mine and licked my lips, chuckling. "I still taste Asmodeus' blood on your mouth. I'd pay good money to have seen his face when you bit off his pride and joy."

What happened with Asmodeus was traumatic, but the trauma of it all eased beneath the brilliance of Belial's eyes as they beamed with pride. "You're every bit the queen I mean to make you."

He rose on his knees, tugging the shirt off over his head and tossing it to the floor. A beat later, he was naked, the viridescent moonlight framing his perfect body in a sinister glow. My heart fluttered in time with my pussy as he crawled back on top of me.

When he settled between my thighs again, his mouth was on my throat, raining down an assault of hungry kisses. Then, he kissed my shoulders, down my arm, until his lips reached the three cuts he'd gouged into my wrist.

He worshipped them with his mouth, each revenant brush of his skin a juxtaposition to the memory of when he'd cut into me, all three moments seared into my mind forever.

Belial had been right from the beginning. He'd delivered the pain he'd promised to bring as my punishment for robbing Catherine's grave. What neither of us had counted on was how much both of us would come to crave the agony.

I turned my head on Leviathan's pillow, my eye catching on the barbequed heads skewered onto the oar.

"Are they going to watch while we...." I trailed off as Belial drew back to look at me with that panty-obliterating smile. He got the picture.

"Don't you want them to watch?"

Against all odds, I found myself grinning ear to ear. I almost wished Asmodeus was still alive to see his brother fuck me, but this would do.

"I do."

CHAPTER SEVENTEEN

RAYVEN

"What would you like me to do to you, Rayven? Tell me how you want to be touched."

I couldn't help but gape at Belial's scared face, taken aback by the sincerity I found behind his eyes.

It wasn't like him to ask me what I liked or how I wanted it. Somehow, he just knew, and he never asked for permission or guidance. He just did it.

It struck me as odd, until I made out the concern etching his features. Was he being careful with me, knowing I'd been through literal Hell in the last circle with the lord of rape and creepy furniture?

"Whatever you want," I breathed out, hot breath tickling his neck and making goosebumps pebble his skin. I loved knowing

I affected him the same way he did me. "So long as it involves you fucking my brains out."

He tilted his head, his midnight hair spilling over his eyes, his silver horn jewelry jingling as the chains and charms shifted. *Fuck me dead*. How could any man be so diabolically handsome?

"Whatever I want..." he repeated my words with a dark chuckle and that suave-as-sin grin. "Careful, treasure. I have a disturbing imagination, and while this is a dream..."

His palm smoothed up my belly and between my breasts, his spread fingers skimming my pierced nipples and making them pebble.

My breath froze in my lungs as his hand traveled up my body and slowly gripped me by the throat.

"This can quickly turn into a nightmare..."

He shifted right before my eyes, his form morphing into a much larger male—horns three times as large, death-pale skin tinted the slightest hint of blue, and a giant skull head with nothing but blue fire filling his gaping eye sockets.

Every time I'd seen the god of death in his full glory, I'd felt nothing but hatred for him.

When I'd learned Belial and the Lord of Bones were one and the same, that hatred turned into something more complex.

Now, all I felt was curiosity and strangely safe caged between his muscular, vein-corded arms. Maybe it was because this was a dream, and the false security of it made the sudden shift in our dynamic easier to swallow.

I stared into those two flaming pits, my chest heaving as my pulse launched into hyperdrive.

His maw opened, and a thick black tongue oozing saliva snaked around between his huge, razor-sharp teeth. It painted a lick over my lips, and I instantly felt how powerful it was.

My frantic heart beat like it was going to burst from my ribcage as I imagined how a tongue like that would feel inside me.

The appendage was about as thick as his cock in his lesser form, more than enough to fill me. My attention moved down his body, trying to make out the outline of what he was packing in this form.

His cloak was draped over us on either side, wrapping his brawny frame in shadows.

Unable to bridle my curiosity, I moved my hand between his legs to grip him over his pants.

Jesus. He was freaking huge. Good thing this was a dream; otherwise, I'd question if I'd ever walk again.

"Like what you feel, my grave treasure?"

Yes. The answer was fuck to the yes. But also, nerves were eating me alive. I was so damn small compared to him. How was this even going to be logistically possible?

"Careful putting that monster anywhere near my mouth. I have a new thing for biting off demon lord cocks." Of course, my mouth had a tendency to run when I was nervous.

I tensed, waiting for the Lord of Bones' wrath.

Instead, he laughed, sounding more like the demon I'd fallen in love with. "First, you have to fit it into your mouth, so good luck with that. But I'll enjoy watching you try."

The place between my thighs buzzed with heat. Since I had no panties on, I knew I had to be soaking Leviathan's bedding. Good thing the spot wouldn't be there once I woke up. The creepy bastard would probably never wash them after that.

Belial flicked his tongue, as if tasting my arousal filtering into the air. His massive hand wedged between my thighs, deadly claws teasing my flesh as he rubbed the pad of his pointer digit over my weeping seam.

"You've thought about fucking me in this form before, haven't you?"

"No," I denied, even though we both knew it was a lie.

He laughed, dark and deep. The sound had the little hairs on my arm bolting up, and thick pearls of arousal leaked from my center, dripping down my ass cheeks.

He caught one of the beads with the crook of his finger and brought it to his mouth. My eyes widened as I watched his tongue split apart and encircle his pointer finger twice.

A growl rumbled from his chest. "You get this slutty little look on your face whenever you see my tongue."

His fingers smoothed over my apex, one slipping inside me, and he laughed at the way I gasped and clenched around him.

"Wetter, too."

"You're a sadistic bastard. Oh *fuuuuck*," I said, punctuating my words with a drawn out moan.

"Sadistic? Oh, dear little human. You haven't seen anything yet…"

I barked a laugh. "Says the bone demon who killed my boyfriend by ripping out his spine like a string in a fucking party popper, made me a crown out of it, and told me I'd become his queen if I didn't make it through his creepy carnivorous garden filled with body parts and perverted ferrymen."

He snorted, pulling his finger out with an embarrassing wet sound and getting off the bed. I rose up on my elbows, scowling at him as the heat he'd built inside me evaporated with his absence. "Hey!"

My indignation turned to morbid curiosity when he reached for his oar.

What in the fuck was he planning to do with that?

He turned toward me with a dangerous flicker in his flaming eyes. "Spread your legs, Rayven."

I tried to snap my legs shut, but he was there kneeling on the bed again, snatching my thigh—he was so huge, his hand fully encircled it—and firmly prying me back open. "This is your new scepter, my queen, decorated with the heads of your enemies."

My mouth opened, but no words came out. He wanted to fuck me with the oar he'd used to spear the Lord of Lechery's burnt heads.

My eyes dropped to the six blistered eye sockets, most of them now empty, as the gooey orbs had melted, creating stacks of gelatinous tears covering Asmodeus' charred cheeks.

I should have been horrified at the notion, but staring at the smooth butt of the oar that Belial held out, I couldn't help but feel this wicked little warmth thrumming between my thighs.

Fuck, what was wrong with me? I was turning into this perverted...well, queen. Maybe Belial's sadomasochistic streak was rubbing off on me.

It wasn't so bad; this was a dream, after all. There were people out there who dreamt of way more fucked up shit than this...right?

After a moment of thought, it dawned on me. Why was I trying to justify it? I didn't care. I was going to be the queen of death, and maybe I would make a pretty damn good one. Because shit like this not only didn't bother me, it turned me on.

My eyes lit with challenge, and I spread my legs wide, letting them fall onto Leviathan's sheets. "Alright. Fucking do it then."

Even with Belial's expressionless skull head, he appeared surprised. After a beat, he recovered with a sinful purr wrapped in silk. "What a perfect little masochistic slut my queen to be is. Look at you. So wet, so eager to be fucked with the heads of the most infamous incubus to ever exist watching you..."

He nudged the smaller end of the oar to my center, sliding it up and down my dripping slit.

Every muscle in my body pulled tight, the anticipation building the longer he stretched it out. He was toying with me, enjoying our little bubble where time and reality seemed to be at a standstill.

My mouth stretched into an "O" with my silent moan as he slowly pushed the bone into my molten center, sinking it in only an inch before pulling it out again.

He held it up, examining the layer of cream I'd left on it, making Asmodeus' dried blood flake.

If this was real, I'd probably find this disgusting, but this was a dream where I could let my darkest desires run free. And Belial would be right there, helping me peel back my layers of inhibitions until I was nothing but bone.

I licked my dry lips as they curled into a mischievous grin. "Suck it."

Belial's flaming eyes flickered, which I now knew was this form's equivalent of a blink. His muzzle turned toward the oar's end that had been inside me a second ago, and I could practically see the gears turning in his eye sockets as he considered it.

"Go on. Your queen gave you an order."

He made a gravelly chuckle that hooked inside my lower belly, and my hand dropped to my apex. My fingers rubbed tantalizing circles around my clit as I watched him bring the oar to his maw and make a slow show of winding his tongue around the handle.

Christ. It encircled the smooth bone three times with enough length for the tip to lap at the mixture of blood and cum.

"I never thought I'd taste you and my most insufferable brother all in the same lick..." he mused with a small shake of his head. "I definitely wouldn't think the flavor of it would make me this fucking hard."

I rose up on my elbows again, intrigued by the mention of his cock. I still hadn't seen what the Lord of Bones was packing below the belt.

"Let me see."

"You want to see?" he echoed, an arrogant grin evident in his voice.

"Back when I still thought Belial was a different person, you made jokes, taunting me. You said your cock would be good practice for the Lord of Bones. So yeah, color me curious."

I worried my lower lip, a sassy response burning the tip of my tongue. "You know... With all this build up, maybe you aren't as big as you let on. Maybe in this form, you're as smooth as a Ken doll. Maybe your cocky attitude about it has just been over-compensation."

He stared at me with this blank expression, which told me he had no idea what I was talking about.

"I am not familiar with this 'Ken', but if he is anything like the other human males on Earth, I can assure you..."

His free hand flattened over his defined abdominal muscles and slid down, his thumb hooking underneath the waist of his pants and pulling them down.

The monstrosity that flopped out was enough to rearrange a woman's insides. It was much larger than his other form. Like his horn jewelry, all traces of his body jewelry had disappeared; there was no cuff, no prince albert piercing.

Instead of disappointment at the absence of his silver, I was relieved. With his sheer size, there was no way I could fit all of him with the cuff and chain to boot. Besides, he didn't need the cuff for added texture.

His lesser form was larger than human guys I'd been with, but other than that—and his jewelry—it was like any other cock. But not in this form. His monstrous dick was ridged along the underside of his shaft, with several smaller ridges branching out from the main one. It looked just like a ribcage wrapping around his cock. The skin on the ridges was lighter too, almost bone white, while the rest of the appendage was that same slight hue of blue as the rest of him.

"Does your Ken's endowment look like this, my treasure?"

I would have laughed if it wasn't for the fact that I was trying to figure out the logistics of how something that huge was supposed to fit inside me. "Um, no. Not at all."

I watched, completely mesmerized, as he spat large gobs of saliva into his hand and stroked his cock, his blazing gaze sparking as he returned his attention to my center. I was furiously rubbing myself, chasing the promise of that first orgasm which was just within reach.

He tapped the oar to my mound, lightly spanking it, and a cry—one of surprise rather than pain—tripped from my lips

My legs spread further, a silent invitation. He took the hint and sank the oar's rounded end into my throbbing, soaking pussy.

"You look so fucking good with your legs spread, taking whatever I decide to fuck that perfect little cunt with. It's almost a shame demons don't have souls. It would be true torture for Asmodeus, knowing he's been dethroned."

"Dethroned?" My breath hitched, the word coming out fragmented as he thrust the oar deeper inside me. My body stretched to take it, my arousal from earlier making it slide in smooth and easy.

"Oh *yes*," he drawled. His fingers drummed over the oar's handle, claws clacking against the bone while his other hand kept stroking his length to the same rhythm he fucked the oar into me. "There's a new queen of lust and bone. In fact..." He paused, silently mulling over his thoughts. "Every head I collect on this oar is a wedding gift. Not just their head, but each realm that comes with it."

"What do you mean, every realm?"

"The second circle is a stinking cesspit of a realm, but without a king, it's leaderless. It's yours now to shape to your will."

I wasn't sure what he meant by 'shape to my will', but that was probably a question for later. Asmodeus' macabre throne had bowed to me. Maybe it was only fitting I try to make the place livable for the souls who called it home.

"Wow, that's—*oh.*" He pushed the oar's handle down so the end inside me angled up, pressing perfectly against my G-spot. I blinked away the stars, laughing and moaning in the same breath. "On the surface, most people just give toasters for a wedding gift. Or a vitamix or something."

"I don't know what those are. Down here, I gift my new queen kingdoms, the heads of her enemies, and orgasms. Countless fucking orgasms."

It was like he'd timed it perfectly, because no sooner had the last word left his mouth, I came. Violently. I thrashed against the Lord of Envy's mattress, my climax wracking my body as vicious pleasure tore through my system.

I clenched around the oar, and he must have felt the way my walls fluttered, because his cock thickened in his hand. In a fit of envy, he pulled the oar out and tossed it to the floor.

It made a sickening, slapping sound as Asmodeus' remains hit the cavern floor.

"That will be the closest another man gets to this perfect little pussy again. Because *it's mine.* Understand, Rayven? You're all mine."

CHAPTER EIGHTEEN

BELIAL

"You're mine." Over and over, I repeated those words as I crawled back onto the bed, trapping her tiny frame between my arms.

I kept saying it not only because it made her shiver in ecstasy, but also as an assurance to myself. She was fucking mine, *not* my brothers', despite their backstabbing plans to take her from me.

I'd do everything it took to get her back, murder being the least of it. Even now, as I wooed my little human in her dreams, I was back on my gondola, sailing straight for Vine's domain.

He was next on my war path to regain my property. It didn't matter that he wasn't involved in the other lords' scheme. He hadn't even been at the All Hallows' Eve Masquerade, but Rayven had passed through his domain, and the Lord of Pride hadn't so much as lifted a finger to help her.

It wasn't like he didn't know the mortal human floating through the Styx, stinking of Limbo, belonged to me. He just didn't care enough to interfere, and he would die for that mistake.

Soon, his would be another head on my oar, and the realm he'd leave behind would be yet another wedding gift for my queen.

Once I'd finished paying Vine a visit in the third circle, I'd make my way to the fourth and collect Rayven from Leviathan. Of all my brothers, he was the only one I'd call a friend, though that was still a bit of a stretch. I did trust him to keep her away from the other demon lords, though. Leviathan hated the concept of sharing just as much as me.

He'd keep her safe for me until I arrived.

In the meantime, I'd keep her mind at ease while she slept.

Blood and darkness, the sounds she made as she came were so fucking delicious, they had my tongue oozing with copious amounts of saliva, a thick rope of pre-cum trailing from the slit of my tip.

She squirmed and flushed that hue of red I loved so much as my fluids dripped onto her skin.

Fuck, I needed her more than ever. That look she gave me when I shifted into my monster form went straight to my dick. For the first time, she didn't look at the Lord of Bones with fear and hatred. She looked at me with *desire*.

Then, when she took my oar, her sweet little mound growing slicker than ever? Dark perfection.

If only this was real. If only I really had her pinned beneath me. Thanks to the plum magic, sex would feel more real than any dream ever could, but at the end of the night, it would still be only that; a dream and nothing more.

I'd ride her hard tonight so she'd wake up throbbing with need for me. The whisper of my touch between her legs would be a promise for what was to come once she was truly in my arms.

She whimpered as I ran my hands over her body, smearing my saliva and pre-cum over every inch of her, leaving her glistening.

Leviathan's bedroom opened to the ocean, and the moon leaked through its shroud of clouds. Unlike the blood moon in Limbo, Envy's was a pale green. Its sinister glow outlined one side of Rayven's body while the flickering light suspended over the bed wrapped her other side in fire and shadow.

I hummed at the sight of her, spread and panting for me, ready for my cock—or at least so she thought. In reality, when we mated in my true form, she'd need more warming up before her mortal cunt could take a demon like me.

She was so sensitive, and I picked up on every goddamn reaction her body had to me. Each tear that leaked from her weeping cunt. Each breath she drew into her lungs, making her breasts heave. Each bat of her lashes and every beat of her heart.

"You're staring at me," she muttered, breathless as she rode out the tail of her orgasm.

My fingers swept over her shoulder, brushing back a lock of her raven hair. "Can you blame me? Look at you. You're fucking glowing with life."

My hand roamed down her body from her shoulder, sweeping over her breast, flicking her nipple piercing before settling on her thigh. "Practically *begging* for death to snuff out that pretty light behind your eyes..."

Her chest hitched with the gasp frozen in her throat, and I laughed, cold and cruel. There was that flicker of fear I'd almost come to miss. I loved seeing her strong and stubborn, but there was something about mortal terror that got my dick hard. That lust for fear was inherent to all demonkind.

"Relax, little human. I've already decided I'm keeping you like this, forever the mortal queen of rot and bone. That way, I'll still be able to feel the beat of your heart whenever I slip inside you..."

"You're fucked," she said, repeating her words the night I'd had her in my bed, when I told her she had the prettiest pussy I'd ever seen—fluttery and warm, unlike any corpse I'd known. Then, I'd promptly fucked her with a wine bottle.

"And your flesh will stay vibrant and fresh." I pinched her inner thigh, and she jerked. My tongue flicked the spot, enjoying the way it burned hot, and my body dipped lower. I traced the scars on her calves—the ones she'd gotten from scaling countless cemetery fences. "I could count your scars till the end time, you know."

She gaped at me with a thunderstruck look. I half wished I was still in my lesser form so she could reach out and touch my scars the way I knew she would.

I rose and carefully wrapped my hand around her throat. "The second I get you home, I'm making you a new collar. You won't have to wear it all the time."

She gave me a hopeful expression that seemed distrusting at the same time. "I won't?"

"Only in private. In our bed."

Her gaze turned suspicious. "You won't have me wear anything in public?"

"Of course I will," I snarled as my attention settled on her frantic pulse drumming a beat against my fingers. "You'll wear my crown."

CHAPTER NINETEEN

RAYVEN

THE INTENSE PULSE BETWEEN my legs, coupled with his words, had me burning up.

I balked at the deadly heat in Belial's eyes. His hands clamped over my hips, and he lifted me, flipping me so I was on the mattress on my hands and knees.

"Bend over for me, treasure. Show me all I own."

That line. Fuck, *that line.*

This wasn't the first time he'd commanded me into this exposing position in my dreams.

But this time was different. Before I could obey of my own will, he took hold of my soul again, like he had in the hall after the masquerade, and forced my head to the pillow with my ass in the air.

I felt like a puppet on a string. And fuck me, it had me so wet and worked up, I could barely stand it. I started to drip with arousal that streaked down my thighs.

Belial took notice and laughed—ugh, that laugh. In this form, he didn't have lips, but I could still hear that arrogant, half-cocked smirk in his voice.

His hands smoothed over my ass, kneading my blazing flesh. He'd worked me up until I was half-drunk with lust, and his fingers biting into my asscheeks had me straining against his hold, trying to push closer to him.

I needed more friction. "Belial, please... I need..."

"You need what?" he teased. "Demon cock? How about you beg me for it?"

"Fuck you," I hissed through clenched teeth.

"You're about to," he cackled as his fingers trailed to my soaked core.

He ran his index finger gently over my center, from my asshole all the way to my clit, his claw grazing the sensitive skin just enough to leave me shivering.

"You're a fucking tease."

"*No*," he corrected with a sharp edge in his grave-deep baritone. "A merciful Lord is what I am. If I don't make sure you're dripping wet for me, I'll ruin your pretty little pussy before I've barely had a chance to play with it."

After a few more moments, he removed his hand and replaced it with the head of his cock, nudging it against my folds.

I half expected him to enter me violently, but he took his time, canting his hips forward at a pace that was somehow even more excruciating.

"Weeping Hells," Belial said behind me in a half groan, half growl. "Do you have any idea how fucking good you look stretching around me?"

My fingers curled into the sheets as he pushed more of himself inside. My body struggled to take him, but he talked me through it as he worked himself into me inch by inch.

"You're doing so good for me, Rayven. Almost there. Fuck—you're taking so much of me."

He was impossibly huge, but he managed to seat all of himself inside me.

"Good fucking girl," he praised, his hunger making his voice thick and wolfish. "You sheath all of me."

Gods, how could this be a dream? It felt so real—everything from his warm breath barreling over the back of my neck to the ridges on his shaft, rubbing me in a way that had drool trickling from the corners of my mouth.

Belial arched over my frame, his muzzle nuzzling into my hair. "How does it feel to have the Lord of Bones inside you, human?"

That was a complicated question. It fucking hurt. Having him this close, even in my dreams, always hurt, but I'd come to crave the pain.

I opened my mouth to respond, but a sharp punch of his hips had nothing but a swollen string of broken curses, laced together on a lusty groan, falling from my tongue.

He let out an evil chuckle as he used his magic to force me up onto my knees. His meaty forearms banded around my middle, keeping me flush to him as he fucked me with deep and un-hurried thrusts. His long fingers curled around my arm, claws drumming against the three marks he cut into my flesh. "All fucking *mine*."

For once, I didn't have a bratty retort to fire off. All I could manage was a sloppy nod.

He released his hold on my arm, only to snatch my chin and turn my head to force my gaze to his. The flames of his eyes filled my vision, and I found myself frozen in unholy awe of the terrifying demon lord taking me from behind.

His head canted, smoke from his eyes twirling through the air between his horns like a crown of haze and embers. "What was that, grave treasure?"

My eyes watered as his skull shoved into my space, his flames making it impossible to breathe as it stung my nostrils. I choked, sputtering in a complicated twist of torturous pleasure. "I—I—"

"If you know you belong to me..." His fingers spread from my chin, his hand swallowing my face as he wrenched my head to his until there was no space left between us. "Use your words to tell me."

"I…I belong to you," I gasped into his palm, stupidly turned on by the monstrous visage peaking at me through his spread fingers.

"That's right. I own every bit of you."

His ring finger moved down my face, slipping into my mouth, hooking under my teeth and rubbing the backs of them. "Your bones. Your soul…"

I choked out a sob as I felt his grip on my soul twist, and my hips slammed back on his cock hard enough to make me see stars.

"Your flesh."

He slapped my ass hard enough to make a loud *crack* that echoed through the Lord of Envy's chamber. Whatever pain I felt from the spank was quickly chased away by overwhelming shockwaves of pure pleasure.

Pulling his finger from my mouth to grip my throat, he chuckled as he caught my expression. "Look at that slutty little look on your face. It's even sexier than that expression you get when you imagine my split tongue inside your sweet little cunt."

"I—I don't imagine that."

"Does your pussy always clench when you lie?" Another firm smack to my ass, the delicious sting pushing me closer to the edge. "Come for your Lord, little human. Drench my cock in your cum." His words were authoritative, demanding my complete obedience. I didn't dare disobey him.

I came with a strangled cry, my every nerve on fucking fire as my orgasm ravaged my system.

He rode me through the intense waves of my release, his thrusts more punishing and frantic now as he chased his own climax.

His maw opened, ropes of saliva dripping onto my shoulders and slipping down my breasts as he panted with every push and pull of his hips. A few beats later, he came, exploding inside me with a demonic snarl.

The warmth inside me was better than it had any right to be in the throes of my own mind.

It wasn't until I went limp in his arms that he released his hold on my soul, slipped his cock out of me, and turned me around so we were face to face, our chests clashing together as he fought for breath. "You did so good for me, Rayven."

He gently laid me down in bed, tucking me in as if I was actually sleeping in Leviathan's bed for the night, rather than the cold cage beside it.

"What now?"

The demon lord rose from the bed, standing over me with a sad air about him. "Now, you wake up."

My pounding heart twisted in my chest. "What about Leviathan?"

"He'll keep you safe."

"Safe?" I shot into a sitting position, scoffing. "Stripping me out of my dress and forcing me into a cage doesn't make me feel safe."

Belial tensed, the cords in his thick neck flexing. "I thought Asmodeus took your clothes."

"No, it was your creepy sea snake of a brother. He made me eat out of his hand. I don't like how he looks at me."

There was a barbed moment of silence as Belial seemed to absorb this new information. "Asmodeus was too thick to understand my powers, but Leviathan is well aware that I am stronger than him. He may make you uncomfortable, but he won't hurt you."

I should have found comfort in Belial's assurance, but that hook in my gut only seemed to dig deeper. "How long will I have to wait?"

"I'm coming for you as fast as I can." He gently guided me back and teased his tongue over the seam of my lips, the closest to a kiss he could give in this form. "You'll be safe in Leviathan's realm until I come to you. I promise, I'm not far."

My heart fluttered at the thought of him showing up for real and saving me, and my attention moved back to the trio of severed heads speared onto the ferryman's oar.

If my suspicions were right, Leviathan's head would be joining the oar soon.

CHAPTER TWENTY

RAYVEN

When I woke, Belial was gone. I lay on the bottom of the cage, staring up at the point where the bars came together, replaying the dream from last night over in my mind.

Too bad I had to wake up, back to my hellish reality where I was hopelessly trapped. I hated feeling so helpless.

This damsel in distress thing wasn't my vibe. While Belial was fighting his way through the upper layers of Hell to rescue me, I was expected to sit here and wait.

I closed my eyes, trying to slip back into the plum dream, but the spell was over. My demon was gone. His absence made my eyes sting, tears welling in the corners.

"Don't cry, pet," Leviathan's voice slithered around me, sticking to my skin.

I looked over, the hot tears spilling down my cheeks, and found him splayed over his bed with his hookah pipe pinched between his fingers. Had he watched me sleep?

"Don't you have anything better to do?" I gritted out.

"No." He took a long drag off his hookah. *What the fuck was this guy smoking like an absolute freight train?* "What could be better than admiring the prettiest thing in the nine layers?"

A chill shot through me, and I dragged myself up, pulling my knees to my chest. It didn't do much, but it gave me a modicum of modesty.

"You could let me out," I offered, batting my eyelashes at him. "That would be better."

His serpent tongue flicked the salty sea air with his laugh. "And risk you running off so one of my brothers can snatch you from me? Not a chance. None of them will ever have you, little human. You're mine. You're never getting out of that cage."

The blood in my veins crystalized. Leviathan had no intention of handing me over to Belial.

A cold little smile curled my lips. This would end badly for him.

"Can I at least have some water?" I snapped at the serpent demon.

Leviathan scooted to the edge of his bed, still admiring me. I was getting used to his constant gaze, but it didn't make it any less fucked. I wished he'd go away for five minutes, or at least take a fucking nap. Anything for a little privacy.

He rubbed his scaled chin, lost in thought for a moment. "I have something else you can drink."

The suggestive bend to his tone had me rolling my eyes. "You're disgusting."

After being forced to suck Asmodeus' cock, the thought of Leviathan touching me made my stomach churn.

He said he wasn't a brute, but would he force himself on me too if I didn't obey?

Slinking to his feet, he sauntered over and stopped next to the cage. He towered over me, his slitted eyes burning into mine with a demented gleam. "Why don't you prove to me just how thirsty you are?"

He reached through the bars, trailing a single finger along my jawline. Dread washed over me, and I shrank away, pressing myself against the bars farthest from him.

"Keep your hands off me if you want to keep them attached. I have this thing where I bite off appendages that venture too close to my fucking face."

"You're always so feisty," he said with a wicked laugh, tapping his fingers on one of the copper bars. "Like a rabid animal. Wild, with feral beauty. I see why Belial was so enrapt by you." I was sure he meant for those to be compliments, but the way they oozed off his tongue made them much more insulting.

"What do you say?" His eyes roved over me hungrily. "Put on a little show for me. Dance for me like you would your precious Lord of Bones, and I'll give you a drink."

He wants me to dance for him?

I doubted it was because he wanted to admire my body. He wanted to revel in my discomfort.

"Why don't you go suck your own dick instead?" I snapped, despite how badly I wanted something to soothe my dry mouth and scratchy throat.

There was no way I was dancing naked in a cage for this asshole. Not on his life.

Belial would be here soon to save me, I knew that—he'd promised me—but I didn't know how long I'd have to suffer before he got here.

How long could a human body survive without water? Much longer than I'd been stuck in this cage, but there was no way in fuck I'd last more than a day or two, not after all the running I'd done since the ball. My lips were already cracked, my mouth feeling like it was full of cotton. The more I thought about it, the drier it got.

Leviathan chuckled as I attempted to lick my lips, but somehow, they remained just as parched. I was so damn—

"Thirsty, are we?" he teased, cockiness evident in his tone.

I stared at him, my throat beginning to ache. I was thirsty when I woke, but as the seconds flicked by, I grew way more parched. Suddenly, my throat was drier than a desert, like something was draining every drop of water in my body.

"What are you doing to me..." My words came out scratchy, cracking mid-sentence.

The demon's wicked smile gave me my answer. Whatever magic he possessed was dehydrating me.

His eyes turned dark, a smile twisting his mouth. "I told you I can be rather persuasive. Now dance, pet."

"I fucking hate you," I hissed out, an ache working its way through me. My whole body was affected, from my dry eyes down to my veins.

"Is hate really all that different from love?" he mused, stroking a scaly finger along one of the copper bars of my prison. "A feeling so intense, it shapes how you see a person. Both can make you believe untruths and trust blatant lies. Whether you hate or love someone, they live in your mind, even when you don't want them to."

Yeah, I fucking hated him.

And I hated that he was making the tiniest bit of sense.

"Now, dance." His order came out sharper this time, and I could see the beast lurking behind his eyes. "Or this will get a whole lot worse before it gets better."

I wanted to refuse. I was fucking sick of having men—asshole demon lords in particular—tell me what to do. The only lord I wanted to obey was Belial, but if I didn't get up and dance, Leviathan would probably leave me as a pile of dust for him to find.

I couldn't stomach the thought.

"The clock is ticking," he sing-songed. "I'd hurry if I were you."

Reluctantly, I stood, mind whirling as I tried to come up with a plan to get out of this. Unfortunately, I was faced with the very real possibility of turning into a shriveled fleshy raisin. There was no time to think.

He had me in his claws, and he knew it.

With a grimace, I swayed my hips back and forth like I would to some basic pop music in a bar, my arms crossed over my chest to shield my breasts from his gaze. My movements came out stiff, discomfort making my skin crawl.

"Happy now?" I asked through gritted teeth.

"You can do better than that." He shook his head slowly. "The Lord of Bones wouldn't be pining for your scarred flesh if that was all. Show me what you do to him."

I hated how he commented on my scars, his cadence making me feel as though they were something to be ashamed of. Belial worshipped them.

My skin felt tighter and dryer by the second, constricting around me and making it more difficult to move.

Fuck.

It's just a dance, that's all, I said to myself in an attempt to ground my nerves. I wasn't much of a dancer, but if it meant Leviathan would stop whatever the fuck he was doing to my bodily fluids...

"Then you'll give me something to drink?" I wasn't sure why I asked. He probably wouldn't tell me the truth anyway.

Still, a yes would make me feel better about the fucked up situation. At least he wasn't asking me to suck his dick or offer him my asshole as payment.

Just a dance.

"I'm a man of my word."

I scoffed, anger bubbling through me. Of course he wasn't. He was a fucking snake.

Too bad I didn't have much of a choice.

Trust him or die.

Dance or suffer.

Those were my options.

With a groan, I dropped my hands as my face flushed with heat. I hoped Belial carved Leviathan into tiny pieces and fed him to sharks or something.

Were there sharks in Hell?

I moved my hips, this time slower, more seductive. I closed my eyes and tried to imagine Belial standing in front of me, hoping it would make the act more appealing, but my skin still crawled. I ran my hands over my breasts and down my waist, hoping it was what the serpent lord wanted.

When I opened my eyes again, he'd moved closer, his face pressed against the bars. He was rocking his hips, rubbing the bulge in the front of his pants against the copper.

"More," he urged, his tongue snaking out to wrap around one of the bars.

Suddenly, I was extra thankful for the cage separating us.

With a grimace, I turned around and bore my ass to him, wiggling it a little before whirling back around. He was smiling, drool dripping off his tongue and sliding down the metal bar, eyes locked on me as his hand slipped beneath the waistband of his pants.

I swallowed hard. Was this demon really about to jack off to me?

His tongue slipped back into his mouth, and his eyes dropped lower. "Run your fingers through that delicious hair." I balked. He wasn't talking about the hair on my head.

"You said dance," I bit out, eyes narrowing on him. I wondered if I'd be fast enough to punch him in the face if I tried. "I danced."

"True, but we're not done." He shook his head.

My mouth was completely dry now, my eyes aching from the lack of lubrication. My muscles ached.

I cringed, wanting nothing more than for all this to be over, but Leviathan's eager eyes were waiting. With shaky fingers, I did as I was told, running my fingers through my pubic hair while he watched. A throaty groan escaped him.

"Lower," he said, licking his lips again.

My throat swelled. "Lower?"

He couldn't mean for me to...

"Touch yourself for me, pet."

"Fuck no," I said, but even as the words left my mouth, my bottom lip cracked, and I tasted blood.

Fuck. Fuck. Fuck.

"Touch yourself," he hissed, his voice wrapping around my throat like an invisible chain. "And all the pain goes away."

I doubted that, but I did it anyway, desperate for him to stop. My fingers slid through my folds and found my clit. I was so far from turned on that I would have been dry even without him zapping the moisture out of me, but I swirled my fingers around my clit nevertheless.

"Yes," he hissed, shoving his pants down until his dick sprang free.

The Lord of Envy's dick was thick with iridescent scales that ran along the base, the rest soft green flesh wrapped in a complicated network of veins. A copper hoop looped through the tip. His hand worked over the rock-hard erection, his eyes never leaving me as he pleasured himself to my writhing form.

I thought about Holga and how she was probably worried sick about me. I thought about the masquerade guests, twirling in their pretty costumes. I thought about taxes. Puppies. Belial's talking furniture. His vast collection of horn jewelry—how the silver spider charm was my favorite. Anything to get my mind off what was happening.

All this for some goddamn water.

"Come closer, pet."

"Fuck you," I choked, my voice hoarse.

"Is that a request?" The eagerness in his gaze turned dark, lustful.

My eyes narrowed on him.

"If you don't want me ripping this cage open and coming in one of those pretty holes, I suggest you come closer," he demanded, his voice sinister.

With my heart in my throat, I inched closer to the bars until the metal pressed against my skin.

Fucking hell, did this feel disgusting. The Lord of Envy was jerking his dick while he forced me to touch myself, but at least that's all this was. He wasn't touching me. He wasn't hurting me—not physically, anyway.

I looked away, trying to focus on anything but the smell of salty seaweed pouring off him, but he clicked his tongue.

"Fucking look at me."

Cheeks heating with anger, I met his gaze again. A second later, he came, warm cum spurting across my stomach, dripping into my navel.

I jumped backward a second too late, desperate to get it off. I didn't want to touch it, but there was nothing in my cage I could clean it with.

"You slimy motherfucker," I growled.

He was tucking himself back into his pants, adjusting them. "Any female of my realm would be grateful to receive my seed, you bratty little bitch."

I wanted to stab him. I wanted to claw his eyes out. I didn't want to wait for Belial to get here to see him ripped apart. I wanted to do it my damn self.

"Now can I have some fucking water, you fucking prick?" I choked, my hoarse voice hardly more than a whisper.

"I guess, since you've been such an obedient pet." He reached through the bars with the hand he'd just finished jacking off with, cupping it like he was offering me something. A second later, water pooled in his palm. "Drink."

I stared down at the liquid, every part of me screaming for me to take the offering despite the little globs of cum floating in it.

Gross.

"Ew. I'm not drinking your dick water, you sick fuck."

"I guess you aren't that thirsty after all," he said, his gaze turning sinister.

Was he going to drain more from me? I wasn't sure how much more I could take before my organs shut down and I collapsed, dead.

With a scathing glare, I put my lips to his hand and allowed him to tip the water into my mouth. It was warm and had a slightly salty aftertaste, but I choked it down.

Thankfully, he refilled his palm a couple of times to let me drink. It wasn't enough—far from it—but it alleviated the ache, for which I was grateful.

"What a good pet." He withdrew his hand. "Maybe I can tame you after all."

Footsteps in the distance cut him off and caught my attention. They were wet slapping sounds that grew louder as the seconds passed, and my heart slammed painfully into my ribcage at the flicker of hope the sound sparked.

Someone was coming.

Leviathan instantly tensed, and the look on his face told me he wasn't amused.

Every muscle in my body tightened as my hope grew, my eyes straining deep into the cavern, searching for a familiar face. All the while, a question burned in the back of my mind.

Had Belial already made it to save me?

CHAPTER TWENTY-ONE

RAYVEN

FROM THE SHADOWS EMERGED one of Leviathan's servants haloed in an orange glow. He wore dark, water-logged clothes and looked like he'd just taken a swim. Water streamed from his stringy black hair, and most of his sickly-looking blue skin was crusted in barnacles. I didn't know if he was a demon native to this realm or a soul sentenced to this layer of hell, but he looked terrified.

A second later, I realized why.

The orange glow I'd seen was coming from a pair of enormous flaming wings attached to one of the most grisly-looking beasts I'd seen, apart from Asmodeus. He was enormous, even bigger than the Lord of Bones by my estimation.

He had heavy muscles packed onto his wide body and rough, armor-like skin as black as midnight. Dark horns curved up toward the cavern ceiling. He wore a thick leather belt around his waist that reminded me of a tool belt, and a leather apron hung between his meaty thighs.

Judging by the swell of energy emanating from him that made my hair stand on end, he was no doubt one of the demon lords.

"I don't remember sending for you, Mammon," Leviathan said, annoyance lacing his tone. My eyes widened at the name, recalling how he'd looked at the ball. This had to be his true form, since this was hardly the same motherfucker who'd helped kidnap me.

A smile bowed Mammon's lips as his blood-red eyes drifted past Leviathan to my cage. They lingered on my naked form, and I curled in on myself again, shielding myself the best I could. I was tired of being ogled like a zoo animal.

"Y-your Majesty, I told him you didn't want any visitors," the servant stammered. "But Lord Mammon insisted—"

"*Silence,*" Leviathan snapped.

The servant bowed and backed away into the shadows without another word.

Leviathan's gaze leveled on his brother, anger flickering behind his eyes. "This better be important."

Mammon cocked a dark eyebrow at him. "You think I'd waste my time coming up to this grimy place if it wasn't?"

The serpent demon made a noise that suggested that was exactly what he thought.

"You have something I want," Mammon continued.

"Take it and go then," Leviathan said impatiently with a dismissive hand wave. "Obviously, I'm a little tied up."

Mammon's intense gaze once again landed on me, and I squirmed. "Let her out, then, and I'll be on my way."

"I think not." Leviathan's tone was vicious, sharp. "She's my pet now."

Mammon took a step closer to me, tsking. "Now, now, Lord of Envy. That wasn't the plan. We agreed to hand her down the line and each have our fun with her."

Leviathan stepped into his path, shielding me from him. "Come on. Asmodeus never intended to let her go, and now that she's mine, neither do I." He obviously wasn't afraid of his brother, which either made him really stupid or really cocky. I hadn't seen Leviathan's true form yet, but something told me he'd still be outmatched.

"How did you even know she was here?"

"Souls whisper, brother," Mammon answered Leviathan while keeping his eyes fixed on me. "They speak of the mortal queen of Limbo. The tortured souls of Asmodeus' realm kneeled to her in fealty."

My heart fluttered at the memory of the souls in Asmodeus' throne room kneeling before me. Had they communicated with other souls? Was word spreading through all the layers of Hell?

A lump formed in my throat at the thought, but I couldn't worry about that now.

"What has me scratching my brain is *how* she got away." Mammon hiked an inquisitive brow at me. "Asmodeus' realm is a fortress. Souls never escape his clutches unless he means them to."

"I bit his dick off." I forced a grin, trying to look intimidating. Maybe neither of them would touch me if they thought they might end up like their three-headed brother.

If anything, it only seemed to heighten Mammon's curiosity. His red eyes nearly glowed with excitement.

"You are a tasty-looking morsel." Mammon stepped around Leviathan and pressed closer to my cell. The flickering torch lights played over his face, distorting his features. "I think you've been kept in this cage long enough."

That, we could agree on.

"I'm taking her to the Forge, brother."

Leviathan laughed dryly and shook his head. "Maybe you didn't understand me before. She's *mine*. The only times she'll ever leave that cage will be the short excursions to my bed."

I hadn't worked out what sin Mammon represented, but I doubted it was pride or wrath. Either one would have probably exploded and ripped Leviathan's head off by now. What did that leave? Gluttony? Sloth? *Greed?*

Something hooked beneath my gut.

I'd put money on Mammon being the Lord of Greed.

"It wasn't up for debate," the winged beast snapped. "I'll make you a deal. Give me the girl, and I'll let you live."

Leviathan just laughed, which intensified the dread creeping up my spine. I was either about to see Mammon turn him into a snake-kabob, or he had a trick up his sleeve yet.

I moved to the far end of my cage, trying to put as much distance between myself and these two as possible, but it wasn't nearly far enough. My back pressed against the metal bars so hard, it hurt.

For a tense moment, no one moved or said anything, the tension so thick, Leviathan could slice through it with his claws. Mammon gripped my bars, ready to bend them apart to free me.

Leviathan lunged for the winged demon lord, who reacted just as quickly and swung a punch at the serpent demon's face.

It was so fast, I was sure I was about to see the serpent hit the ground. He dove to the side, dodging the blow, and his body began to shift even before he righted himself.

Leviathan's legs disappeared, replaced by a long, reptilian tail. His claws grew longer, his muscles twisting and contorting as he tripled in size. What was left was a hellish naga creature, half man, half snake. My eyes popped as I watched him whip forward, hitting Mammon straight in the chest.

They tumbled backward on the stone floor in a tangle of limbs, fists, fangs, and claws.

Leviathan's sharp nails raked across Mammon's impossibly thick skin, doing minimal damage that I could see, and the fire demon grappled with the thrashing tail. One of his blazing wings brushed against the silk sheets of Leviathan's bed. The whole thing went up in flames in the blink of an eye.

Leviathan roared, his fist connecting with Mammon's face, and I screamed as flames licked dangerously close to the cage.

As if disturbed by the Lord of Envy's rage, the ocean outside began to crash harder, waves washing into the cavern and soaking the floor. A white crest crashed into the bed, putting out the fire a second later and leaving a crispy, drenched heap behind.

In the midst of the brawl, there was a crackle of red magic, and a giant iron hammer appeared in Mammon's hand. He swung it—hard. It cracked Leviathan in the side of the head, sending him sprawling across the stone.

The demon Lord of Envy twitched on the cave floor but fell still a moment later and didn't move again.

Seeing the serpent demon's body splayed on the ground, I found my voice and finally screamed.

Mammon's eyes snapped in my direction.

"As I was saying..." He approached the cage, still wielding the giant hammer in one hand. It was nearly as tall as I was, with multiple faces and ornate demonic runes carved into the handle. "You're coming with me."

I tried to back up, but there was nowhere to go. "I'm not going anywhere with you."

I had to stall. Belial couldn't be far away now...

Mammon laughed as he gripped the copper bars. Fire blazed beneath his touch, and the metal glowed hot before melting enough for him to bend them.

The bars groaned, and I screamed, "Leave me the fuck alone!"

He ignored me and warped the metal until there was a space big enough for me to fit.

"Come here, morsel," he said, grabbing me by the forearm and yanking me out of my prison. I stumbled, trying to wrestle my arm out of his hold, but to no avail.

On the one hand, I was thankful to be free. But Belial had been right—as much as I hated it—that the cage had been the safest place for me to wait for his rescue. He'd told me to stay put in Leviathan's realm until then.

By the time he got here, I'd be gone, pulled deeper into the depths of Hell.

"Let me go," I screamed, pulling against his iron-like grip. I clawed, kicked, scratched, and bit at his hand until he grabbed me by the waist and tucked me up under one of his arms. He probably would have thrown me over his shoulder if not for the wings; they'd burn me alive.

"You're a light little thing, morsel," he said, carrying me as easily as if I was a bag of groceries. I swung my legs frantically, desperate to connect with something, but it was no use. "We're gonna have to fatten you up for sure."

My insides turned. I didn't want to know why he'd want more meat on my bones or why he kept calling me 'morsel'. Whatever he had planned for me, it wasn't good. It wasn't good at all.

I screamed again, making eye contact with a helpless water demon servant as we marched by.

"Help me! Please!" I begged, but he simply watched us go with pity in his eyes.

I couldn't blame him. What was he going to do against a fucking lord of Hell?

"Put me down. I can walk just fine," I argued, still kicking as we headed deeper into the cave. I wasn't sure where he was taking me exactly, but maybe I could give him the slip if he just put me down.

Mammon laughed as though I'd told a joke. "Did you forget? I've seen how much of a runner you are. Gonna keep you safe and sound until we reach the ship."

Ship? I balked, wondering why the fuck there would be a ship. Then, I remembered the demon ferrymen. I might not have seen one of the ferries yet, but Belial told me they existed. Were there other lords with vessels that could sail the bloody waters?

Mammon's boat was little more than a glorified sailboat and hardly qualified as a ship, but I wasn't about to tell the Lord of Greed what I thought of his little dinghy.

It was made out of metal, with black sails and iron details. He dropped me to the deck the second we were on it, and I screamed when a creature darted toward me. A small, ugly, beady-eyed, goblin-looking creature quickly wound a chain around my naked body and locked it into place around a pole.

It then hobbled away to the steering wheel, barking orders at the rest of the crew as they hobbled into view. I tried to move, but the chain weighing me down was too heavy.

"You'll be glad you're naked," Mammon said, grabbing the wheel and guiding the boat down the Styx. "It's hot where we're headed."

"Your realm?" I asked, hoping he would elaborate.

He only leveled me with a glare, his red eyes flickering. "The Forge."

CHAPTER TWENTY-TWO

BELIAL

THE DEMON LORD OF Pride screamed in unholy agony as I tore his head off, but all I could hear were Rayven's screams as she came on my cock.

Vine's death came quickly, and I took no joy from it, unlike when I'd murdered Asmodeus.

He begged me to spare him, but I denied his request. He'd done nothing to help Rayven when she passed through his realm, half-drowned in the Styx. He'd known her soul belonged to me, yet he stood idly by.

I tuned out his last screams, replaying my time in Rayven's dream.

She'd taken me so perfectly.

I'd manipulated the dream to ensure she could fit me. When we truly mated, it would be harder for her little pussy to take me in this form, but her reaction made me hopeful.

My little human had a penchant for pain. I'd just have to tease and work her up so she could take me, and I'd savor every moment.

With Vine's head added to my oar, I made my way through his palace back to the Styx, flowing through his throne room.

Cecil and Holga were huddled on the gondola bench, watching as I approached. They said nothing when I climbed into the ferry.

"The Lord of Pride…" my librarian muttered, his toothy eye sockets gaping at the latest edition to my collection.

I thought I'd feel a twinge of guilt for Vine's death. Now that it was done, I felt nothing. That's what Rayven did to me.

The only life I cared for was hers now.

So, when I pulled my ferry up to dock outside Leviathan's cliffside palace, I maintained my steely indifference to the prospect of his death as well.

Of all the lords of the nine realms, I would have thought Leviathan would be the one to remain loyal to me. But what Rayven told me had me second-guessing my faith in my relationship with the Lord of Envy.

If I found out he was in on the kidnapping, there'd be Hell to pay.

I demanded directions to Leviathan's chamber from a servant soul who cowered as I loomed over him. With a shaky hand, he pointed me in the right direction, and I swept past him, charging down the hallway carved from stone.

It always struck me as odd how I was the lord of death and bone, yet I seemed to be the only one who couldn't stand living in the ground. I took several sets of stairs carved from stone until the narrow corridor opened to the ocean—Leviathan's chamber being the only part of his home above sea level.

The black sea reflecting the ominous green glow of Envy's moon was strangely beautiful, but there was no time to admire the view. I was on a mission, my sole focus rescuing Rayven and taking her back to Limbo, but a prickling feeling of unease swept through me when I stepped deeper into the room.

It was destroyed, his things disturbed, his bed half-torched.

My jaw tightened, and my eyes, hot and full of fire, locked with Leviathan's. The snake was lying on his singed mattress, curled up in his naga form with his tail wrapped around his humanoid torso.

There was no sign of Rayven anywhere—only the lingering traces of her scent.

The copper cage he'd kept her in was lying on its side, its bars melted and bent out of shape, an indication that a fire demon had been here.

My fists clenched, and the fire in my eyes sockets leapt high. *Mammon.*

I approached the bed while I surveyed the wreckage of his room. There was blood on the ground, but judging by the scent, none of it was Rayven's. Another glance at the serpent demon told me who the blood belonged to. Mammon had beaten Leviathan badly. He was bruised and burnt all over, with a bad head wound that indicated he'd been struck by the Lord of Greed's infamous war hammer. "What happened here?"

If the serpent demon was surprised to see me, he didn't show it. "Mammon happened, that fucking brute. I tried to stop him."

My heavy boots crunched against the ground with every step as I closed the distance between me and my brother. "Tried to stop Mammon from doing what, Leviathan?"

"I tried to stop him from taking your mortal pet."

"My mortal *queen*," I corrected him with a growl that had him flinching. "And you should have fought harder."

I moved to kneel beside the battered cage, fingers brushing over the melted bars.

I'd missed her...

Fuck!

It couldn't have been by much. I could still smell the flames of Mammon's wings, and something else clung to the air. My attention landed on a small white puddle on the ground beside Rayven's cage.

I swiped a finger through it and held it up.

Hellish rage blasted through me, turning my insides to ash when I realized it was cum. Fresh serpent demon cum.

Rising to my feet, I spun around and charged towards the bed, murder bright in my eyes. "What did you do to her?"

"I—"

I didn't want to believe he'd betrayed me, but I already knew the truth. His reaction to me—his pounding heart, the fear in his eyes, the way he trembled as I stormed toward him—told me everything. The traitorous bastard gave himself away before the lie even slithered off his forked tongue.

"I didn't hurt her!"

"Lies!" I roared. I snapped my fingers, and my oar appeared in my hand with a spark of shimmering blue magic.

Terror washed over the Lord of Envy's scaly physiognomy when he took in the heads of Vine and Asmodeus.

"Tell me what happened from the beginning, and you can save yourself from becoming the next addition to my little collection here."

Now I was the one lying. The lord of the fourth circle had sealed his doom the moment he'd decided to betray me.

"When you sent the invitations, Asmodeus tried to get all of us together to kidnap your new human pet. He said she was too distracting for you, that you'd get on with your job without her to occupy your time," he explained, fear growing in his eyes with every word he spoke. "We were supposed to pass her down the layers until she arrived at the ninth circle."

Fury painted my vision red, and fire thrummed through my system as I glared daggers at the demon I'd once called my friend. "You fucking viper."

"What?" He flicked his nail, nervously reaching for his hookah's mouthpiece. He was trying to act innocent but was failing miserably. "I never intended on giving her up to Mammon or anyone else. I was going to keep her safe in that cage. For you."

"For me?" I repeated, the two words sounding every bit like the punchline it was. "You're full of shit."

Leviathan's forked tongue licked the air with his indignant hiss. "I'm on your side, Belial! I'm loyal to you, not the others."

"If that's the case, why didn't you tell me about Asmodeus' plan, if you knew what he intended to do before the ball? Why didn't you try and stop him when he and the others kidnapped Rayven? Why didn't you call for me when you pulled her from the Styx? And why..."

I snatched his tongue in my hand before he could pull away and wrenched him off the bed, jamming my finger—the one oozing with cum—in his face. "Why is your filthy snake cum on the ground?"

All the blood drained from his face. He couldn't speak since I was still gripping his tongue, but his muffled cries indicated he knew what was about to happen.

"You fucking traitor," I snarled into his face. "You're lucky I don't have time to draw out your death. But I promise you, I'll be back for your body. I'm going to skin you and fashion your scales into a pretty dress for my new queen."

The naga squirmed and thrashed, his tail uncoiling from his torso to try and wrap around me. My blue flames engulfed my body, and he screamed, managing to wiggle away. I stomped after him, dragging my oar of heads behind me, my manic laughter filling the cave.

He slithered toward where the cavern opened in an attempt to slip into the sea, but I slammed my oar down on his tail hard enough to break the bone. He screamed, and the ocean swelled with its lord's pain, a wave rising and crashing down over me. My flames created a shield around me, and I held my ground as the inky waters raged through the cavern.

I gripped Leviathan's tail, pulling it like I was winding up a rope. He screamed as I dragged him through the fire, inch by inch, his water doing little to soothe the burns.

By the time I got to his head, the fire had consumed his entire body. With his dying breath, the water receded into the ocean. Laying limp on the ground, he looked up at me, eyes full of hateful tears. "You were my brother."

I glared down at him, maw opening to release a bellow of a laugh. "You're right. You *were* my brother."

I placed my boot on his head and slowly applied pressure until there was a sickening crunch of his skull giving out beneath my sole, and his serpentine body went limp for good. I lifted my boot after an eerily still moment, the rush of the water breaking against the rock the only sound as I stooped to cut off my favorite brother's head.

"Now you'll be nothing more than a bitter memory and something to hang in my queen's closet."

CHAPTER TWENTY-THREE

BELIAL

Our gondola tore down the Styx so quickly, it caused the crimson current to roll and slosh. We were in a narrow channel, surrounded by stone as we ripped through Leviathan's realm.

The flames in my eyes raged bright and would have illuminated the tunnel on their own if not for the flaming torches scattered along the way.

I glanced at my oar as I pushed it behind the gondola, urging us to move faster down the river. The blackened remains of Leviathan's incinerated head stared back at me from where he was speared beneath Asmodeus.

Mammon would be next. When I got my claws into the Lord of Greed, I'd rip him apart slowly. Painfully. Bone by bone.

Nothing less would suffice.

I knew I'd missed Mammon and Rayven by mere minutes.

I could catch up. I *would* catch up.

"M-my Lord," Holga's soft voice could barely be heard over the violent rocking of the ferry and the clashing of the Styx on the rocky cavern as we barreled down it. For her soft cadence, she might as well have been yelling.

The terror shaking her voice told me she wanted me to slow down, but I ignored her. I couldn't afford any distractions, not when I was so hellishly focused. Above all, I couldn't afford to slow down.

Rayven was nearly within my grasp.

After a minute or two, the narrow channel opened wider, the rocks spreading and thinning until they disappeared. We were nearing the end of Leviathan's realm, surrounded by swirling darkness, drifting closer to the fifth layer of Hell, Mammon's domain.

I was beginning to think I'd made a grave mistake taking time to kill Leviathan. I'd been quick, but maybe the handful of minutes I spared doling out his Judgement had cost me.

My heart sank, and my hope of catching up to them was all but gone when I saw it: the stern of a boat in the distance. It was much larger than the ferries used to usher souls to the lower layers of Hell and looked to be made of iron.

Of course, it would be.

Mammon never missed an opportunity to utilize his iron forge. He'd made numerous things over the years in his fortress, filling his realm with iron constructs. It had already been cluttered when I visited over five hundred years ago—there was no telling how much the greedy bastard was hoarding now.

It seemed he'd made himself a boat. He'd probably fashioned it to get to and from Belphegor's realm, considering they were fucking. Under different circumstances, I would have laughed, but the thought of my backstabbing brothers only made me row faster.

My muscles burned with the pace I was setting, but I was slowly closing the distance. Holga's bones chattered as she shook below me, Cecil still doing his best to comfort her. The closer we got, the more violent the water became, choppy waves rolling toward us as the ship cut through the bloody current.

All I had to do was catch up and slaughter the crew, and Rayven would be mine.

Could she see me? Did she know she was minutes from being saved?

"I'm coming, treasure," I muttered beneath my breath.

A massive stone wall materialized, split in half by a giant archway over the Styx. My muscles coiled, recognizing the entrance to the Lord of Greed's realm.

"Rayven!" the sound that tore from my lipless maw hardly sounded like myself. It was raw, pained. If the crew hadn't realized we were on their tail before, they did now.

Mammon's fiery eyes whipped in my direction, and his flaming wings flexed before he barked orders. The iron boat began to pull ahead, widening the gap between us. A growl rumbled up my throat, and I rowed faster, but it wasn't enough to close the distance again.

I was so focused on catching up and saving my little treasure that I didn't notice the massive iron bars dropping from the archway up ahead until they were nearly halfway down. If they closed completely, they would block our entrance into the fifth layer.

There would be no way through with the ferry.

Mammon's boat picked up more speed, and something jerked in my gut. It didn't look like they would make it in time. I held my breath, wondering if I would have to jump ship to save Rayven. If Mammon's boat was destroyed, there was a chance.

They sped closer, the gate dangerously low. I kept rowing as fast as I could, unholy fury fueling every stroke, but the iron boat slipped beneath the bars just before they slammed into the river.

"No!" I dove off the side of the ferry and rushed to the gate, grabbing the bars and trying to lift or bend them. To my surprise—and horror—they didn't budge. "What kind of magic—"

The question died in my throat when I submerged myself, hoping there was enough room for me to squeeze underneath it, but the bars ran straight to the bed of the river.

I couldn't get through.

Resurfacing with a roar, I threw my head back, my cloak slapping against the water's surface. I gripped the iron gate's girthy bars and tried to bend them again, but to no avail. The gate was several thousand pounds at least—even I, strong as I was, couldn't budge it.

Through the gaps in the metal, I could see the boat shrinking, Mammon's sadistic laugh carrying on the air. I set my flaming eyes on him as they disappeared into the distance, my rage palpable as I harnessed my magic to destroy the hurdle keeping me from my queen.

The explosion of blue magic blew straight into the gate, leaving it unfazed, without so much as a scorch. I tried again, reaching deep into my pool of power, but again, it was pointless.

"Fuck, fuck, fuck," I growled. My magic wasn't working on this iron monstrosity, probably because it was Mammon's metal. Iron was stronger than silver.

Panic hooked in my gut.

"My Lord, let me try," Holga piped from the ferry.

If my magic didn't work, I didn't see hers being able to break through the gate, but it was worth a shot. I didn't have any other ideas, and Mammon's boat was drifting farther away with every passing second.

A flicker of magic sparked from her fingers, but that failed too.

I slammed my fists against the enormous gate with a snarl, and dust rained from above. Still, nothing seemed to affect it, which only fanned the roiling inferno burning through me.

Mammon had been busy at work over the last five hundred years, fool-proofing this realm, apparently. If there was no way in, there was no way out.

I punched the metal again with an animalistic roar just as a severed hand grabbed hold of my robe.

"Master," a head with one eye bubbled. "Please, pass Judgement again. *Please...*"

A torso without arms bobbed toward me, and several other voices whispered, joining the first.

"Lord of Bones... Lord of Souls, please..."

I growled, swiping my claws at the souls to get away from them before climbing back into the boat. The begging whispers ceased the moment I was out of the water, and I ran a blood-soaked hand down my skull, thinking.

How the fuck was I supposed to penetrate the impenetrable?

Magic and strength had failed me. What other option did I have?

"M-my Lord." It was Cecil this time, his teeth-filled eye sockets watching me apprehensively. "Perhaps I could assist."

I glared at him, wondering what the ancient librarian could possibly do that Holga and I hadn't been able to accomplish. I'd known him for so long, millennia at this point. He wasn't hiding anything from me; I would have known.

"How?" I tried to keep my patience, but it was an arduous task.

"The library," he answered slowly, thoughtfully, like Cecil always did. Normally, I appreciated his careful, articulated thoughts, but right now, it made me want to toss him off the gondola. Was he suggesting we return to Limbo to riffle through soul books?

The Library? I didn't see how that could help us here. "We don't have time to turn back, if that's what you're suggesting."

"If magic and brute strength don't work, an engineer could probably help," he said.

I glared, anger burning beneath my skin. I was definitely going to throw him overboard.

"Ah yes, because I happen to have one of those in my fucking pocket." I rubbed the patch of bone between my eyes in irritation since I didn't have a nose to pinch in this form. I was losing the last shred of my patience.

Cecil trembled and shook his head. "You have a few in the castle library. I could fetch one and see if they can work out the mechanism."

This ancient sack of dust and bones had officially lost his marbles—if he'd had any to begin with.

Sensing my growing frustration, Cecil cleared his throat and pushed his wire-rimmed glasses up his barely-there nose. "Allow me, Sire."

Holga and I watched in awe as he produced a dinner-plate-sized portal with a flourish of his skeletal hands. It grew, stretching outward until it was tall enough for him to slip through. Inside it, a sliver of the Library of Souls was clearly visible.

Admittedly, I was impressed.

Cecil had some limited powers when it came to the library, but he rarely ventured from the vast hall, much less the castle.

Had he always had this ability and just never had the chance to utilize it?

"So you're going to bring me the soul of an engineer…" I ventured a guess, my eyes landing on his proud expression, "who will be able to get this fucking gate open?"

He nodded once.

"And if it doesn't work?" I bit out.

"What do you have to lose?"

"*Everything.*" The fury in my voice was unintentional and made both servants flinch. My voice softened with a sigh that felt every bit as heavy as my chest. "I could lose everything, Cecil."

"We'll find her," Holga assured me with the gentlest tone she'd ever directed toward me.

"Go," I urged Cecil. My eyes slid from the soul librarian to the portal. "With haste."

Without another word, the librarian slipped through the portal. It closed a second later, blinking him out of sight.

CHAPTER TWENTY-FOUR

RAYVEN

EVERY WHISPER OF HOPE shattered with the clang of the gate closing, and I felt my heart breaking all over again as Belial's gondola melted into the darkness. Tears stung the corners of my eyes, a scream burning up my throat.

"Belial!" The sound was immediately swallowed by the hot, acrid air as we drifted deeper into Mammon's domain.

I stared into the distance, even though any trace of Belial was long gone, hoping to see him on our tail again. I was desperate for him to get to me.

He'd been so close to saving me, and now...

"By the time Belial catches up, it'll be too late," Mammon's voice mocked my internal thoughts, making my skin itch.

I whipped my head in the Lord of Greed's direction, already working on a fiery retort, but the words died on my tongue when the forge came into view behind him. My mouth dropped in an involuntary O as it loomed, unlike anything I'd seen before.

It was an enormous stone fortress stretching several stories high, the tips of its spires disappearing into pitch blackness. An enormous iron statue of Mammon was erected in front of it, his legs parting over the River Styx to let the bloody water enter.

We sailed into the structure, Mammon's boat moving along the outer perimeter of the stone, my eyes shifting quickly to take it all in. It was a circular space, with a giant opening in the middle where the floor should have been. It was also hot as fuck, my lungs burning with every inhale.

When we docked, Mammon grabbed hold of the end of my chain and dragged me off the boat.

It was difficult to walk with the weight of the iron links around me, but I managed. The stone was hot beneath my bare feet, the air scorching my skin. It felt like we'd walked into an oven.

Following in the Lord of Greed's wake with goblin creatures on my heels, I inched my way nearer to the opening in the floor, curious to see what lay below. The sight had my stomach cartwheeling.

Nearly fifty feet beneath us was a lake of lava, bubbling and boiling. One wrong step was all it would take to die a very painful death.

My eyes traveled upward, above the molten magma, to a raised concrete dais. Four sets of stone steps led up to it, which a few goblin creatures were currently hobbling up and down. I expected to see giant anvils or other forge tools, but there was only a giant cauldron over a roaring fire.

What the fuck?

I imagined a bunch of iron workers making weapons or something in Hell's very own forge...not cooking fucking soup.

"You're just in time for a feast," Mammon announced, sounding proud. He stopped short and whirled to face me, one of his flaming wings nearly brushing my arm.

"A feast?" I peered at the dais again in time to see a goblin dump a sack of various vegetables into the cauldron. Another stood on a ladder, stirring the concoction with a giant spoon.

As they worked, they sang a song, the lyrics creepy and the tune off-kilter. "Toil, toil, burn and roil, in the demon's brew you're sure to boil."

What kind of macabre Hocus Pocus fuckery is this shit?

"Yes, a feast. How else would we celebrate?" The cocky look on his face gave me the impression I was missing something, like the invisible dots were laid out for me but I hadn't yet connected them.

Were they celebrating...me? I nearly laughed as soon as the thought crossed my mind.

"What's the occasion?" I asked when he didn't offer any type of explanation.

Mammon merely laughed, the sound grating against my eardrums. "You, and the new era you bring."

A new era? Celebrating me? No way this motherfucker kidnapped me and was now throwing me a party. Something wasn't right.

Seeing the question plain on my face, Mammon continued. "Without you distracting the Lord of Bones, we will finally get the souls we're rightly owed. My realm will once again be filled with the screams of degenerates. Definitely worthy of a celebration."

"So you're eating...soup?" I asked in disbelief, looking between him and the giant cauldron. A goblin was tossing in giant clumps of leafy greens.

"Of course not. That's just an appetizer." Mammon jerked on the chain, making me stumble toward him, and leered down to meet my gaze. "You're the main course, morsel."

Main course?

I barely had time to register it before Mammon wheeled around and jerked on the chain, leading me toward a set of doors in the stone. They were massive, much like the ones in Belial's castle, and led into a long, narrow dining hall.

The longest table I'd ever seen was set and ready for the feast, fruit-laden trays spaced intermittently down the center with iron candelabras and bouquets wrought from metal. There were at least a hundred chairs tucked up against the table, though only three were filled.

Sitting at the head of the hall, his white hair spilling over his shoulders, was Belphegor. To his left sat a demon with pale, wrinkly skin and one large, cyan eye in place of a face. The large eye locked on me the moment I entered the hall. To his right was a demon with at least a dozen eyes and a teeth-filled, gaping maw, his many arachnid-like legs folded around him.

The power buzzing through the room was palpable, and I knew who the strange demons were before Mammon opened his mouth.

"It wouldn't be a celebration without the Lords of Wrath and Sloth joining us," he said, gesturing to his guests. "They were quite intrigued when I told them about our mortal morsel."

"Belial is going to skewer you fucks when he gets here," I snapped as Mammon dragged me down the hall. I wasn't sure what his plan was, especially since he claimed I was the main course, but I wasn't going to roll over and take it.

"Belial can't do shit if he can't get in," Belphegor's voice whipped through the silent space.

The demon was still in the feminine bombshell form I'd met at the ball, but now, he wore a strappy leather number that showed more skin than not. "He'll give up trying and crawl back to his realm. You'll see. Or maybe you won't..."

He examined his long nails, looking bored. "Considering you won't be here much longer."

His eyes flicked up, gleaming at me from beneath his snow-white lashes. In this form, he was beautiful, and somehow, I got the gut feeling he was more dangerous than Lust, Envy, and maybe even Greed.

My eyes narrowed on him. "He'll never give up." I didn't feel like arguing with any of these dickheads, especially over Belial's obsession with me.

They would all see, and they would all pay.

Belphegor shoved his chair back, the legs scraping against the stone floor with a wail. Then, he trotted his way over, balancing on six-inch stilettos I would have broken my neck trying to walk in. All the while, the other demon lords observed quietly, making my skin crawl.

Belphegor stopped in front of us, towering over me with the added height, taking me in with those nearly black eyes.

"We'll see about that." He glared down his nose at me, a phantom smirk tugging at the corner of his plump lips. "There won't be a point once you're ingested anyway; he's wasting his time."

I swallowed hard. "*Ingested?*"

Oh, fuck. That's what Mammon meant by me being the main course. This crazy fuck meant to literally eat me.

Was he going to plop me in the cauldron? Filet me in front of his servants? Eat me whole?

I wasn't sure how he'd manage the last one, but I wouldn't put it past him.

"Yes," Belphegor confirmed with a huff. "It wasn't my idea. Personally, I could think of more *entertaining* ways to get rid of you."

"Enough," Mammon snapped, cutting Belphegor off before thrusting the end of my chain at him. "I want you to get her ready."

He might as well have been handing Belphegor a dirty diaper for the disgusted face he made. "Get her ready? You want me to tenderize the meat or something, Mammon?"

He chuckled darkly. "I cherish that demented mind of yours, but no. Bathe her; get her nice and clean."

"I'm not your goddamn handmaid," the white-haired demon seethed, snatching the chain from him. "If it wasn't for that giant cock of yours, I'd tell you to make one of your filthy gremlins do it."

"Aw, come on, Belly. Don't be like that..." he cooed in a lovey-dovey tone that would have made me sick if I wasn't already feeling nauseous, what with learning I was about to be eaten.

Oh *God*. That cauldron was for me. They intended to boil and eat me.

"Don't." The venom in Belphegor's voice cut him off as he raised a slender, manicured finger. "I told you not to call me that."

Mammon cackled and dropped his voice to a rumbly whisper. "You don't seem to mind when I'm balls deep in that sweet ass of yours, brother."

Rolling his eyes, Belphegor turned and dragged me through the hall, his eyes set on an iron door in the corner.

I wasn't sure where he was taking me—from the outside, it didn't look like there was much space for bedchambers or bathrooms—but I was relieved to be away from Mammon. The sheer heat pouring off his flaming wings had made my skin tender.

Whatever Belphegor meant by 'more entertaining' things to do with me, it had to be better than Mammon's plans to have me for dinner. It was the thinnest silver lining, but it was silver, nonetheless.

The iron door opened into a surprisingly wide corridor, which must have led out of the actual forge and into a castle I hadn't seen on the way in. It was a little cooler here, but still hot enough to make me sweat. Much more of this, and I'd be half-boiled before I even reached the pot.

I expected us to walk in silence, but a steady stream of mumbling seemed to come from Belphegor as we turned down a second hallway.

"Such a waste," he muttered, his long white hair dancing as he shook his head. "He has never been the brightest though."

"Are you talking about Mammon?" I attempted conversation, eager for information. If I could find out something—anything—from Belphegor that might help me get out of this hell hole, I'd take it.

"Yes, he's so...*greedy*." Belphegor huffed a laugh. "As if that's a surprise, but it has to be *his* way or no way."

He shoved open a door to reveal an empty bedchamber, dragging me toward the ensuite. My stomach dropped, realizing Belphegor would be the one bathing me. I didn't like that thought at all, especially not after all the other fucked up things his brothers had done to me.

"If you run, I'll turn you into bloody confetti." He flashed his manicured claws that would definitely slice me into ribbons. "Got it?"

I nodded, shifting uncomfortably while he dug between his ample breasts and produced an iron key. He promptly fit it into the padlock attached to my chains, and they clanged loudly to the floor.

For the first time since the chains were put on, I could breathe.

"It really is a shame." He tsked his tongue as he crossed to the clawfoot tub and turned on the water. It was so hot, the room immediately filled with steam. "We could have so much more fun."

His hungry eyes roved over me for much longer than I would have liked, and I crossed my arms over my chest in an attempt at modesty.

I had no idea what kind of sadistic torture Belphegor could dream up, but I couldn't imagine many things worse than being eaten. In fact, I was willing to bet that however Belphegor wanted to play, it was a million times better than being boiled to death and digested by a demon lord.

If I could just convince Belphegor of the same thing, maybe I'd have a shot out of here. I at least had to try.

"What kinds of things?" I asked, forcing innocence into my words.

Belphegor's eyes snapped up to meet mine, and I froze. He was impossible to read, especially since the form he presented himself in wasn't his true one. He was a shapeshifter, the ulti-mate demon of deception. For all I knew, his entire personality was a guise and he didn't even care about Mammon.

"So many things." The corner of his pouty lips lifted into a smirk. "Would you like me to show you?"

CHAPTER TWENTY-FIVE

Rayven

My throat tightened as Belphegor eyed me through the steam collecting in the bathroom, and I wondered what he meant. Whatever it was, it couldn't be good.

But it has to be better than being eaten... I kept telling myself that as he started for me, an evil glint in his death-black eyes. For every slow step he took toward me, I took two back.

He giggled as if he found my fear amusing. "Come on, you asked what I had planned for you. Don't you want a taste?"

No, I didn't want a taste. If it involved any of his body parts, they would promptly get bitten off. Maybe he hadn't heard what I'd done to Asmodeus yet...

Though maybe it was better if he hadn't.

"Fuck you," I spat at him, and he laughed, the unsettling sound reverberating off the bathing chamber's stone walls.

"Don't you know that's basically demon for yes?"

There was something about the way he regarded my naked body that had a little voice in my head screaming for me to run. Despite barely knowing the demon, I couldn't shake the foreboding sense that this lord was worse than every one of his brothers I'd met so far.

Except for maybe Belial. No one was more intimidating than the Lord of Bones.

Belphegor chewed his lip in deep thought as he seemed to consider what happened next. He was hard to read in this form, but it was obvious what had him torn.

Obey Mammon and prepare me for the cauldron in the main chamber, or rebel and act out whatever twisted plans he had in mind for me instead.

It was a testament to how fucked my situation was that I hoped for the second option.

After what felt like an eternity, it appeared he thought better of defying Mammon. He turned around and took a seat on the stool at the foot of the bath.

I watched him carefully, a fist-sized lump in my throat as he swirled the bath water with a claw waiting for the basin to fill.

Paired with the sticky hot air in the bathroom and the unsettling silence, I was practically stewing alive in the tension.

There was a noise outside the door—the shuffle of small feet and hyena-like snickering. Belphegor's glare whipped toward the intruders and, with an irritated sigh, ushered them in.

Two goblins scuttled inside, bowing clumsily to Belphegor at least half a dozen times while their little heads craned in my direction, ogling me with their large, yellowed eyes. The first goblin carried a woven basket filled with various scrub brushes and hand towels. The second held a tray of what I assumed to be bath salts and soaps. The scent of rosemary had my stomach grumbling.

My stomach flipped when, on closer inspection, I made out an array of items you'd use to prepare a hunk of meat for a meal: oils, salts—not the bath variety—and various herbs and spices.

"We're here to assist with the preparation of the meat, Lord Belphegor."

Assist? As in, bathe me? Oh hell no. If Belphegor bathed me, I could at least try to pretend it was Holga instead.

The goblins were shriveled, warty little creatures with curling yellowed fingernails and rancid breath. They leered at my naked body, their ratty little loincloths tenting with their erections.

The thought of them touching me had me edging away until my back hit the bathing chamber's cold stone wall.

The only way out was the single doorway the goblins blocked off. Even if I made it out of the bathroom, where would I go? This entire place was a prison.

Belphegor snickered at my reaction, clearly finding my disgust amusing, but to my relief, he took the basket of brushes and loofahs and waved the goblins away. "Get out. No one touches the Lord of Greed's royal meat but me."

Bile burned in my throat at being referred to as the "royal meat."

He placed the basket on the ground beside his seat and dipped a pinky into the water, testing the temperature.

"It's too hot. Unless you're trying to boil me before you dump me into that cauldron," I muttered, trying to keep the fear from my voice. It was pointless, though, considering how my body wouldn't stop shaking no matter how hard I willed it to stay still.

"You're terrified, aren't you?" Belphegor's small smile sent a violent chill through my core.

"Your heart is beating like a little rabbit's caught in a snare. I feel so sorry for you, *poor thing*." Belphegor's smile indicated that he didn't feel sorry for me in the slightest.

I bared my teeth, and he laughed again. "Well, you still have more spunk than any human I've met. I suppose you'd have to have something special about you to wiggle your way inside Belial's icy heart."

Was that jealousy I caught in his tone?

"Maybe you're just putting on a brave face because your soul is still in the hands of your precious master, which is really too bad." Belphegor poked his bottom lip out in a fake pout. "That means once Mammon sucks the last bit of marrow from your boiled bones, there won't be anything left to torture."

"Belial isn't going to let you do shit with my body."

"Oh, honey." Belphegor's snowy brows furrowed, as if he almost did feel sorry for me now. "You're not stupid enough to think he's going to reach you in time, are you?"

He snorted at my expression. "This realm is a fortress. I'm sure he'll try his best, considering how hard up he seems to be for your scrawny little body. That was quite the show he put on at the masquerade. Chaining you to his throne? The way he looked at you... Either he had his ferryman's oar stuffed down his pants, or he was thinking about bending you over his throne, right there in front of everyone."

A moan crawled up his throat, and his white lashes fluttered. "Mmm, now *that* would have been a show."

With the claw-foot basin full, he cut the water, and his gaze slithered back to me. His plump lips pursed as he considered me. "You must be quite the little fuck to keep a monster cock like Belial's standing at attention."

I cringed, and he threw his head back, his mocking laughter making the little hairs on my nape rise.

"Oh, don't give me that pathetic look. Unlike my brothers, I'm not interested in that little mound between your thighs."

Something akin to relief flooded my system, releasing some of the tension in my chest. If he wasn't bullshitting me, then whatever his plan was, it didn't entail eating me, boiling me, or raping me.

As much as this demon made alarms go off in my head, he was the lesser evil as far as his plans with me went. I just had to convince him to defy Mammon and get me the hell out of here.

"You said earlier you had a better idea on how to make use of me. So why are you going along with the feast?"

Belphegor's brows furrowed as his hand hovered over the tray of herbs. He opted for a mixture of salt and rosemary and tossed it into the steaming bath. "Mammon always gets what he wants."

"But aren't you a demon lord too?" I asked, my eyes bouncing between him and the tub. "Why should Mammon get his way and not you? Is he better than you, or is that just what he likes to think?"

The white-haired demon's lip curled and his nostrils flared. "I know what you're doing. You're not going to drive a wedge between me and my Mon-Mon."

Mon-Mon? Oh, barf.

The demon lord gave an irritated flip of his snow-white hair while drumming his manicured claws against the edge of the now-full tub. "This is boring me. Get in so we can get this over with."

He stirred the water with a slender index finger, musing through a devious smirk, "Maybe your meat will taste good enough to make this worth it."

Fuck.

I should have figured it wouldn't be easy convincing Belphegor to go against the Lord of Greed. Luckily, I had an ace up my sleeve.

My mind went back to my last bath, the one I'd shared with Belial just two days ago, but I tried not to linger on the memory too much. This wasn't the time or place to daydream about how Belial had joined me in the water. It definitely wasn't the place to dwell on how he'd helped me discover my latest concerning kink after nearly drowning me and forcing me to come before he let me breathe.

Instead, I turned my thoughts to what he'd told me about his brothers and how Belphegor and Asmodeus used to fuck. It was a risky move—one that could easily backfire—to bring it up, but I had to try. I needed to know just how devoted Belphegor was to the Lord of Greed if I had any hope of changing his mind.

"Oh, I wouldn't want to drive a wedge between true love," I said, forcing innocence into my voice.

Belphegor's scowl deepened. "I didn't say shit about true love. Mammon's too much of a selfish prick to keep my interest for long."

I swallowed down my flicker of hope and kept up my innocent act. "Don't you think you deserve better?"

"What could a human girl ever know about love between demons?"

"I know that, just like with humans, love doesn't always last, does it?" I steeled my nerves before I pressed on. "Just like with Asmodeus. It ended with him, so naturally, it will end with Mammon too. Why not end it now and keep me all for yourself?"

Belphegor flew to his feet, and even in the steam, I could see his shape flicker. Just for a moment—if I'd blinked, I would have missed it—he morphed back to his true form. He was a handsome, lithe male, with a sharp bone structure and that same silky hair that moved like water reaching past his waist.

Ugh. Why were most of these assholes so damn beautiful?

"How dare you invoke the name of the Lord of Lust, you little rat?" His tone dropped to a deadly hiss, and violence radiated from him that was just as visceral as the steam spiraling off the bath water. "Especially after what you did to him."

Oh. Shit. *He knew.*

Belphegor knew I'd bitten off Asmodeus' dick.

I wondered if he knew Belial had killed him yet.

"I said. Get. In. The. Bath," Belphegor gritted out, punctuating each of his words with a growl.

Whatever thin veil Belphegor had drawn to maintain that he was the sane one of his brothers was gone now. I saw the rage in his face, and I knew he was just as psychotic as the rest, maybe even more so.

"Go on," he purred through a smile I didn't trust. "Force my hand. I can make you get in the bathtub." His voice came out alarmingly soft and almost seductive, a threat wrapped up in velvet. "I can make you do whatever I want..."

I was still shaking, but now, it was in fury, not fear. "I'm sick of you demonic fucks. What the hell did I ever do? Last week, I was just minding my own goddamn business, trying to pay my damn rent. Now, here I was, dragged to the underworld against my will. I've been nearly eaten by carnivorous trees, half drowned in mud, chained and caged like a fucking animal, and almost raped. So you know what? You all can get fucked."

Of course, Belphegor was going to take that as a challenge when in reality, I was just tired of being treated like a piece of meat being fought over by a pack of wolves.

I was definitely tired of feeling so damn helpless.

"Alright," Belphegor purred. The steam in the enclosed room was so thick now, I could barely see him through the haze. All I could discern was a swelling shape getting bigger and bigger.

The shifter was taking on a new form.

When he stepped closer to me, the steam rolled around him in tendrils, heightening the dramatics of the reveal.

I slapped my hand over my mouth to keep myself from screaming when three heads emerged. It was eerie seeing Asmodeus again. It was a perfect likeness, as if he was back from the dead.

"How about I give you a bath like this?"

CHAPTER TWENTY-SIX

RAYVEN

My muscles seized and my breath ran thin as I found myself looking at Belphegor's likeness to the Lord of Lechery.

Logically, I knew the lord of the second circle was dead, but seeing this perfect imitation of him had the primal part of my brain lurching into a full-blown panic.

"I... No... Get the fuck away from me."

"Aw." Belphegor's trio of lips pursed into mocking pouts. "Our feral little rat isn't so brave now that she's cornered. Come here."

His claws curled, beckoning me closer. "Maybe I'll pluck off one of your body parts and send it to As in a pretty bow-wrapped package as a condolence for his loss. Maybe your tongue?" His eyes gleamed with malevolence as they dropped to the apex of my thighs. "Or that little nub between those folds? I'd make it quick."

"Fuck you!"

"Hmm, you're right. Asmodeus would probably much prefer your pretty pierced nipples. Once I sever them, I can fit them in his metal. I think you'll look so much better in gold than silver anyway."

"Don't you fucking touch me, or—"

"Or what?" The demon stalked closer, looking terrifying with the whirling steam winding around his goat's horns. "Are you going to threaten me with what Belial might do? Don't make me laugh. I'd give up every soul in my charge to have his hands on me."

"He'll rip your fucking head off is what he'll do."

"Maybe once I'm dead. But I know Belial. He'll tease out my end, edge out every last fucking breath until I've paid for all my sins. And there isn't enough oxygen in all the nine realms for that. It will be slow..."

He licked his lips, and a moan-like sigh slithered up his throat like it was the most erotic thought he'd ever had. "Such a slow, sweet fucking death by the Lord of Bones himself."

Normally, the erection tenting his loincloth would bother me—especially considering he was getting a boner by fantasizing about how Belial might kill him—but seeing that this version of Asmodeus still had his cock intact helped ground me.

This wasn't the brutal demon lord who'd assaulted me. It was just an illusion.

I forced a smirk. "Maybe I'll just kill you myself then. If I'm going to be the queen of death, I should practice killing people, right? The Lord of..."

My words trailed off as I realized I didn't know what sin Belphegor lorded over.

"Gluttony," he seethed, appearing pissed as hell that I didn't already know.

Right. I should have guessed that. "The Lord of Gluttony would be a perfect first kill for the queen of death."

"You're not going to be the queen of anything, little rat. Mortals are vermin. Living or dead, they don't deserve to rule any part of Hell, most certainly not Limbo."

"Oh, vermin, am I? Then it really will be embarrassing as fuck when I kill you, won't it?"

My heart pounded in my ears so hard, I could barely hear myself think. This was when I needed to shut my mouth. Taunting a powerful demon king was not wise; even Belial would advise me to hold my tongue until I had some kind of upper hand.

Belphegor's three menacing grins chilled me to my core "I'd like to see you try."

He surged forward, leaping through the screen of steam. I tried to get away from his swinging claws, but he was too fast, his arm sweeping around my middle and hauling me into the air.

I screamed and scratched at his back, but it was like clawing aged leather. It looked soft and supple, but he had a natural armor to his skin that made it extra durable.

He threw me into the tub, water sloshing everywhere as my ass slammed painfully against the bottom, spikes of pain shooting up my spine.

I coughed and sputtered, trying to get the water I'd inhaled out of my lungs.

If it wasn't bad enough that the water was hot enough to scald my skin, I now took notice of the rusty iron cuffs mounted to the rim of the tub. Oh great. So this was the bathroom where they washed all the 'guests' destined to be the *royal meat.*

The demon lord gave a cruel laugh when he caught me staring wide-eyed at the cruel hunk of metal. "You should be used to these. Rumor has it, the Lord of Bones loves manacling his whores before fucking them."

"That's none of your damn business."

"So it's true then?" With the way his eyes lit up, you'd think I'd told him Santa Claus was real and that he was bringing him Belial for Christmas, wrapped in nothing but shiny paper.

Belphegor grabbed a scrub brush and went to work on my skin, dragging the scratchy loofah end over my sensitive skin. I squirmed in his grasp, wincing in pain, but he hardly seemed to notice.

"What is it about you that fascinates him so?" he wondered aloud as he scrubbed me. "It can't just be your black hair or your warm little cunt. I can shift into whatever I want. I can look like anything..." His words trailed off as he hastily dumped a bucket of water over my head, making me sputter again. "It can't be your soul. Otherwise, he wouldn't be at Mammon's gate, looking like he's gunning for the Lord of Wrath's gig."

His tongue swept over his lips, wetting them in thought. "I wonder if it's that mortal heart." His curious gaze dropped to the place between my breasts. "If I tore it from your chest, how long would it stay beating?"

I shivered, moving to shield my tits from his hungry gaze, and he leaned so close, his breath spilled over my neck with his next words. "I bet he gets off on the feeling of it beating when he's buried inside you."

Suddenly, without warning, he snatched my shoulder in one arm to keep me still and thrust the brush between my legs. I yelped as the rough material of the loofah scraped over my most sensitive parts.

"Settle down, little rat, or I just might have to drown you to shut you up. Mammon doesn't need you breathing to eat you."

I wanted to spit into his face—or maybe take a go at lunging at him and biting off one of his noses—but I thought better of it. It was clear he hated me for my relationship with Delial. It was painfully obvious how jealous he was. But maybe there was still a chance at convincing him that his plan, whatever it was, was better than letting Mammon have me for dinner.

"What? What happened to your fight, little rat? I was just starting to have fun with you."

"I don't know what you want from me," I seethed, trying to ignore the fiery pit of rage building in my chest and failing miserably.

"I want you to entertain me," he said, as if the answer was obvious. "I've been around for so long, rat. It's the same fucking thing every day, and there aren't any new souls to torture anymore, thanks to you and that human woman Belial was obsessed with before."

I bit my tongue so hard, the metallic tang of my own blood bloomed in my mouth. Of course, the demon lords blamed me for the lack of souls Belial judged these days. They couldn't fathom that sometime in the last thousand years or so, the Lord of Bones had grown a heart, that he would rather create afterlives in his library instead of throwing the souls en masse down the Styx.

After an awkward moment of silence and aimless scrubbing, its only purpose seeming to be to make my skin ache, he tossed the brush to the floor with a bored sigh and stood. To my horror, he climbed into the bathtub.

"What are you doing?" I screamed, instantly fighting to put space between us. He stood there, looming over me, his tented loincloth swinging dangerously close to my face.

"I warned you I might bathe with you. What's the matter? Does Asmodeus make you uncomfortable?" A chuckle rumbled in his chest, and the water sloshed as he stepped closer. "Come on, little rat. You must have a masochistic streak to enjoy our Lord of Bones' bedroom preferences."

"You can't exactly compare the two, can you?" I spat, backing up until my back hit the porcelain. "One is a monster, lying dead in his disgusting pit, alone and rotting. The other is a fucking *god*."

I wished I could gulp back my words, but it was too late. I'd let it slip that Asmodeus was dead, and judging by the look on Belphegor's face, this didn't come as good news.

"So, the Lord of Lechery is dead," Belphegor mused, his dark eyes bright with loathing. "Belial's handiwork, no doubt."

I steeled myself, waiting for the hammer to drop, because there was no way he wasn't going to blame me for Asmodeus' death.

"He's coming for all of us, isn't he?" It seemed like more of a rhetorical question, but something dark flashed behind his eyes when the words left his mouth.

Suddenly, he bent down, snatching my hair and throwing my head back until it felt like my neck might snap.

I wanted to be brave. After all I'd been through, after getting bent over and forced to take all this shit I never asked for, I wanted nothing more than to look the Lord of Gluttony in his eyes—or rather, Asmodeus' six beady eyes currently staring me down—and spit in them.

Now that he knew the real Asmodeus was dead, the ferry had probably sailed on convincing Belphegor not to let his boyfriend eat me.

So, if I was going to die, I wanted to die fighting.

But there was something about looking into the three demonic faces of the demon who'd assaulted me with my neck precious millimeters from being snapped that froze me over.

Belphegor sneered at the naked fear on my face as he forced his hand between my thighs.

I thrashed as hard as the excruciating hold he had over me would allow, but he anchored my head back further, forcing me still as he cupped my mound.

"How many of us are going to die all because of Belial's obsession with this mortal pussy?" I gasped when he spread my lips and ran a teasing finger up and down my opening. "I don't fucking get it. It's just like any other fucking cunt..."

I would have sold my soul to another devil all over again to have my twat grow teeth in this moment and chomp off Belphegor's hands.

My jaw clenched. My nostrils flared. Pure hatred swept over me like a fever, making me feel cold despite the scalding hot water I was half submerged in. "I didn't ask to be kidnapped. Your precious Lord of Rape is dead because you sick fucks couldn't keep your hands off me. If you'd left me alone, none of this would have fucking happened. Now, Belial is on a war path, and you're going to die like fucking dogs."

I expected Belphegor to double down on his rage, but instead, that amused smirk locked back in place as he lowered me back into the water. "Well, what's done is done. If we're going to die, might as well have ourselves a little *celebration*. Seven thousand years or so, give or take a few centuries, is a decent run."

Before I could dare ask him what kind of celebration he had in mind, he forced my wrists into the manacles bolted to the sides of the bathtub. A chill shot up my spine at the iron locking into place with a loud *clink*.

There was a splash as Belphegor—still in Asmodeus' form—fell to his knees in the bath before me and grabbed the basket of herbs and spices. He cackled as he dumped the whole thing over my head and started massaging the salty mixture into my skin.

His touch was rough and lingered in the places he noticed made me thrash the most.

"Hmm, wonder if we should cut these out before we throw you in the cooking cauldron," he mused, plucking at one of my nipple piercings. "I'll leave them for now. It will be something for Mammon to pick his teeth with later."

CHAPTER TWENTY-SEVEN

RAYVEN

As fast as I could blink, the three-headed demon's image melted away, replaced by Belphegor's preferred feminine form. He stepped out of the bath, water dripping from his shapely form and little black dress—if it could even be called that with how little fabric there was. It was soaked through and clinging to his skin.

Leaning toward a small oval mirror mounted to the stone wall, he wiped the film of steam from the glass to admire himself. "I look so damn good, Mammon is going to want to eat us both."

He turned back toward the bath, mischievous fire burning behind his black eyes as his claw-tipped fingers unlocked the manacles clamped around my wrists.

Before I could react, he grabbed me by the arm and yanked me out of the tub.

I slipped and stumbled, his nails digging unforgivably into my skin as he dragged me across the bathroom. Blood beaded at the puncture wounds, which only made him smirk.

"There," he said, looking back so his glowering eyes could roam over me. "I have a feeling you're going to taste fucking delicious, little rat."

I was thankful he no longer resembled Asmodeus, but that didn't alleviate the pit of dread in my stomach. Now that I'd gotten a glimpse of the beast lurking beneath his exterior, I didn't know if his feminine mask was much better.

I stared at him, trying to bury the images of Asmodeus bathing me, his rough hands violating my skin as they roamed, but they were branded on the backs of my eyelids. He'd scrubbed me thoroughly, but now, I felt dirtier than before he'd bathed me.

Belphegor was a horror.

While the other brothers were obviously awful and relied on simpler methods of torture, the Lord of Gluttony could sink down into my deepest fears and make them appear. He could twist reality, and even though I knew it wasn't real, my racing heart and the icy dread spreading through my chest *were*.

Belphegor excelled at creating bone-chilling terror with his shapeshifting powers, and I was afraid he'd have more tricks up his sleeve before he was done with me. Whatever they were, they were sure to be horrid.

I'd been so certain the Lord of Gluttony couldn't be worse than the other demons I'd dealt with so far, but now, I wasn't so sure. Was being driven insane by psychological torture—along with whatever other kinds Belphegor could think of—really better than being eaten? Probably, but the thought didn't comfort me the way it had an hour ago.

"Come on, rat." He jerked on my arm, dragging me back through the bedchamber and into the corridor. I was still wet, leaving a trail of seasoned bathwater in my wake; I was marinated and ready to be boiled.

My throat tightened as we headed for the dining hall, the prospect of my violent death causing my pulse to race. My panicked breaths came faster, my mind whirling, trying to come up with a plan.

There was no plan.

Even if I gave Belphegor the slip, what the hell was I supposed to do? I was trapped in a fortress. There was no way in, no way out. If I got away, I was only prolonging the inevitable.

"Whatever you were planning to do with me before, it has to be better than eating me. You said so yourself—once the meal is done, I'm gone. There's nothing left to torture once my soul lies with the Lord of Bones." My voice was a little shaky, but I tried not to sound afraid.

Belphegor's eyes slid over to me, and he licked his grinning lips. "Your screams earlier said otherwise. Although, I must say, your fear is *delicious*. Tastier than your mortal flesh could ever be."

My stomach twisted into painful knots. Thoughts of Asmodeus touching me, rubbing his filthy fucking hands all over me, had me tasting bile, but I had to do this. At the very least, I had to buy time for Belial.

"If only Mammon saw things your way for once," I said. Belphegor's jaw twitched at my words, but he said nothing. "Fear is infinite. You could torture me forever and never get tired, but if Mammon eats me..." I swallowed hard, shoving my fear aside. "The fun stops now."

"You're not wrong," he said, an amused look twisting his features. "And you've only gotten a taste of what I can do."

"But Mammon knows best, I guess." I shrugged, my eyes casually searching the hall for any sign of the Lord of Greed or the other demon lords. They must have been outside, tending to the cauldron, making sure everything was in perfect order. "It's probably best if you obey him. I wouldn't want to be on his shit list, that's for sure."

Belphegor whipped around abruptly, nails digging into my arm hard enough to make me wince. Pure, unbridled rage burned behind his dark eyes.

"I do not *obey* Mammon," he growled, stooping to leer in my face. "I do what I want, not what some demon oaf demands."

"Right..." I drew out the word as I rolled my eyes, ignoring the pain shooting down my arm from his tightening grip. "Obviously. I mean, he told you to bathe me and you did, told you he was going to eat me and you went along with it. Sounds to me like he has you on a short leash."

If looks could kill, I would have been dead on the spot. I'd struck a nerve.

Belphegor's lip twitched as he stared me down, looking internally conflicted. I held my breath, hoping he'd take the bait and decide to keep me for himself. All he had to do was defy Mammon and sneak me out however he got here.

To my disappointment, he turned and continued leading me out of the hall.

"The sooner Mammon swallows you, the better," he spat.

My chest deflated when the cauldron came into view, and the moment we stepped out the door, a wave of demented cheers erupted through the forge.

Goblin creatures cheered and cackled as Belphegor led me toward the dais, bowing out of his way and murmuring amongst themselves. A few reached out to touch me, and I jerked away from their grubby little hands.

I looked around and found Mammon, giant fiery wings ablaze, sitting on an imposing iron throne at one end of the forge, watching the spectacle unfold. Rather than tossing me in the cauldron himself or skinning me alive for his subjects to watch, it seemed he was going to let Belphegor do his dirty work.

On either side of him were the demon lords I'd seen earlier. Now that the demon with the gigantic eyeball for a head was standing, I could tell he was less humanoid than I'd originally thought. His body seemed to be made of braided cords of tissue, winding together to make his form. Rather than hands or feet, his extremities ended with tentacles.

The spider-looking demon with no eyes seemed like he'd doubled in size now that all his legs were spread wide, and he bared his several rows of razor-sharp teeth at me as I stared. I had every intention of staying as far away from his creepy limbs as possible.

"Our feast is about to begin," Mammon's amplified voice echoed through the forge, followed by a fresh wave of cheers and hollers from the goblin creatures.

"Feast! Feast! Feast!" they chanted, more and more voices joining the chorus as we approached the stairs leading to the dais.

I tensed in Belphegor's hold, pausing at the base of the steps, my eyes glued to the cauldron overhead.

There was still no sign of Belial, and I didn't have a backup plan. As much as I hoped for a last-second salvation, I couldn't see my way out of this.

"Up," Belphegor snapped, dragging me up the stairs. If I fought and he let me go, I'd fall to my death in the lake of lava. If I went along with it, I'd be boiled to death.

Either way, I was cooked.

Personally, falling to my death seemed less painful and more dramatic than being slowly boiled alive. Mammon also couldn't eat me if I was swallowed by magma, so that was another hair-thin silver lining.

The air wafting up from the lake of lava below was scorching, burning my skin. The bottoms of my feet were raw against the hot stone, and every inhale left my lungs feeling scorched.

Belphegor dragged me all the way to the top, shoving one of the goblin servants out of his way, nearly sending him to a fiery death below. The top of the cauldron was as tall as I was and just as wide, but Belphegor was tall enough to peer inside. He watched whatever was in the cauldron for a long moment, his gaze intense.

His fingers were still locked around my arm, but he didn't move to throw me in or drag me up the ladder. He didn't do anything at all.

What is he waiting for?

"Well, get on with it," Mammon's commanding voice echoed through the forge, followed by another wave of cheers. "Don't keep your brothers waiting, Belly."

My stomach dropped.

"Belphegor." I wasn't sure why I said his name; I'd learned my lesson about trying to appeal to the better nature of demons, and I was fairly certain Belphegor didn't have a better nature. I'd already done my best to convince him to defy Mammon, to get me the fuck out of the forge, but he seemed loyal to the Lord of Greed. Or at least he had moments ago.

Was he...changing his mind?

Another minute ticked by, my bones rattling with nerves as I awaited my fate.

"Belphegor," Mammon's voice whipped through the air, snapping the shape-shifting demon out of his daze. "My precious meat isn't going to cook itself, and I don't have all day. Throw her in already."

A muscle ticked in Belphegor's cheek, and his eyes narrowed. I stiffened, prepared to fight if he turned around to grab me. If I was going over the edge of the cauldron, I might as well pitch myself off the dais. I refused to be eaten.

"I think..." Belphegor said, his voice carrying despite the low tone, "not."

"What did you say?" Mammon rose from his throne and stalked forward, his eyes glued to us.

I caught my breath, worried that if I moved or breathed too suddenly, everything around me would explode. I'd already watched two demon lords battle it out over me. Was I about to witness another fight? And whose side would Eyeball and Spider guy take?

"Belly, do what I asked," Mammon gritted out, his fiery red gaze landing on me. "Don't make me do it myself."

Belphegor scoffed. "If you wanted it done, you should have done it from the start. I'm not taking any more orders, *Mon-Mon*. In fact, I've changed my mind. I'm going to keep this little mortal for myself."

"What are you—" Mammon yelled, but his voice cut off abruptly when Belphegor planted the bottom of his stiletto on the side of the cauldron and pushed hard. It wobbled back and forth, the liquid inside sloshing loudly.

"Stop! Belphegor! What are you doing?" Mammon was beside himself, too caught off guard to do anything more than gape as Belphegor kicked the cauldron again.

This time, it tilted farther, just enough for some of the water to slosh out the side.

"I'm doing what I should have done a long time ago, Mammon," he gritted out. "It's over, babe."

The third kick did the trick. The cauldron fell off its stand with a clang and toppled, pouring a gush of boiling broth down the dais. Goblins screamed, fighting to get out of the way, but many weren't fast enough. They crumpled beneath the wave, their skin blistering the moment the hot water hit them.

Most of the soup spilled into the great pit in the middle of the forge, hitting the lake of lava with a violent hiss. Smoke billowed, wafting up the hole and swallowing the dais, obscuring my view.

"Belphegor!" Mammon yelled. His flaming wings flickered through the smoke as he took flight, but Belphegor was already dragging me back down the stairs.

If I wrenched my arm free, I could have lost him in the smoke. I could have darted off and found a place to hide, but without the shapeshifter, my chance to escape disappeared. If I wanted to live—and be subjected to whatever twisted fucking torture Belphegor had planned—I had to get out of the forge.

This was exactly what I'd wanted, for Belphegor to take me for himself. It was my only chance at survival, and I reminded myself of that fact as Mammon barked orders, commanding his servants to find us.

My pulse fumbled as Belphegor finally released his death grip on my arm. He was shifting again, into something large and animalistic. My eyes strained through the smoke, struggling to make out his newest shape.

White fur spread over his body, giant, pointy ears growing from his head, and large wings sprouted from his sides where his arms had been with skin so thin, you could see the complicated network of veins running through them.

The giant white bat launched into the air, his feet grabbing me by my ankle and ripping me off my feet.

The acrid air thrashed my hair and whipped my face as we dipped dangerously close to the lava.

Mammon's bellowing roar ripped through the fortress as he seemed to spot us through the smoke and launched after us. Even with me in tow, Belphegor seemed lighter and faster, sailing through the air as Mammon's bulky, flaming form failed to keep up.

With the combination of the heat, the speed at which we were flying, and all the blood draining to my skull, darkness closed in. As unconsciousness swept in to take me, the last thing I heard over another of Mammon's cavernous growls was Belial's silk-wrapped baritone calling my name.

CHAPTER TWENTY-EIGHT

RAYVEN

THE MOMENT I OPENED my eyes, antlers came into view. The familiar charms and chains draping the bones had tears rolling down my cheeks instantly.

"You're crying... Why are you crying?" The panic in Belial's barrage of questions had the tears flowing faster. "Who hurt you? Was it Mammon?"

"I'm fine, I—I think. I just hate that this isn't real. You're not really here." This was another dream, the power of the plum magic uniting our minds while I slept.

"No, treasure, but I'm coming for you." The sincerity in his storm-gray eyes calmed some of the crushing sadness churning through me. "Cecil procured the soul book of a renowned engineer, who is sure he can break a mechanism in the gate. He's working quickly and won't be long now."

At the mention of Cecil, I swiveled my gaze around, but there was no one here. It was just the two of us on a gondola, bobbing in the middle of the River Styx, the enormous iron gate of the fifth circle looming over us.

"Cecil's here?"

He nodded. "Holga too."

There was a platform on the back of the gondola, where I ventured the ferryman was supposed to stand while he ferried souls around, pushing his oar behind him. I could practically see Belial standing there, leaning against his oar decorated with the heads of his brothers, eyes glazed over as he immersed himself in my mind. All the while, Cecil bickered with the engineer at the front of the vessel.

"I'm surprised you let them come."

"They insisted." A smirk played at his scarred lips. "Good thing, too. I wasn't anticipating the gate; it's new. Well, new as in built after my last visit several centuries ago. With Cecil's quick thinking, I'll be inside soon. I'll kill Mammon, and we can go home and put this nightmare behind us."

Home.

At my agonized expression, Belial's strong arms gathered around me. He sat down on the bottom of the gondola with his back against the ebony wood, pulling me into his lap.

Normally, I'd feel ridiculous in this kind of position, since he was cradling me and gently rocking me like a baby, but after all

I'd been through, I needed the comfort of his embrace. "What happened? Tell me everything, Rayven."

"I..." My voice trailed off as I recalled my last moments of consciousness, of Belphegor transforming into a giant white bat. My stomach lurched, a sinking feeling sweeping over me. I had no idea what happened after I blacked out, but I had a good guess. "I'm not in the fifth circle anymore. Or if I am, I won't be for long. Belphegor—"

"Belphegor?" Belial's handsome face took on a chilling expression. "What did he do to you?"

"Mammon was going to eat me. There was this big cauldron—goblins everywhere. There were two other demon lords too," I said with a chill. "One had a big eyeball for a head, and the other is some sort of spider monster."

"Paimon and Baal, the Lords of Sloth and Wrath." Belial spat the names like they were trash in his mouth. "Fucking traitors, all of them."

"Belphegor saved me." I frowned. No, that wasn't right. I didn't feel saved at all. "But whatever he has planned for me..." I couldn't put words to what I expected the shapeshifter to do, simply because I hadn't the slightest clue. All I had to go off of was the sinking feeling in the pit of my stomach.

I knew my gut was right when I caught a flicker of something I could almost sense as fear behind Belial's luminous eyes. "If Belphegor hurts you before I'm able to reach you..."

He couldn't seem to bear the thought long enough to finish the sentence. "I'll kill him, no matter what, but his head won't be the last on the oar. It will be mine."

"What?" I froze, ice prickling through my veins. "You mean you'll kill yourself?"

"My war path isn't about punishing the demon lords who kidnapped you. I'm punishing every demon who's hurt you. I'm pretty fucking sure I'm at the top of that list, little human."

I hadn't thought about everything he'd done to me in the last couple of days—because getting kidnapped and dragged down through the layers of Hell had a way of distracting a girl—but I hadn't exactly forgotten all the fucked up shit he'd done. Killing Mark and making me a crown from his spine. Making me take a bet I could escape his carnivorous, corpse-filled garden in three days or else I'd become his queen—a bet I could never win in the first place. Manipulating me into thinking his second form was a different person, making me trust him. Making me fall in love with him.

I hadn't exactly forgiven him, but he was making it damn difficult to stay mad at him.

"What is that little pout for?" he snickered, that imperious, smug-as-fuck attitude returning to his face in the form of a panty-melty smirk. "Mad that I plan on killing myself once you're rescued? If it would make you happy, I'll let you do it."

"I'm not fucking killing you," I snapped. "I agreed to stay, didn't I? I want to be your queen. *Your queen.* I'm not interested in ruling your dusty old realm, or the eight others below it, alone."

"You're so damn beautiful when you're pissed off."

I snorted. "I wish looking hot as fuck while kidnapped felt like more of an upside."

The corners of his smirk twitched, almost wavering. It felt more like a mask than the one he used to wear around me. His mouth curved upward but, in spite of that, he looked so sad.

I reached up, my fingers brushing his jaw and cupping his cheek. His hand slipped behind my neck, his thumb swirling slow and gentle circles against my nape. Somehow, the intimacy felt new but familiar all at the same time.

"What's wrong?" I muttered, searching his eyes. It felt like a stupid question given the circumstances, but there was something more weighing on him.

"I'm not used to feeling this helpless. I don't like sitting around and waiting. I'm the God of Death, for fuck's sake. My mate's life shouldn't rest on the shoulders of a mortal soul." He buried his head in his free hand, his black hair spilling over his fingers. "I shouldn't have left you alone, not with those monsters in the castle. What was I thinking?"

I blinked at him, feeling a strange ache in my chest. He was upset with himself. I'd never seen him like this before.

"Belial..."

"When I get you back home, I'm crowning you queen. Then, I'm going to teach you magic."

Another blink. "Magic? What kind of magic?"

"An ancient arcana so powerful, no one will dare defy you. Your enemies will fall to their knees in fear, your allies in fealty."

"What about you?" I arched an eyebrow at him. "Will it be magic powerful enough to bring even a god like the Lord of Bones to his knees?"

His face lifted from his palm. There was that half-cocked smirk again. "You've proven you don't need magic for that. But yes, even me. I'll train you to protect yourself against anything and anyone. Including me." He brushed a featherlight kiss to my brow. "Especially me."

"You wouldn't have to train me to protect myself against you if, you know, you didn't act like a freaking psychopath half the time."

Belial's gaze darkened, and his smile spread wide. "Where's the fun in that, though?"

"You're deranged."

"You don't know how right you are." It was still weird seeing his bare face. I'd gotten good at reading his eyes, but without his mask, I could read him like a book. The scars on his lips twitched with the smile he was holding back. His brows quirked like he was thinking back on all the things he'd done to earn him that title.

"The fuck I don't," I huffed with a toss of my eyes. "You've made me kiss your boots while I was drowning in quicksand. You half drowned me in a bathtub. You've fucked me with a wine bottle while I was chained to your bed. You've spanked me in a graveyard—"

"Maybe I just crave giving you what you want, the things your human sensibilities won't let you ask for."

I opened my mouth to argue, but his hand had moved from the back of my neck to curve around my throat, gripping me firmly enough to cut off my rebuttal. "You were the one masturbating on the grave of an old servant of mine."

My mind went back to that day in the labyrinth, when Belial had spanked me then put me on my knees and throat fucked me. He'd come, and he'd left me high and dry. So, I'd taken matters into my own hands there on one of the graves.

He leaned closer until his marred face filled my vision and his breath tickled my lips. "You looked fucking beautiful, your gown torn, my cum still dripping down your chin with your fingers stuffed into that pink little pussy. So needy for the Lord of Death to come back and fuck you stupid against that grave for all the monsters in my gardens to see."

His eyes gleamed as he whispered in a tone that made the little hairs on my nape bolt up. "How's that for deranged?"

My throat bobbed with a swallow, the menial movement feeling almost impossible with Belial's hand around my throat. Everything about his possessive touch, his filthy words, and his dark, leering gaze felt desperate, like all he wanted to do was reach through my dreams and pull me back out on the other side of reality.

His hand slipped from my throat and roamed over me, memorizing the planes of my body with an ache in his touch that burrowed into my bones and sunk into my marrow.

"I fucking need you," he groaned, the pain in his voice making me shiver. "I miss you so much."

I worked my bottom lip between my teeth, peering up at him through my lashes. "Tell me what you miss about me."

The smile he'd been holding back broke loose. "I miss your bratty mouth."

I blinked. "You do?"

"Of course," he said with a chuckle, as if it was obvious. "No one has the stones to speak to me the way you do. It's fucking electric."

His hands wandered, long fingers fitted with an assortment of silver rings flexing as he squeezed my breasts.

When he plucked at my nipple piercings and a moan rumbled from my lips, he laughed. "And I miss the sexy little sounds you make when I play with your perfect tits…"

His hand wandered lower, slipping between my thighs. I bit back a gasp when his fingers pinched my clit—light enough not to hurt and firm enough to send a rush of pleasure through my core.

I squirmed in his lap, and he laughed, the silken sound turning my pussy molten, arousal dripping onto his fingers.

"And I miss how responsive you are to me. You're always so wet for me, and your skin…" He muttered a curse under his breath as his eyes skated over my naked form. A full-bodied blush was sweeping over me like a fever. "Seeing your flesh dressed in this delicious hue of red makes my cock fucking ache."

A series of gasps and moans tumbled from me as he continued to rub my clit. He oscillated between lightly circling it, waiting for me to squirm with the need for more friction, and then moving in and plucking on it until I was twitching from the overstimulation.

A devilish yet somehow studious expression was etched into his scarred features as he worked me up until I was trembling with pleasure, like my impending orgasm was the most serious business he'd attended to all day.

"That's it, treasure. Make a mess on your Lord's fingers," he said on a dark purr. "I want to watch you suck them clean once you're done."

The swirling warmth between my legs mounted, and I reached for him, grabbing onto his antlers. A rumbling growl rose from his chest at the contact, encouraging me to hold tight.

His silver earring, the one shaped like a small dagger to match the one he'd given me in the labyrinth, brushed the back of my hand. I wish I still had it. It was probably still lying on the floor of his bathroom back in Limbo. Not that it would have done me much good. I doubted I would have been able to summon him outside his realm anyway.

Tears pricked my eyes, and whether it was from the fact that I missed Belial so much it hurt or the mind-shattering bliss wracking my body, I wasn't sure.

They rolled down my face, and he arched over to kiss them away. His tongue slid over my skin, and it was surprisingly cool against my burning cheeks.

"I love when your body weeps for me, Rayven," he whispered against my skin. "In every conceivable way."

His fingers stroked me, knowing just where to press and pull. It was like I was his instrument and he knew every chord, every note to make me sing.

His thumb covered my clit to free his index and middle fingers, sinking them into my pussy a second later. He pumped in and out of me at a pace that had a bead of drool dribbling down the corner of my mouth.

"Oh, God!" I whimpered and clamped my lips shut the instant the words left my mouth. He hated it when I called out that name and not his.

Belial's eyes narrowed, and I waited for my punishment, but his lips only spread into a sinister smile. "You know full well that I am your god now, Rayven. You sold your soul to the Devil. You worship me now."

CHAPTER TWENTY-NINE

RAYVEN

His fingers curved inside me to tease that hidden spot. The pleasure rose to a crescendo, and I came with a strangled cry that didn't even sound like me. I shook in his arms, and he held me tighter, pulling out of me only when the intense wave of sensation passed.

He held his fingers up and spread them to demonstrate just how wet I was. A string of arousal connected both digits until it snapped and oozed down his middle finger. Holding them to my lips, he looked at me expectantly.

My lips parted, and he pressed his fingers inside, his face twisting into a sexy expression as he watched me suck myself clean from him.

"That was beautiful, grave treasure," he praised. "So fucking beautiful."

"Fuck, that was good," I sighed. "I needed that."

He gave a dark laugh, and it shot a chill through me. "Oh, we're not done. That one was for you. Now, this is for me."

Before I could ask him what he meant, he gripped me by the back of my neck, pulling me out of his lap and positioning me so I was on all fours on the bench.

My breath hitched as he placed a knee on the bench behind me, so close that the hardness in his pants jabbed my ass.

"Hands on the edge of the gondola," he instructed. His grip tightened on the back of my neck and guided me so I was leaning over the boat's edge, my face hovering over the water.

There was a barbed moment of silence. He teased out the seconds, the bastard taking pleasure in watching me squirm in anticipation. My fingers clutched the black lacquered edge of the gondola, nails tapping nervously against the elaborate silver filigree decorating the wood.

A flood of renewed heat surged through me as the sounds of rustling fabric met my ears. I tried to turn my head, but his grip tightened on my nape and kept me held down. In a small act of mercy, he canted his hips forward, allowing me to feel him undoing the laces of his pants.

When he sprung out, his thick length fell into the valley of my ass. My skin pricked, and a tiny "oh" slipped from my lips when he spit on my backside and rubbed his cock up and down my ass cheeks, spreading his saliva to slide easily over my flesh.

He went still for a beat as he seemed to weigh his next move. "Keep your hands on the edge of the ferry, Rayven. Don't move."

The moment Belial's hand lifted from the back of my neck, I turned to see him pulling his silver cuff off, unclasping the chain that connected it to his Prince Albert piercing.

His stormy eyes narrowed when he caught me looking at him. "Stubborn little human. You never listen."

He dropped the silver onto the floor of the gondola with a clank and thrust his ringed fingers into my hair, shoving my head over the water, my face precious inches from the flowing crimson current.

Every sinew in my body stiffened when I felt him press into me—but not into my pussy. Instead, his head forced its way through the tight ring of muscle, the place I'd yet to have any man.

"Wait!" I choked out, the sting of him stretching my asshole making my voice raspy. "N–not there!"

My protests were met with a soft chuckle as he eased another inch of himself inside me. "Didn't I tell you I'd be claiming every one of your holes? You're lucky I'm taking your ass in a dream spell first. Consider this practice."

"Fuck, it hurts!" I snapped, but I couldn't bring myself to use my safe word. The pain only heightened the pleasure ebbing into my system, gripping me as tight as Belial's vice-like grip on my neck.

"Stop fighting it and let me in—Weeping Hells, you're so damn tight."

His steely baritone was wrapped up in fire and silk and masculine hunger. It sent a bolt of electricity through me, the delicious cocktail of pain and pleasure warming my entire body.

The Lord of Death was being surprisingly delicate with me as he worked himself inside at an excruciating pace, slow and careful as he waited for my body to adjust before sinking more of himself into me. Plus, he'd removed his jewelry, probably to minimize my discomfort.

As my body relaxed, I started to give into the comfort he instilled.

"I love you, Belial." It slipped out of my mouth. I didn't mean for it to, but it did.

He stilled, and his thumb rubbed gentle circles on my jugular without relinquishing his hold on me. "I love you too, little human."

His spine bowed, his large hands coming to grip the lip of the gondola beside mine as he draped his hard muscle over me, his chest pressed against my back. "Does this mean you forgive me?" His words were as soft as the sweet kiss he planted on the skin below my ear, making me melt beneath him.

I opened my mouth, and when no words came out, I closed it again. I couldn't tell him I'd forgiven him yet. I missed him. I loved him. But I still carried a hurt in my heart that held me back from telling him what he wanted to hear.

"I said I love you," I bit out, venom threading my every syllable. "What more do you want from me?"

"Fucking everything, Rayven."

Before I could respond, he drew back—just enough for the tip to stay lodged inside me—and then he rammed himself back inside so hard, it nearly sent me toppling into the water below.

His hand on my neck steadied me, but before any kind of relief set in, he shoved my head into the River Styx, forcing me below the rushing current while he fucked into my ass at a feral rhythm that had me screaming into the thick river water. Bubbles erupted from my mouth, precious air releasing in my panic.

The fingers in my hair wrenched my head from the water, and I gulped down huge mouthfuls of air to fill up my burning lungs.

"You are going to be a good little soul and come for the ferryman while he fucks you in the ass. If you don't come, you'll drown. And don't think I'll stop fucking you when you do. How's that for depraved?"

"Belial—" Before his name could fully leave my mouth, my head was shoved back into the river.

The water rushed up my nose and filled my mouth. It tasted bitter, a flavor I couldn't begin to describe, like death and something else completely foreign. Bits of bodies rushed past, tickling my cheeks. Something tried to grab onto the few strands of my long hair that fell into the water, maybe a passing soul that desperately tried to cling to something, anything to prevent its journey deeper through the Nine Hells.

Belial's free hand came around to massage my clit in frantic little strokes, building up another orgasm—this one promising to be intensely violent.

"Come for your Lord like the good little soul you are, Rayven." Belial's voice was muffled, but his words were surprisingly clear for my head being submerged under water. "Come, and I'll let you breathe."

This was a dream. I didn't need to breathe, but fuck me, it felt like I was on the brink of drowning. Knowing I was perfectly safe only added an extra bite to the swirling pleasure building between my legs.

As cruel as he was being, I found myself desperate for every second of his sweet torment.

His fingers knew every pleasure point on my body, and the hot pain from his thrusts had turned into a warmth that devoured all of me.

Paired with the burning in my lungs and his muffled voice demanding I come around his cock, how could I not?

A wave of intense bliss shredded through me, making me jerk violently, my hands so sweaty, they slipped on the boat's edge.

Belial's fingers flexed tighter into my hair and yanked me out of the water in a spray of red, strands of sopping wet locks whipping through the air.

I sputtered and choked, precious oxygen flooding my lungs.

Belial laughed at my struggle to regain breath, all the while continuing to fuck into me with quick, punching thrusts.

"Look at you, so fucking sexy when you're dripping for me," he said with an amused drawl, punctuating it with a quick smack to my ass.

"Fuck you!" I snapped through gritted teeth, even though we both knew full well just how much I was enjoying this twisted moment.

"Oh, sweet little human. Don't pretend you don't love this game. Now, are you going to be my good little mortal and come for your Lord again?"

My eyes widened. "Again?"

"Again." With the way he held my hair in his fist, I couldn't turn to look at him, but there was no missing the sneer in his voice. "And this time, give me a little bit of a challenge. I want to rip this next one out of you."

CHAPTER THIRTY

BELIAL

BLEEDING, WEEPING HELLS. RAYVEN'S screams were the sexiest sounds I'd ever heard, especially underwater. The sound of her strangled breathing, her choking, the way she fought me while her hips pressed back into my pelvis, begging me for more...it sank straight to my balls.

The spell I'd put on the plum was powerful, ancient arcana. Every lick, every pinch, every bite in the magic-induced dream would feel true to life.

I could make her feel good even while we were miles apart. Even realms apart, if Belphegor had managed to steal her away from Mammon and drag her deeper through the Hells.

No. I couldn't stand to think about that right now.

Gritting my teeth, I foisted the storm of dark thoughts—and all my fears of what could happen to Rayven if I didn't reach her in time—to the furthest reaches of my mind. Right now, I was helpless to do anything but wait for Cecil and his soul to find a weak point in the gate's construction.

So what better way to pass the time than to play with my favorite mortal's dreams? Even though she put on a brave face the way she had since I'd dragged her to my realm days ago, I knew she was terrified.

She needed a distraction, and I needed to drown myself in her as much as fucking possible. I savored every sweet cry that fell from her perfect lips, every flex and flutter of her inner muscles as they gripped my dick tight, every gasping breath.

I threw all of myself into tormenting her in that wicked way that had her pussy sopping, thick pearls of arousal rushing down her legs and making her flesh glisten in the dull red light that illuminated the Styx.

I adjusted my hold on her raven hair, wrapping the long trusses around my wrist like a leash before sinking my fingertips back into her scalp, my nails scraping her flesh hard enough to leave angry red welts just visible beneath her roots.

Wrenching her head back, I pulled her up on her knees so her back was flush against my chest and pressed the supple flesh of her cheek against my ruined lips. "Fuck, there's nothing that makes my dick harder than when I see your pretty skin turn red and bloody for me."

"O–of course you like it, you depraved fuck," she huffed. Her eyes dropped to the rushing waters below, beads of crimson clinging like dew to her dark lashes. "It's the color of death."

My mouth curled with a smile against her cheek, and when I laughed, my breath washed over her face, making her blush deepen in hue. "Oh, but that's where you're wrong. Red is the color of life..." Keeping one hand anchored in her hair, I took my other and dragged a sharp nail down her jawline.

She shivered, and the baby hairs on her nape rose as I sliced the shallowest of cuts into her flesh. Her gaze darted back to me, side-eyeing me as best she could with the way I had her held as I lapped up the bead of blood dripping from the fresh wound.

"Only the living bleed," I purred, the sound melting into a growl as the taste of her blood bloomed across my tongue. "Why do you think I had such an aversion to seeing you dressed in black when you first arrived in Limbo? That's the color of death, and you, my bratty mortal, are very much alive."

"That's funny." The corner of her mouth lifted into a messy, lopsided grin, strands of her wet hair clinging to her bloody face. "I think I wear death well."

To emphasize her meaning, she writhed her hips, which had my dick throbbing inside her tight little ass.

"That you fucking do."

I shoved her head back into the water and smirked at the bubbles rushing to the surface as she struggled to breathe. We'd already played this game once before in the bathtub back home, and I'd gotten stabbed for it, but she couldn't fool me.

She fucking loved when I catered to her darker, more twisted appetites. There was still a part of her human sensibilities that felt a hint of shame for getting off on things like this. I'd strangle that part out of her yet.

I spit on her backside—normally, there wasn't as much saliva as there would be in my Lord of Bones form—but since this was a dream, I could tweak the details. I could do anything, be anything in this altered reality, though all I wanted was to fuck my little human senseless.

Large gobs of saliva slid down between her ass cheeks and oozed around where I penetrated her. With a few more thrusts, I coated my shaft in the makeshift lube.

This was a dream, so we didn't necessarily need the extra lubrication, but I liked the way her skin shimmered under the film of my saliva and the obscene sounds that filled the air as I fucked into her.

The swirling pleasure mounted. My balls drew up. My ministrations grew more frantic as I chased my release with feral desperation.

I smacked her ass. Once. Three times. Five. I kept spanking her, addicted to the little rush of bubbles every time my hand slapped the round globe of her ass. With every strike, she clenched around me.

With her ass thoroughly pinked and covered in several welts in the smeared shape of my hand, I turned my attention back to her clit. I pinched it with just enough pressure to have her clenching in that telling way.

She was coming.

Fuck. The dark magic I'd cast to make it so I never had to leave her heat again.

My hand left her clit to grab her by the back of the neck and wrench her head from the water one final time. She came, hard. An animalistic sound crawled up her throat, wet and garbled and thick with pleasure.

It was with that that I unloaded into her ass. I pulled out before I'd finished dumping the copious amount of seed inside her, just for the pleasure of watching the milky ropes ooze from her ass, connecting us before they snapped and coated the backs of her thighs.

My fingers encircled my shaft, and I pumped myself a few more times, draining the last of my seed from my balls before wiping my head on her ass cheek. Then, I gathered her in my arms, spinning her around to face me.

"You did so fucking good for me, treasure."

She coughed, bloody drops of water streaming down her flushed face. "You keep calling me that, like you think I'm some kind of prized possession."

I adjusted her in my arms so her feet didn't touch the bottom of the gondola and locked her eyes with mine, holding them while I dragged my tongue over her clavicle and lapped up the drop of water pooling at the hollow of her throat. "That's exactly what you are."

My little human gave the tiniest of huffs. "Do you abuse all your favorite things?"

She was too thoroughly fucked to argue much, but she'd always use the last bit of her breath to be defiant, down to the very end. I fucking loved that about her.

I dragged my lips up her throat, nipping her soft flesh along the way, gentle but firm enough to make her gasp and squirm in my arms. I kissed up her neck, her chin, then paused when her lips were level with mine.

"Yes," I said with more sadness in my tone than I'd intended. "I'm the god of all things dead and forgotten. It shouldn't be shocking that I'm not the most attentive keeper. But with you..."

I reached up to wring the excess water from one of her soaking locks of hair before tucking it behind her ear. "With you, it's different. Ever since I caught my little thief scuttling around in the Petherick tomb, I can't stand to think of anything else."

"That's why your brothers kidnapped me." Her tone turned somber, her gaze distant, even as the last tingling sensations of her orgasm worked through her and she twitched in my arms. "They think you'll get back to your job if I'm not around to distract you. They don't know you at all, do they?"

I laid us down carefully at the bottom of the gondola and tucked her against me. She snuggled close, her face buried against my chest. Her heart was beating so hard, I could feel its thrum against my stomach.

Staring down at her head, I gently stroked her hair as her breathing steadied and her muscles relaxed. She was right. My brothers had known me for millennia, and yet, they didn't know me at all. This human had known me for not even a full week and somehow knew me better than they ever would.

My fingers threaded through her hair, combing out the tangles and idly winding a strand around my knuckle. "They may be my brothers, but they've never been family."

Family. Ha. That word had little meaning to me, and the thought of it only stirred the smallest twinges of loneliness. That was how it had always been for as long as I could remember. Even in my human life, from the little I could recall, I'd been alone, a soldier with no one to wait for me had the war not taken my life.

But maybe it didn't always have to be that way.

My attention dropped back to Rayven in my arms, and I found her peering up at me through her dark lashes. Registering the anxiety churning behind her doe-like eyes, I frowned and pulled her closer. "I'm not going to let them hurt you."

She was looking right at me, yet her gaze was distant. "I don't want to wake up."

A creature like me barely registered pain, but the ache in her voice sent an invisible dagger straight through my heart. The tears rolling down her cheeks gave it an extra agonizing twist.

"Shouldn't you be able to summon me or something, now that you have my soul?"

"That's not how it works, Rayven." My voice came out hardly more than a rasp. "But by the nine Hells, do I wish that wasn't the case."

"What if Belphegor kills me before you find me?"

I bared my teeth, and every sinew in my body went rigid. Even the thought of Belphegor taking Rayven's life, the thing that belonged to me and me alone, sent me into a rage. "He won't. I'll fucking kill him."

"You're going to kill him anyway! That won't stop him from...." Her words began to wobble, and she trailed off. The tears had stopped, but then something worse happened. Her expression shifted, not a hint of emotion on her face. She looked resigned, like she was making peace with whatever Belphegor planned to do with her once she woke. "I guess it doesn't matter if he kills me. You'll just resurrect me, right?"

A sharp sensation hooked into my gut.

There was pain worse than death.

Knowing Belphegor, his plans to torture Rayven would be more complex than the other demon lords. Chances were, he wouldn't kill her.

The Lord of the Gluttony was probably the worst of them all because he would hurt her in ways I couldn't fix with magic.

I couldn't bring myself to tell her that. All I could do was flash her that smile she hated to love and reach down, tugging ever so softly on her nipple piercing, just enough to make her gasp.

My mouth crashed down over hers to capture her sexy little mewl. I nipped her lower lip and growled into her mouth, "That's right..."

My hand slid up her arm, and my thumb rubbed over the three marks I'd cut into her flesh. "You'll never escape me. Even gods can't keep you from me. No matter how deep through

Hell they drag you, I'll find you. I'll decimate anything and anyone who stands in my goddamn way. Do you fucking understand me, little human?"

Days ago, Rayven would have cringed away. She would have fought me. She might have even willingly gone with my brothers if it meant escaping me.

Now, my vow seemed to comfort her. "Alright. When you get here, I want you to hold Belphegor down…"

Knowing the shapeshifter, he'd enjoy that too much. I bit back the thought and let her finish.

She drew back and pinned me with this mischievous look that had me hard again.

"And I'll be the one to cut off his head. I'd say we should fuck on his headless corpse to celebrate, but from what I know of Belphegor, I think he'd like that too much."

CHAPTER THIRTY-ONE

BELIAL

"My Lord, the engineer has found a weak point in the gate."

A bony hand on my arm gingerly shook me from the immersive daydream.

The spell shattered, Rayven's image fading as she slipped from my arms. I reached for her, crying her name, but it was too late. Consciousness came slamming back, and I was plunged into cold reality.

I'd been standing at the back of the gondola on the platform designated for the ferryman, leaning on my oar in a magic-induced trance while using Asmodeus' over-cooked bull head as a pillow.

It was like being wrenched out of a dead sleep, my senses crashing into me in a blink. Before I even fully processed what was happening, I reflexively lifted my oar from the water and swung it toward the offender who'd disturbed the dream spell.

I registered Cecil's terrified features just as my oar made contact with the skeletal servant.

A curse dropped from my lips as my hand snatched out, catching the librarian by his yellowed cravat before he could topple into the River Styx. Relief wrinkled what was left of his aged skin.

I pulled him back into the boat, setting him to his feet with a scowl. "That's a good way to get your soul shattered, Cecil," I grumbled.

Cecil's tooth-laden eye sockets clacked together like they always did when his nerves took over. "F—forgive me, Lord. I was just saying that the engineer, he's finished."

Finally, the soul found a weak point. A chain and a pulley hung above the gate—mechanisms so small, I hadn't seen them, despite my thorough inspection. It was hard to believe they were integral to the iron monstrosity.

A quick blast of magic snapped the chain, and weights that had been concealed by the stalactites overheard plummeted into the river of souls. The gate slammed open with a deafening thud that rained dust from the cavern's ceiling.

I straightened, brushing dust from my cloaked shoulders before taking my stance back on the ferryman's platform. I guided our vessel through the gates of the fifth circle of Hell while Cecil ushered the soul back through the portal with promises of a new soul book for him to live out his eternal paradise as a reward upon our return.

The gondola drifted through the gate, and suddenly, the air was sweltering and sticky. Even the Styx burned almost magma hot, and the water started to boil and bubble with heat, making everything smell of death and rot.

It had been centuries since I'd visited Mammon's realm, yet that was still too soon for my tastes.

Holga shivered on the bench beside me, even though she didn't have skin or nerves to sense the hellish atmosphere. "This place is filled with horrible energy. It's as bad as the second circle."

"Mammon is not unlike Asmodeus." My voice dropped to a hateful growl. "They're both cruel and stupid, though if I had to choose, I'd say Mammon wins out by a couple of brain cells."

Here, in the Lord of Greed's domain, the souls in the Styx were restless. Faint, spectral hands reached from the boiling river, grasping at the gondola as we passed. Holga screamed, zapping a bit of magic at the occasional hand that managed to grip the sides of our vessel.

Using my oar, I knocked back the growing heap of souls gathering around us. Their collective, tortured moans did nothing to shake my sympathies. If these souls were here instead of in the safety of my soul library, it meant they deserved every bit of the torture in store for them in the lower realms.

A towering replica of Mammon loomed as we approached the forge, and my face screwed up in annoyance. The fucker was even uglier wrought from iron.

We sailed between the statue's legs and into the massive structure, the dock workers and various enslaved souls stopping their work to watch our approach.

Whispers of disbelief rose from the gathering crowd as I shifted back into the Lord of Bones. None of my ferries had passed through these parts in ages, and seeing one operated by the Lord of Limbo himself was unheard of.

I docked next to Mammon's hideous river boat, noting the two vessels that bobbed in the water beside it. One of the vessels was a long, thin gondola like mine, veneered and stained in a poison-colored hue of green. A silvery substance clung to the hull, sitting on top of the water like an oil spill.

If the mercury—the Lord of Sloth's metal—wasn't a dead giveaway that the vessel belonged to Paimon, the demons native to the seventh circle minding the boat in their master's absence were. They had giant eyeballs for heads, and their limbs were covered in a network of skinless muscle and sinew.

The vessel beside that looked just like a Viking ship, the sails bearing what I knew was the Lord of Wrath's sigil rolled up tight with many thralls, legendary warriors in past lives, waiting for Baal's return.

Fuck. Paimon and Baal were here too. What in the nine Hells were they up to?

The foreboding feeling in my gut spiked, pushing me to move faster. I commanded Cecil and Holga to remain seated while I cast a protective charm on the gondola. The souls among the slaves on the docks would likely keep to themselves, but among the workers was an alarming number of goblins.

I fucking hated goblins. They were stupid, hideous little fucks, dirty and crude. Mammon loved them, thought they made fantastic servants since they bred like rabbits. Sheer numbers always appealed to wannabe warlords like the Lord of Greed.

I ascended the steps, my oar acting as a staff, and the goblins parted as I passed. They bowed and groveled as they poked and shoved at each other, all eager for a turn to offer me their worthless greetings and respects.

"It's the Lord of Bones," one hissed.

"Why is he here?" another grunted. "He never leaves his realm."

"Must be here for the feast!"

At the mention of a feast, my attention perked up.

"He's not here to partake in the feast. I heard he'd rather fuck the royal meat than eat her."

"Imagine that, wanting to fuck yer own dinner."

Royal meat? A heady coalescence of dread and outrage thrummed through my system and made the flames in my eyes burn bright. I inhaled deeply, barely making out the hint of smoke, fire, and something savory beneath the hot stink of Mammon's realm.

Without giving the wretched little creatures the honor of my full attention, I sent a powerful wave of magic down the steps with a wave of my oar.

Screams filled the air, followed by the loud splat of bodies falling into the boiling River Styx below.

The souls drifting in the crimson current would latch onto the creatures, drowning the ones who didn't succumb to the heat before carrying their remains downriver.

The goblins who remained fell dead still, leaving only the echo of my footsteps as I made my way into the Forge.

Rayven had said he planned to eat her, but I'd clung to the sliver of hope that she'd been misled. Maybe it was a good thing if Belphegor had managed to steal her away.

Oh, the destruction I'd wreak if I found out Mammon ate her.

I'd break him in half and suck the marrow out of his bones before tossing them into the Styx like common garbage if he touched her.

Hells, I'd probably do it anyway.

I'd always hated Mammon.

As I made my way around the courtyard, it was clear all hell had broken loose well before my arrival. A giant cauldron on a dais was tipped over, the fire beneath it all but burned out. A savory-smelling broth covered the ground, and the sickening aroma of burnt goblin flesh tainted the air.

I strode through the havoc, kicking a twitching goblin out of my way with a snarl as I stormed past Mammon's gaudy iron throne. My eyes were set on a towering set of double doors that led deeper into the forge. There was no sign of the other demon lords out here, so they must have retreated inside.

The goblins minding the entrance scrambled to attention with my hasty approach. They grabbed the intricate iron handles and pulled the doors open, a loud groan echoing through the forge as they slowly swung outward.

The Lord of Greed loved gorging himself on all the luxuries being a Lord of Hell afforded him, almost as much as Belphegor. The banquet hall was a large room that took front and center and wasn't hard to locate.

I burst into the hall in a swirl of my cloak and twisting smoke, my gaze immediately falling to the demon lords seated around the absurdly long table, which had been set for a large feast.

Mammon stood to the left before a grand hearth, staring into the flames, his blazing wings turned toward me. Baal sat at the end of the table with his spider-like limbs folded neatly around him, and Paimon's enormous blue eyeball glared at me, gleaming with silent curiosity.

"I don't remember sending you an invitation to my feast, Belial." Mammon didn't even bother to look in my direction.

Baal muttered something flippant, but his words didn't register. I was too busy sizing up Sloth. His massive head stared at me with an unblinking gaze.

The demon lord of the seventh circle didn't lord over the sin of sloth because he was lazy. What he lacked in physical strength, he made up for with his mystic ability to warp time, even slow it to a stop with a single glance.

I'd need to kill him first.

I donned a manic grin and stepped out from the shadows that clung to the edges of the banquet hall and into the torchlight.

Baal and Paimon both took notice of my oar, and what—or rather, who—decorated it at the same time.

"It's rude not to invite all your brothers to your little gathering, Mammon. Don't worry, I brought them all with me so we can enjoy this feast I heard goblins chattering about."

CHAPTER THIRTY-TWO

RAYVEN

My vision was blurry when I opened my eyes, and I blinked furiously until it focused. Once again, I was in a place I didn't recognize, but at least I wasn't in the Lord of Greed's domain.

The sweltering air no longer threatened to choke me with every inhale. It was faintly chilly here, but not unbearable like Asmodeus' realm had been. The cool air licked at my skin, a welcome relief after being in the Forge.

A quick glance around the room told me I was in Belphegor's realm. The place embodied the sin he lorded over: gluttony.

It was a large space that reminded me of an underground cavern, but unlike the previous realms that were dark and carved into regular stone, the walls here seemed to glitter. It looked like hundreds of crystals had been crushed and dusted over the stones to make them shine.

The room itself was spilling over with so many things, it was hard to focus on any one in particular. There were several sofas shoved against the walls, nearly buried beneath mountains of jewel-toned throw pillows. Several shades of dark fabric draped from the ceiling overhead, and an enormous circular bed occupied the center of the room. It was piled high with black blankets and multi-colored pillows.

Everything, no matter which direction I looked, seemed to shimmer or shine with excessive decadence. It seemed wildly befitting of Belphegor.

But there was too much fucking stuff. I was already feeling a little claustrophobic, like the objects filling the room were crushing in on me even though they didn't move.

After the minute it took to digest my view, I realized I was upright, my hands manacled above my head on a black leather St. Andrew's cross, the kind you'd find in a BDSM dungeon.

My immediate instinct was to tug at the chains, even though I knew it wouldn't do any good. The shackles didn't budge.

"Fuck." My eyes swept over the room for any sign of the Lord of Gluttony.

To my relief, he was nowhere in sight, but that didn't mean much. I half-expected one of the piles of pillows in the corner to shift and reveal him at any second. He could have been hiding anywhere, and I wouldn't have noticed.

A muffled sound nearby made me jump, and I inhaled sharply. Heart thrumming in my chest, I craned my neck to see another cross, identical to mine, a few feet away. A slender, familiar-looking woman was splayed out across it, completely naked.

She was human, but her pale form was tinged blue and a little transparent. She was like a projection, though her body was still solid enough to be manacled in place.

My chest seized.

She was a soul.

Her eyes were closed, her head drooping to one side.

I studied her face and its familiar features, the ones I'd memorized from her painting in Belial's castle. Her cheekbones, her thick black lashes, her pouty lips, her jet black hair—she was unmistakable.

Shock shot through my system, a shiver vibrating up my spine. It clicked who she was.

Catherine.

It was the soul of Belial's first pet, the one who'd fought tooth and nail to get away from him—the woman whose tomb I'd robbed, sealing my fate as the Lord of Bones' next mortal captive.

My mouth was dry as I watched her, warring emotions clashing within me.

"C-Catherine?" My voice was hoarse, but she stirred at the noise, her dark eyes blinking open to lock with mine.

For a moment, neither of us spoke, both drinking in our reality. The recognition in her eyes told me she knew exactly who I was, even though I'd never seen her face in person. She'd never seen mine either, as far as I knew, but I'd spoken to her through the dagger.

My heart clenched. Belphegor had obviously stolen her soul somehow when he and the other lords kidnapped me. He must have picked up Catherine's dagger after they'd kidnapped me since I'd used it in a sad attempt to fend them all off. He must have extracted the soul from inside the blade.

"Are you alright?" I shouldn't have asked. I shouldn't have cared, but seeing her tied up, just as helpless as myself, pulled at my heartstrings. Concern wavered in her eyes before they darted around the room, probably making sure the coast was clear.

"I'm okay," she said, though she didn't sound so sure. Her gaze snapped back to mine again. "You should have killed yourself when you had the chance."

Her words were shocking, but there was no malice in her voice. She truly meant it. The poor woman had tried so hard to get away from Belial, to escape from Hell. Even after her final suicide attempt, when he'd laid her body to rest, she'd never truly found peace, not while her soul remained in his realm.

She didn't want that same fate for me.

Yet, here I was.

The only difference between our situations right now was that I'd given my soul to the same demon lord she fought so hard to flee.

I'd do it all over again too.

So maybe this was my punishment for being the twisted fuck I was, for failing to get away from the demon lord who'd kidnapped me from the surface and killed Mark. But what about Catherine? Did she deserve whatever it was Belphegor had planned for us?

Sure, I'd be full of shit if I said I wasn't at least a little apprehensive about seeing her. Despite her hating Belial, she'd captivated him for years. She was the source of so much heartache, regardless of whether it was her fault.

The fact that Belial had ever been infatuated with her at all was enough reason for me not to like her, but still. That didn't mean I wanted her to suffer.

How long had she been chained up like this? Had she been here all this time, or had he manacled us together?

A hundred more questions galloped through my racing mind and then slammed to a halt when a door creaked open somewhere, announcing that we weren't alone.

Panic flashed over Catherine's face. My throat seized as the steady clack of high heels on marble echoed through the crowded chamber, and my attention whipped across the room to see Belphegor slinking toward us. A revealing little dress—if it could even be called that—made of countless little bronze loops created a chainmail effect, delicately clinging to the feminine frame he currently embodied.

"I see you've had time to get acquainted." He smirked, his eyes locked in my direction as he weaved between towering piles of clutter. "Who would have thought I'd be so lucky? I have not one but two of Belial's most treasured pets. I'm honored."

Okay, so he knew who she was. Fuck.

My eyes shifted from Belphegor to Catherine, and the horror on her face told me everything I needed to know. He'd done more than just keep her chained up. Whatever he'd done to her, whatever she'd seen, it obviously terrified her, and her bottom lip trembled.

"Please," she begged, her voice faint. "No more. Please, leave me alone."

Belphegor merely chuckled, but he wasn't paying her any attention. His gaze was fixed on me, an eager hunger brewing behind his eyes.

"I have so much fun planned for the three of us," he said, his voice heavy with venom. Something told me that whatever he had planned, it wasn't going to be fun at all. Painful, maybe, but not the enjoyable kind Belial had taught me to crave.

I swallowed hard, the blood freezing in my veins as he skirted around the bed in the middle of the room. It was hard to imagine how anything in this cavern was functional, including the bed, with how much shit was piled on top of it, and I didn't want to find out.

Stopping in front of me, Belphegor flashed a wicked grin and trailed one of his manicured fingers along my collarbone. I flinched away from his touch, but the cuffs binding my wrists and ankles didn't allow me to put more than an inch or so between us.

The Lord of Gluttony had made sure I couldn't escape him. "What are you going to do to us?" I asked, afraid to know the answer.

He laughed, tossing his snow-pale hair over his shoulder. "Nothing I won't thoroughly enjoy."

I didn't like the sound of that at all.

The demon's coal-black eyes flicked in Catherine's direction, and she winced like he'd struck her.

There was something about the way he regarded her that made my skin crawl and my blood boil.

Obviously, the sick fuck got off on terrorizing people.

"Leave her alone," I demanded, sounding way braver than I felt. I didn't owe Catherine anything, especially since she tried to make me jump out a window when I first arrived at the Lord of Bones' castle.

But a tug in my chest demanded I say something in her defense.

"You said you wanted to play with me," I said, steeling my nerves. "Now's your chance, but you have to leave her alone."

Belphegor tsked his tongue. "Oh, little mortal, you don't have any bargaining power here. You're both going to be my toys for however long you keep me entertained."

His head canted to the side, his eyes narrowing. "Who should I turn into this time? You had so much fun with the Lord of Lust."

I shivered, realizing he was planning on shifting again. I was afraid I'd never forget the way he'd touched me as Asmodeus, shackling me to the bathtub, running his fingers along my folds. The thought of his hands on me again had me tasting bile.

"Maybe I'll turn into Mammon this time, seeing as he didn't get to have his fun with you," Belphegor teased, his manicured nail trailing down my chest, carving a hair-thin line of blood between my breasts. "A demon like him would split you open and jerk off into your pretty pool of guts. Knowing him, he'd be able to finish inside you before your insides even had a chance to stop twitching."

As horrible as that sounded, I couldn't think of anything worse than him turning into Asmodeus and raping me repeatedly. He'd already said he wasn't interested in fucking me. Had that been a lie? Had he changed his mind?

"Or, I could turn into the Lord of Wrath and see how you handle both his spiked cocks," the demon lord mused, tapping his fingers on his chin. "So many options. Eternity is a long time, but I have enough ideas to last a few hundred years."

Nausea churned my stomach at the thought of being stuck in the Lord of Gluttony's realm for that long, but I couldn't think about that.

Belial was on his way. He was coming for me. He'd figure out a way through Mammon's forge and come for me.

"Belial will rip your head off and wear your skin like a cape, you bastard," I seethed.

Suddenly, Belphegor's eyes lit up, nearly glowing as a wicked smile curled his lips.

"Silly me," he said, taking a step back. "You must be missing your precious Lord of Bones, aren't you? Don't worry. I can help with that."

Before I could even open my mouth, he shifted, his shape changing and filling out.

His white hair turned into an unkempt black shag, his breasts into perfectly defined pecs. Antlers sprouted from his head, a smooth black mask with faded embellishments appearing out of thin air.

When he finished morphing into this new shape, my heart was in my throat, making the simple task of breathing damn near impossible.

Standing before me was Belial, identical down to the arrogant smirk quirking his mouth.

"That's better, isn't it, mortal?" he asked in the velvet-wrapped baritone that normally made me melt. Hearing it now was like being shocked by a high-voltage fence.

I jerked against the cross, my chains rattling as surprise and horror and a dozen other complicated emotions rushed through my veins.

Belphegor's eyes sparkled in amusement with his chuckle. "Now we're ready to play."

CHAPTER THIRTY-THREE

BELIAL

Mammon finally glanced up from the fire and turned to look at me. His line of sight went straight to the oar gripped in my fist, and as he struggled to identify the burnt heads impaled onto the bone, I released a dark, guttural laugh that shook the banquet hall.

"Don't you recognize your own brothers?" I gestured to each brutalized and beaten head I'd collected as I made my way through the Nine Hells. "Asmodeus. Pine. Leviathan. We're all here. One big, happy fucking family. Well, minus Belphegor…"

I strode further into the hall and grabbed a knife sticking out of a wheel of cheese, stabbing a chunk and shoving it into my maw. "And what I'm presuming was meant to be the main course."

It might have been a trick of the fire, but for a moment, I could have sworn I saw a flicker of fear behind his infernal eyes.

I thought about burying the knife in one of their hearts for a beat before dismissing the idea. While it would be hilarious to kill one of them with a cheese knife, it wouldn't be efficient. I needed to dispose of these bastards quickly.

"Just tell me where she is, and I'll consider sparing all three of your miserable carcasses."

"We don't know what you're talking about," Mammon sneered. "The soup was the main course. Belphegor broke up with me and kicked it over, so eat what's left and get out. Whatever else you're looking for isn't here."

My fist tightened around my oar so hard, I was afraid the bone might snap in half.

Mammon was a pathetic liar. Even without Rayven's warning, I could have seen straight through his words. The way he tensed, a muscle ticking in his jaw as he narrowed his eyes on me, told me everything I needed to know.

No matter what, I wasn't leaving this room without three new heads added to my ever-growing collection to the family tree.

There was no denying I was being a cruel and selfish bastard for indulging in my rage.

I knew she wasn't here. There was nothing stopping me from turning around and going straight to Belphegor's realm, but leaving them alive would probably come back to bite me in the ass. Since my teleportation abilities didn't work outside Limbo, we'd have to come back this way, and I didn't trust these three not to ambush us on our journey back. I had to eliminate the threat now.

I took another stride closer to them, walking along the length of the table while pretending to peruse the food, occasionally stabbing a grape or bits of cheese onto my knife before stuffing it into my mouth.

The way Mammon's eyes kept pinging between me and his giant war hammer propped against the side of the massive fireplace didn't go unnoticed. He was determining how much space I'd have to close between us before he went for it.

Paimon and Baal tensed with my approach, and when I sat a few chairs down from them, I was sure they were all wondering the same thing as Mammon: should they kill me before I could add their heads to my oar?

None of them moved as I fixed myself a plate of food, but they seemed to relax.

"Shame about your human pet, Belial," Baal spoke up, his voice a mix of garbled syllables and clicks. His attention slipped to my oar leaning against the table, the Lord of Lechery's blackened heads gaping at him and Paimon. "Heard Asmodeus kidnapped her from your All Hallows' Eve Masquerade, but it looks like you got your revenge. Mammon's right—you should eat and go home."

I swept a clump of what remained of Asmodeus' flaxen hair off the table with a growl-laced chuckle. "Bullshit. I won't be satisfied until my queen is back in my arms."

"Your queen?" Mammon laughed with a snide grin that had no humor in it at all. "You can't make a mortal the Queen of Death."

I chewed my food, tamping down my anger as he just about gave away all the shit I already knew.

Brutes like him loved to talk, and if you let them talk long enough, they'd always tell on themselves.

Paimon shot Mammon a look of warning with his giant eye. Since the demon had no mouth, he couldn't talk. Not that he needed to—everything he was thinking could be said with a look.

The fire demon, catching the Lord of Sloth's gaze, started to backtrack. "Not that it matters anymore, right? She's gone. Belphegor probably had his fun and disposed of her. Knowing that depraved bastard, there won't be much left of her body, so might as well go back to your realm."

"You're right," I muttered, fighting tooth and nail to keep my cool demeanor in place. "She was just a distraction anyway, right? So what if she's dead? Mortals are supposed to die." I twirled the cheese knife between my fingers, my voice taking a dark bend. "I say, good riddance."

Perhaps I wasn't such a bad liar after all. That, or Mammon was dumber than I'd given him credit for, because even under his garish armor, I could see his muscles relaxing. "Finally, you've come to your senses. Shame you had to kill some of our brothers before you did, but that means more for us to rule. We can divvy up the realms between us."

There was a sudden shift in the room, and the other demon lords seemed to eat up the obvious lie. Was it easy for them to buy, since they couldn't grasp the concept of loving anything other than their power?

That had to be it. They couldn't understand my obsession with my mortal pet, so it was easy to believe my feelings for her were but a passing infatuation.

"Slave! Ambrosia for my brothers!" Mammon roared, his gravelly voice echoing through the hall. A second later, a soul with a chain around his throat shuffled in with an iron pitcher. By the time he finished pouring all four of us goblets of the rare liquor, Mammon lost his patience. As the soul took too long navigating the perimeter of the comically long table, he threw him into the fire.

He couldn't shatter souls like I could, so the soul would live on, feeling every bit of the fire as it burned for however long it suited the Lord of Greed.

Mammon took a seat beside Paimon across from me and held his goblet up for a toast. "To mortal meat," he said, his smile stretching from ear to ear as the soul's screams from the fire added to the hellish ambiance.

Tipping my drink to theirs, I said nothing as the other two repeated Mammon's words.

I knocked the goblet back, dumping the meager amount of ambrosial alcohol down my throat. There was a reason it was called the liquor of the gods. It was warm and tasted of heaven, unlike anything else in existence, in the underworld or otherwise. There was a time when I thought the liquor was the closest a demon could ever get to true paradise.

That was before I captured Rayven.

"Speaking of mortal meat," I began, setting my empty goblet down, "have you ever fucked a human pussy while it still throbs with life?"

Mammon's flaming brows quirked. "No, I haven't, but I have eaten fresh mortal flesh. It tastes fucking delicious. When you cook them before they're fully dead, you can taste the fear. Gives the meat a nice flavor."

Disgust had my jaws snapping together, teeth clacking, but to the other lords, it seemed to come off as enthusiasm.

Rayven was right. These monsters were so self-absorbed in their own interests that they hadn't learned shit about me, even after all this time.

"Shame. I was looking forward to tasting some. I've heard your feasts are the most opulent things in the Nine Hells, Mammon."

"And what a feast it would have been today if Belphegor hadn't fucked me over. I think you would have enjoyed the royal meat I had prepared."

Mammon snickered as he took the last gulp of his wine. "In fact, I know you would have. Too bad she's not here anymore. Imagine if Belphegor hadn't ruined things. You would have walked in to see your human pet spread out on my dinner table, trussed and stuffed like a roast pig..."

There it was, the undeniable slip-up I'd been waiting for. A heavy pause settled over the hall, tension choking the room, and Baal exchanged a nervous look with the Lord of Sloth. Mammon, oblivious to the mounting unease, kept running his fucking mouth.

"I would have saved you the best part—her pussy—since you were such a fan of it while it was still alive."

I couldn't keep up the façade a second longer. My blood went cold then molten hot all in the same furious inhale I dragged in.

With a roar, I grabbed my oar and hurled it at Paimon in a blink. He was fast—considering he could bend time at his will—but the fates must have been on my side, because he wasn't quick enough.

The handle speared his giant eyeball, but instead of blood, shining, liquid mercury gushed from the fleshy sack that had been his head a breath before.

The Lord of Wrath let out one of his infamous war cries as he watched his brother slump onto the table, dead in an instant, my oar poking out the back of his eye like a spear on the battlefield.

He leapt onto the table, his spidery legs chittering on the wood, sending plates and cutlery flying as he rushed me.

One of his legs lunged at me, the barbed carapace sharp enough to run me through. I grabbed it and wrenched it around until there was a sickening crunch, followed by a howl of pain.

I thought about using it as a weapon, but I tossed it aside and resorted to stabbing him in the eye too, burying the cheese knife into one of his many spidery eye sockets.

Seeing that Baal was seconds from going down, Mammon jumped out of his chair and went for his hammer. I shot at it with a blast of fiery blue magic, sending the war hammer flying out of his reach. It only bought me a few extra moments, but when one was locked in hand-to-hand combat with the demon Lord of Wrath, a few seconds was plenty.

I wrenched the knife from his eye with a spray of blood and fluid. No steel inside this body, just blood and bone.

Perfect.

Another screech. Some of his many legs, or at least the ones still attached, slammed into me and sent me skidding back on the table, plates and food clattering to the ground in a great havoc that had the goblins outside clamoring to get through the doors.

Skidding to a halt on the table, my attention locked on one of the few things that hadn't been knocked off the table in the chaos.

An iron candelabra with half-burnt candle sticks, their flames still flickering.

Unlike Mammon, Baal was an experienced warlord and warrior. Still, he was cocky, too used to winning.

With me on my back, he made the assumption that I'd lost. The spider demon lunged at me again, another of his sharp carapace legs slamming toward my head—the easiest way to kill a demon lord—but he was too slow, and without Sloth to slow time for him, he had no chance of winning this.

I grabbed the candelabra and slammed the base into the small hole I'd already made in his head. It slid through like hot metal through butter.

It was almost too easy. I laughed at the shocked expression that would be frozen on his head forever before his body slumped on top of mine, lifeless. The Lord of Wrath was dead.

I dumped his body off the table and leapt to my feet, finding Mammon standing in front of the hearth, his great hammer held at the ready.

"All this for what?" he growled out, following my movements by shifting his hammer in my direction. "Has the Lord of Bones and Rot nothing better to do than obsess over an insignificant hunk of meat with a heartbeat?"

With a swipe of my tongue, I wiped a bit of Baal's blood from my bony face, grimacing at the bitter taste. "No, Mammon. All this for a chance at a life I don't fucking loathe."

"Life? *Life?* What business does the Lord of Death have with life?" the fire demon mocked, his armor clanging as he started to close the distance between us with his heavy-footed strides.

"I'm the God of Life and Death. I may not breathe life into bones," I said, positioning myself to lunge at Mammon, "but I decide who lives and dies, and you... you're going to die."

CHAPTER THIRTY-FOUR

RAYVEN

Icy terror flooded me as I stared at Belial's visage. His storm-gray eyes, the ones I'd lost myself in countless times, watched me through the holes in his mask, an evil glint nearly making them glow.

I felt sick, my stomach twisting into knots at the sight of him.

"No, no, no. You're not him." It was the only thing I could say as I stared at Belial's likeness. It looked so much like him, the same way Belphegor had portrayed Asmodeus, but I knew it wasn't real.

Belial wore a black, lantern-sleeved shirt and tight black pants that hugged his impressive bulge perfectly. Everything about him was familiar, aside from his scent. The smell of sweet, ripe strawberries was missing, replaced by Belphegor's perfume-soaked skin. The illusion was otherwise uncanny, with the exception of bronze charms decorating his antlers instead of silver ones.

I focused on those inconsistencies, reminding myself it wasn't real; Belial wasn't really here.

"Rayven," he said, the low, familiar rumble of his voice making my stomach flutter.

I squeezed my eyes closed and shook my head. "No. Fuck you. You're not him."

"Don't be like that, little human," Belphegor said, tsking his tongue. "Aren't you excited to see me? You should be dripping with arousal to see the demon you've been pining for standing before you, just a touch away."

I felt his eyes slither down the length of my naked body, which was still stretched out on the St. Andrews Cross, completely exposed to him.

"This is what you wanted, isn't it?"

It was true that I was desperate to see Belial. Not in a dream, like he appeared to me before I woke, but here, in front of me. I wanted him to appear more than anything I'd ever wanted in my life, but not like this. Never like this.

I'd considered a lot when I convinced Belphegor to betray Mammon and take me for himself, but I hadn't counted on him using Belial against me.

How stupid of me to assume anything less. At least I wasn't being eaten, but it wasn't a good sign that the fact no longer felt as reassuring as it once had.

The Lord of Gluttony taking on Belial's form shouldn't have unsettled me as much as it did.

Seeing him in the flesh made me want to scream and cry and wrap my arms around him all at once.

The complicated emotions knotting my chest turned heavy, like an anvil sat on my ribs, when Belial's illusion pulled his black mask off and tossed it aside. Seeing his beautiful, scared face lit my body on fire, and a terrifying spike of desire and fear twisted through me.

"Fuck you, you sick bastard," I cried, trying and failing to tear my gaze away from him. From his dark brows to his marred lips, everything about him was the demon I loved.

Judging by the laugh that followed, Belphegor knew just how deeply seeing him like this affected me, and he was enjoying himself way more than he had any right to.

"Oh yes, this will be much more fun than parading around as one of my ex-lovers," he chuckled. "Is your heart racing out of fear? Or because of what I can do to you in this form?"

He reached for me, grasping my chin and forcing my gaze to his. His gloved thumb stroked my bottom lip, and I hated how soft and gentle the touch was. It was a lie.

"Keep your fucking hands off me," I growled.

A wicked smirk curved his lips. "How about I touch myself then? Unfortunately, I haven't had the chance to fuck Belial yet, but this will do for now."

He slid his gloved hand over the front of his pants, his cock twitching beneath his touch. I didn't know what I would do if he whipped out his dick and started stroking it in front of me. Would I find it hot because it was Belial's likeness? Or would I be thoroughly fucking disgusted?

I shook my head, trying to banish the demented thoughts from my mind. I didn't like where this was going at all.

Belphegor made a show of unlacing the front of his pants, shoving down the material until a thick, unpierced cock sprang free.

It was strange seeing Belial with a cock that didn't belong to him—the shape and length weren't quite right—but a shiver still rippled up my spine when the demon in front of me moaned in pleasure as he gripped the shaft.

The sounds, the delicious moans and groans, were all uncanny. If I closed my eyes, I wouldn't be able to tell the difference between this fucked up illusion and the real noises Belial made when he was inside me.

"Do you like what you see?" Belphegor asked, sliding his hand up the shaft of his cock and dragging it back down with a hiss.

"No, and I wouldn't mind chopping it off," I spat, dragging my gaze to glare into his storm-gray eyes. "For old time's sake."

"I have a better idea," Belphegor cooed, stepping closer to me with his fingers still wrapped around his dick. I whimpered as he lifted his free hand and brushed the backs of his fingers against my cheek.

"I could sink my cock into something besides my hand," he said, leaning close enough that he was just a kiss away. His breath fanned over my face, but it was nothing like Belial's. He stepped even closer, dragging the head of his cock up my bare thigh.

A scream lodged in my throat. Even if I yelled and cried, it wouldn't do any good. No one was going to hear; no one was going to save me.

If he fucked me in Belial's form, I didn't think I'd ever recover. Every time I fucked the real Belial, I'd think of this moment and cry. Even if I closed my eyes and did my best to convince myself it was really him, pretending I wasn't being raped by his shapeshifting brother, it would taint every single time Belial touched me from here on out.

"Come on, little human. Don't you want to play? I'm a demon lord. Causing pain is in our nature…"

His fingers trailed up to coil the patch of hair between my legs around a ringed finger. "And I know you *crave* the Lord of Bones' brand of pain."

That damned voice… It sunk into my marrow and seeped into my system like poison.

"Get fucked!" I squirmed, trying to escape his touch, but it was no use. I was completely at his mercy. My legs trembled and would have given out if I wasn't manacled to the cross.

"No?" he hummed, his free hand dipping between my legs, dancing over the skin of my inner thigh, dangerously close to my pussy. Goosebumps pebbled my skin, discomfort tearing its way through me as his fingers lifted to brush the three cuts Belial had made on my inner arm before falling away. "Well, if you're sure. I can think of someone else who'd love to have Belial's fat cock inside them."

He tucked his dick back into his pants and stepped away from me, marching over to Catherine.

My stomach dropped as he reached up to unfasten her wrists, and her shrill scream pierced through the chamber as she fought against him.

"No!" I gasped, my heart slamming to a stop. I thrashed, jerking against my restraints, fighting with every ounce of my strength, but it was in vain. "Stop! Leave her alone!"

When she was free, Belphegor wrapped her long hair around his hand and dragged her to stand in front of me, turning her so she was on full display. His other hand came around to cup one of her breasts, eagerly dipping lower to tease over her exposed skin.

"Please, don't touch her," I begged, my voice coming out ragged and raw.

As much as I didn't want him to touch me, seeing Belial's hands on another woman had my heart ripping at the seams. It wasn't real—I knew that—but it didn't make it feel any less difficult to watch or soothe the jealousy burning through my veins. It didn't numb the pain tearing me apart.

Aside from the visceral pain I felt at seeing Belial's hands on her, I couldn't let Belphegor torture Catherine. Judging by her reaction, he'd done enough to her already. She hated Belial, and assaulting her in his form would be the ultimate penance for a crime she didn't commit.

"Do whatever you want to me," I said desperately, jerking against the shackles holding me in place. "Fuck me, do your worst, but..." I couldn't believe I was saying it. "Leave her alone."

He yanked her hair harder, making her cry out, and craned her neck until she was staring up at the ceiling. With a dark chuckle, he ran his teeth over her throat, letting his tongue dance out over the pale skin.

My stomach pitched to my feet and ice prickled up my spine. "Keep your fucking mouth off her."

"You had your chance, mortal," he teased, dipping lower to bite her shoulder. She jerked, trying to fight and get away, but he only twisted his fist tighter in her long locks until she submitted. "Now you get to watch while I play with the Lord of Bones' other precious pet. I bet she'll scream just as prettily as you do."

His hand dipped between her thighs and slipped between her labia, his fingers harsh and careless against her skin. "He certainly has a type. You both have long, raven-black hair and moon-pale skin. The same frantic little flutter of her pulse pounding inside her..."

She screamed, shattering the rest of my heart, and he thrust two fingers into her entrance.

"You sick fucking bastard!" I cried.

I wanted to close my eyes and block out what was happening. I wanted to scream until the sound of Catherine's cries faded into nothing, to save myself from having to watch the demon I loved hurt her, touch her, *rape* her.

But as much as I wanted to, I couldn't look away.

Tears burned my eyes and streamed down my cheeks as he fucked her with his fingers in front of me, a sick fucking grin distorting his scarred features.

"You take my fingers so well," he muttered in Catherine's ear, the sound of Belial's voice making me sick. "I wonder how you'll take other parts of me."

"No!" I screamed, but he was already pulling his fingers out of her and dragging her backward toward the bed. "Stop! Don't do this!"

My words went unheard as he shoved her down onto the mountain of blankets, shifting the fabric around until he found what he was looking for: more manacles.

Catherine fought against him, kicking and thrashing as he fixed her wrists in the restraints, but she was no match for his size and strength.

"Now, now, that's no way for a good little pet to behave," he said, clamping a massive hand over Catherine's mouth to muffle her screams. She trembled as he painted a lick down her neck, catching her nipple in his mouth.

"Belphegor, *please*," I begged for both of us. I couldn't stand the sight of Belial pinning another naked woman down while she screamed for him to set her free. It was worse than anything I'd faced so far in all the layers of hell.

If I had anything in my stomach, I would have thrown up. Instead, I could only choke on the bile burning my throat.

Belphegor crawled off the bed, peeling off his clothes and tossing them to the floor while Catherine screamed herself hoarse. I felt so hopeless, so fucking helpless, watching and not being able to do anything.

It's not him.

Through the tears blurring my vision, I watched him pry her thighs apart and settle there. Pain lanced down my arms as I strained against my cuffs.

I had to get free. I had to help her. I had to do *something* besides stand there and watch the visage of the demon I loved rape this pour woman's soul.

"You should be happy to serve your lord," Belphegor rumbled in Belial's deep baritone as he lined his cock up and pressed his hips forward. He sank into her slowly at first, gradually picking up speed. His mouth moved over her skin, his tongue dancing over her chest, up her neck. "It's an honor to be bedded by the Lord of Limbo."

My heart clenched as I tried to block out his words, squeezing my eyes closed as he picked up speed. Even though I wasn't watching, the sounds of flesh against flesh and the heartbroken whimpers coming from Catherine turned my stomach to acid and had detailed images forming in my mind.

I couldn't escape it, and neither could she.

CHAPTER THIRTY-FIVE

RAYVEN

It's not him, it's not him, it's not him.

I repeated those words to myself, over and over. They were the only anchor I had to remind myself that the horrifying rape unfolding before me wasn't being committed by Belial.

One last, pathetic little "please" left me before I clammed up. Trying to appeal to any sense of mercy wasn't doing good, not with this demon. He didn't have a merciful bone in his body. Besides, I was pretty sure begging him to stop only encouraged him.

The monster was getting off on my and Catherine's pain.

I hated that this was what I'd asked for. I'd practically begged him not to let Mammon eat me.

It's not like I could have known this was what he would do.

I never expected *this.*

How fucked was it that I almost wished I was back in the cauldron, boiling among the vegetables?

That wouldn't have saved Catherine's soul, though. Belphegor would still have her. He'd still be doing this to her even if I wasn't here.

When I opened my eyes again, Belial's wolfish gaze clamped on me, watching my reaction as he fucked the soul beneath him.

My head pounded with panic, and my pulse roared in my ears. I couldn't move or think or breathe as he dipped lower, eyes still locked with mine as he pressed his mouth to Catherine's.

I opened my mouth, this time a scream ripping out, the noise unrecognizable. "You're a fucking monster!" My brain had short-circuited, and they were the only words I could manage.

"And we know how you feel about monster cock," Belial said, his thrusts becoming more erratic. "Don't worry. Your living cunt is next. Now, be a good girl and watch as I fuck her cunt and fill it with as much demon cum as she can handle."

The minutes crawled by, the never-ending repetition of flesh slapping against flesh dragging on for what felt like forever. Belphegor's disgusting grunts and groans drowned out Catherine's broken sobs, and his dirty talk in Belial's voice had me sick to my stomach.

My heart was breaking, and there was nothing I could do to escape the agony.

I was in my own personal hell.

If I closed my eyes, Belphegor only moaned and groaned louder, making it impossible to tune out what was happening. I couldn't even fucking disassociate long, because he'd call my name in Belial's voice, ripping me from whatever whisper of a daydream I'd been trying to cling to.

I was helpless. Hopeless. I felt more alone than ever.

And I couldn't even bring myself to miss Belial, what with Belphegor doing his damndest to completely decimate the positive feelings I'd managed to build for the Lord of Limbo after his betrayal.

"Look at me, mortal," Belial's voice purred. The sound wriggled beneath my skin and burned through me like acid. I squeezed my eyes shut, not wanting to obey a single order from Belphegor, but his next words flipped a switch inside me. "Please, look at me, little human."

My body reacted to the soft plea without my permission, and I opened my eyes to see Belial's face tense with his climax. His brows furrowed, his mouth dropping into a familiar O as a stuttered moan escaped them. My knees gave out, pain lancing my wrists like a hot knife where the manacles held me up

"Fuck you!" I screamed.

It's not him, it's not him, it's not him.

I reminded myself again as tears spilled down my cheeks, but the words no longer brought me any comfort. After watching him fuck Catherine's soul for so long and hearing his voice over and over, it felt too real. The agony, the jealousy, the despair. They were all real.

When he pulled out of her, Catherine didn't move, her eyes swollen shut from crying, her body scratched and bruised from his abuse.

Finally, I thought with an exhale of relief. *It's over.*

He'd probably do it again, maybe more than once, but at least for now, the worst was over.

"Now, get the fuck away from her," I growled.

With an evil smirk, Belphegor moved to undo her wrists, shoving her off the bed in a swift motion once she was free. His antler charms swayed and clinked together, a sound I'd come to love. Now, it just made me want to shrink in on myself.

Catherine hit the floor with a thud, her hair falling in front of her face like a mourning veil. I waited for her to move, but she didn't.

My stomach sank as Belphegor got to his feet, turning in my direction to stare at me from the middle of the room. His cock was already thickening again, like the rage in my eyes had suddenly skyrocketed his libido. He licked his lips, and fear vibrated up my spine.

"Don't look so relieved, mortal," he mused, pacing closer to me. My eyes remained locked on him, a sinking feeling in the pit of my stomach. I knew his next words before he said them. "We're only just getting started. It's your turn now."

I tasted bile.

He stopped in front of me, wrapping a hand around his cock and pumping it a few times. It was hard again in a few seconds.

"Don't you fucking touch me," I gritted out, fully prepared to fight if he took off my wrist restraints.

I didn't have a weapon, but I had nails. I'd claw at every part of him, bite him. If he put his cock in my mouth, that would be the second appendage I'd bite off in the last several hours.

"Oh, I'm going to touch you," Belial's voice purred, making me shudder. "And you're going to like it. I know you love to be fucked by your precious Lord of Bones. Who wouldn't?"

He reached up and undid one of the restraints around my wrist.

"And I've been dying to feel that warm cunt—"

I swung as soon as my arm was free, but he expected it, catching my wrist in a swift motion and pinning it down by my side. He leaned in closer, close enough for his warm breath to roll over me, and smiled maliciously. "Feisty little mortal. Don't lose that fire, because I'm going to do my best to extinguish it."

He undid my other wrist, grabbing my arm before I could attack him, and dragged me away from the St. Andrew's cross. I kicked at him, legs flailing, jerking violently against his hold, doing everything I could to get away.

I couldn't get in that bed. If I did, I wouldn't be able to fight him off.

He'd do exactly what he did to Catherine to me.

My stomach knotted painfully.

"Let. Me. Go."

Belphegor turned and grabbed me around my waist, throwing me over his shoulder with ease and marching toward the bed. I clawed at his muscular back, punching and hitting him until he flipped me onto the mattress. I bounced violently, the mountain of pillows and blankets covering me.

I flailed, trying to clear a path to escape, but the bed dipped with a new weight, and Belphegor swatted the pillows away as he climbed on top of me.

His meaty thighs pinned me in place while he restrained my wrists again. I kicked, thrashed, and fought with every ounce of energy I had left, but it wasn't enough. I felt so weak, sapped of all my strength.

Fighting seemed hopeless, and Belphegor's evil look urged me to surrender. "Stop fighting me. Give in."

No, that wasn't right. The real Belial wanted me to fight; he admired it when I fought back.

He'd want me to keep fighting now.

I screamed as he leaned down, his face so close to mine, I could feel the warmth of his breath roll over my skin. His perfume-soaked scent stuffed its way down my throat, choking me. He might have looked just like my demon lover, but he was a vile monster.

I spat in Belphegor's face, a pitiful gob since my mouth was so dry, but it made contact with his eye. He sat back, the bronze charms on his antlers clinking together. He looked thoroughly unamused.

It was another hairline crack in the illusion. Belial loved it when I spit on him.

"Don't act so ungrateful," he said, dragging one of his fingers along my jawline before dipping it lower, tracing over the hollow of my throat. "You enjoyed watching Belial fuck that pathetic mortal soul. I bet you're already dripping, aren't you?"

"No!" I yelled as he slid lower, ripping my thighs apart with his meaty hands. A wicked smile curled his lips.

"What a pretty pussy." This time, his voice came out more like his own than Belial's. "When I fuck Belial later, maybe I'll borrow this. I'm sure he'd enjoy a familiar flesh sleeve when he's fucking me."

I growled, thrashing and trying to wriggle away from him, but he remained firmly planted between my legs. With a smirk and a flick of his wrist, he produced a glinting silver blade—Catherine's dagger—and placed the point of it between my tits, just hard enough to pierce the skin.

"Stop fighting, or I'll run this through your heart and fuck your corpse." The humor in his voice, coupled with the evil glint in his gray eyes, turned my blood to ice.

I didn't move as he dragged the blade tip down my stomach and tapped it teasingly against my mound, making my heart jump into my throat. For a moment, I thought he might take the blade to my labia, but he swiftly flipped the dagger around and pressed the hilt against my entrance.

"Maybe I should stuff you full of something else first," he missed, pressing the cold metal against me until it slipped inside.

I screamed, kicking and writhing, trying to get away but afraid to be sliced up by the blade. My scream grew louder as the hilt sank deeper inside me, the edges of my vision darkening before I squeezed my eyes closed.

A sound like an explosion made my eyes fly open, and I frantically searched the cavern around us for the source of the noise. The dagger handle slipped out of me, and Belphegor froze.

"What the fuck?" he asked, obviously caught off guard.

That made two of us.

Something deep in the stone sounded like it was erupting, the rocks cracking and crumbling.

My pulse detonated as thunderous booms followed, and I could only imagine what the hell was about to burst into the room to see me in all my glory, splayed and naked, shackled to the bed.

Then, it occurred to me...

"Belial!" I screamed, my voice hoarse as hope soared high in my chest.

A second later, a door flew off its hinges, tumbling through the room and crashing into a table covered in glittering trinkets. They shattered, raining and tinkling to the ground as the Lord of Bones appeared in the cavern. His oar, stacked with all the heads of his brothers—a few new ones having been added to the collection—was clutched in one hand.

The God of Death was a terrifying visage of vengeance and wrath.

"Belial…" I whispered his name like a prayer on the lips of a priest. Relief flooded me, so intense that a fresh wave of tears washed down my face and a sob cracked my chest.

He'd come for me.

Just like he promised, he'd literally fought through hell to get to me.

He was here, and I was finally, *finally* safe.

The blue flames in his eye sockets burned bright, swinging left to right as he took in the scene before him. His line of sight snapped from Catherine's form on the ground to Belphegor kneeling between my thighs and then finally landed on me.

Time seemed to stop as he took in the scene of me naked and chained to the bed with Belphegor on top of me. The violence and anguish rolling off him in powerful waves chilled me down to my core. An unholy growl escaped him, making the entire cavern quake and the glittery crystal dust rain down on us.

"You have to be the most moronic demon in history to kidnap and rape my queen. Unlike our brothers, I think I'll raise your body back from the dead once I destroy you."

Belphegor's face, which still bore the likeness of Belial's lesser form, lit up. "Oh? Will the Lord of Limbo use my corpse as he pleases as punishment for my transgressions?"

"I'd rather cut off my own dick than touch you, Belphegor. Your corpse will be at the mercy of my queen. Your maggot-infested carcass will serve as a reminder of what happens to those who fuck with the Lord of Bones and his Queen of Carrion."

CHAPTER THIRTY-SIX

BELIAL

OF ALL THE DEMON lords I'd slain to rescue my human, Belphegor's death would be the most satisfying. "Your head is going to make the perfect centerpiece for my little collection here." I gestured to the oar clutched tightly in my grip.

The demon Lord of Gluttony slowly rose from the bed, grinning like a maniac with my stolen face.

"Can't you wait for me to shift first?" Belphegor's velvety drawl in my own cadence had me baring my teeth. "Then again, I've heard whispers about how twisted your appetites are. You hole up in that castle of yours, acting like you're better than us, but you're just as sick and depraved. Maybe you want to cut off your own head and add it to the family there, since you've always belonged with us."

He'd have to try harder than that if he wanted his taunts to have any effect on me. "I don't care what shape you take. Once I get my hands around your throat, I'm tearing your head off. Keep my shape for all I fucking care. I'm still mounting it to my queen's new throne once we get home."

Knowing Rayven, she'd probably like having my head as the centerpiece of the throne I'd build her next to mine. Maybe after this was all over, I'd cut off my own too.

I deserved it after everything I'd done. I would never apologize for kidnapping her or tricking her into giving me her soul, but I'd spend the rest of eternity begging for her forgiveness for lying to her. On top of that, I'd allowed her to be dragged through the bowels of Hell.

Seeing her lying in Belphegor's bed, absolute fear and disgust etching her features with the shapeshifter looming over her—*in my likeness*—had rage and guilt ripping through me in equal measures.

And Catherine. Oh, Gods. *Catherine*. Seeing her face again did nothing but stir up painful memories. There was a reason why I'd laid her body to rest in her family tomb, but I'd been a selfish bastard and held on to her soul. For what?

I could have made her a book in the Library of Souls with all her favorite memories...the ones without me in them. I could have put her soul to rest within the pages Cecil would carefully attend for the rest of eternity.

But no, I'd been too bitter to give her that.

Now, it appeared as though Belphegor had managed to extract her soul from the dagger and use her to torture Rayven.

"What have you done to them?"

I could barely keep my voice straight. Rage ate at me like a wildfire, consuming everything. Any detail of this fucked up scene I'd walked into was enough for me to tear down this entire realm with my bare claws. The bruises on Catherine's body. The way Rayven was manacled to the bed, naked and shivering. The wet sheen covering Belphegor's poorly crafted emulation of my cock.

He'd raped at least one of them.

I stormed further into the room, eyes frantically scanning Rayven's body for any signs of abuse. Since her soul was in my possession, I could feel her pain, but maybe it was just emotional torment—Belphegor's specialty—I felt bleeding through the bond.

My eyes frantically scanned Rayven's body, looking for bruises. Handprints. The telltale sheen of cum. I lurched toward the bed, and Belphegor immediately scrambled back onto the mattress, crouching over Rayven.

Something primal and ancient clawed at me, and I roared at the other demon in warning. The shapeshifter only snickered as he gripped Catherine's dagger and brought it to Rayven's throat.

"One more step, and you get to see me slit her throat." He pursed my scarred lips in mock contemplation. "Hmm. You know what? Now that you're here, we can make *this* much more interesting."

His form shifted, my familiar features melting away as he shifted and contorted into a larger shape. His shoulders broadened, two extra heads sprouting from them. A few seconds later, I was staring at Asmodeus' likeness—at least, what he'd looked like before I charred him to a crisp.

"I can slit her throat and fuck the hole, maybe hear what pretty gurgling sounds she makes," Asmodeus' annoying ass voice teased.

I snarled at him, the flames in my eyes leaping high, and he laughed, donning a cocky smile I knew well. "No? Too kinky for you? Alright, Lord of Bones..."

Belphegor's shape was changing again, taking on a new form. My faint pulse—the one I barely remembered I had—slammed against my sternum as I watched the Lord of Gluttony take on the perfect likeness of my human.

He had the same long, black hair, the same doe eyes. He even had the same plush, fuckable lips. The same piercings decorated her body—a loop through her septum and the little bars of metal adorning her nipples, only in place of the silver barbells, they were bronze—Belphegor's metal.

"What about this?" He stretched over Rayven with feline finesse, a dastardly smile bowing those lips that had haunted every part of my mind for the last week. "Does this make your dick hard, brother?"

He arched his spine, his tits pressing against Rayven's while he stooped to kiss her lips.

She bit his lower lip, drawing blood. It dripped down his chin—her chin—and peppered her sneering face. "Fuck you."

"That's exactly what we were going to do before we were interrupted, little rat. But maybe your Lord would like to join in."

He turned his body, exposing his version of Rayven's pussy to me. I didn't like how similar they were. That meant he'd gotten close enough to get the details down.

The disturbed ways I imagined killing him would make a medieval torture master blush.

My mind spun as I ran through all the ways I could kill him, but each one of them risked him slitting her throat. I could bring her back to life, but the magic was tricky and painful.

I didn't want her to hurt more than she already had. Not like this.

"What do you want from me, Belphegor?"

The demon's eyes lit up. Thinking he'd already won, he sat up on Rayven's tummy, thighs clamped around her waist, and gave an excited little wiggle. Seeing the body I craved straddling the woman I loved was doing strange things to me.

That was exactly what the bastard intended, though, so I kept my attention focused on Rayven's real face. She was looking at me, tears filling her angry glare. "Don't give him shit, Belial. He's just going to trick you."

"It's all right, grave treasure. Everything is going to be all right." My attention dropped to Catherine's body on the ground. She'd gone completely still, undoubtedly unconscious, but I added on a "both of you" just in case she could hear me.

"Grave treasure?" Belphegor sneered at the nickname for my human. "More like tomb rat. But I suppose I can see your obsession with her. Her screams *are* delicious."

"Tell me what the fuck you want," I repeated on a growl, even though I already knew the answer. If I kept him talking, I bought time until I could get him away from Rayven and kill him.

"I want you to give me the other hells." His attention went straight to my oar. "Now that they're without rulership."

He licked his grinning lips, and his tongue snaked out to fiddle with the ring looped through his nose. "And we'll seal the deal with a fuck. Then, you can take her and your old pet back to Limbo. I'll even stay like this if it pleases you, Lord."

If it pleases me. "The only thing that would please me is seeing your head on my fucking oar, Belphegor."

He flashed me a smile that was all teeth. "Kinky."

"Fine. Whatever you want," I gnashed out through gritted teeth, not meaning a damn word of it. "But you'll need to unchain her."

Rayven's eyes shot wide, and she opened her mouth to protest, but Belphegor's hand slapped over her lips, muffling her protests. "I'm not going to unchain your slut until we're done."

I growled again in disapproval. The sound affected both versions of Rayven, goosebumps covering both sets of their breasts. "Then we don't have a deal."

My hand dropped to grip the semi-hard mass between my legs. I wasn't proud that I was getting hard, seeing as I got no pleasure seeing Catherine and Rayven in pain like this. But if Belphegor excelled at anything, it was the art of the mindfuck. Even though I knew it was him, he still had the appearance of my naked pet.

"If I'm going to fuck you, it's not going to be on top of her," I pressed. "Get her out of the goddamn bed, or you can kiss control of the other realms goodbye. Imagine what everyone will say when they find out you gave up the other circles because you couldn't give up control over one tiny fucking thing."

"Fine. Put that one over there." He gestured to Catherine with a nod and pointed to a sofa piled high in lavish pillows.

"But this one—" He patted Rayven's cheek, hard enough to make me bristle. "This one goes back on the cross. You can untie her when we're done, but she's going to watch us in the meantime."

CHAPTER THIRTY-SEVEN

Rayven

She can watch us in the meantime.

No, no. no. This wasn't happening. Just when I thought things couldn't possibly get any worse.

Please, don't do this, I begged Belial with my eyes, but he wasn't looking at me anymore. He was scooping up Catherine and taking her to the sofa. As he went, he kept the muzzle of his flame-eyed skull pointed at Belphegor and the dagger clutched to my throat.

Catherine moaned and mumbled something unintelligible as Belial laid her carefully among the sofa cushions.

She'd passed out, which was probably a mercy after everything her poor soul had endured.

My breaths turned short and sharp when Belial came back to the bed. For a moment, Belphegor didn't move, remaining straddled on top of my pelvis. He giggled evilly, wiggling in a way that ground against me, making my body burn.

"Sorry you don't get to join in on the fun, rat," the shapeshifter sing-songed. "Guess your demon lover isn't into group activities. Shame."

The moment he pulled the dagger away, he turned into a white cat and jumped on Belial's shoulder. The sinews in the Lord of Bones' neck tightened, and I knew he thought about grabbing the cat and breaking its neck. Instead, his hands went to me first.

He undid my manacles and hauled me off the bed into his embrace.

If I'd been told a week ago, hell, even three days ago, that I would feel this safe in the Lord of Bones' arms, I would have laughed myself to death.

Now, I melted into his subtle warmth like I was sinking into a warm bath.

"Did he touch you? Did he hurt you?" The Lord of Bones' guttural timbre was etched with a heady mixture of concern, fear, and violence.

The white cat was purring on his shoulder and rubbing up against one of his horns, but Belial paid him no mind. Right now, he only had attention for me.

"No, I'm okay," I told him, even though it felt like a lie. I didn't feel okay at all.

He carried me to the cross and paused. I looked up to see his muzzle pointed at where he'd made his explosive entrance to the cavern. He was probably considering our escape; what was stopping him from just leaving? Why in the world would he strap me back to that cross and give into Belphegor's demands?

He wouldn't.

As if reading my mind, he started for the door, and Belphegor, who'd been a cat a beat before, transformed into his male form—his true form, the one I'd seen for a blink in Mammon's bathing chamber. He had the same long, silvery hair as his female form, perfect bone structure, and a bronze lip ring decorating the center of his upper lip.

His arms flung around Belial's meaty shoulders, having to stretch onto his tiptoes to reach. He released a manic giggle against his skull. "Where do you think you're going? We haven't even begun to play yet."

Belial's body tensed against mine, every muscle in his sculpted torso drawing tight. The blue flames in his eye sockets flickered, burning brighter, and I could sense the inner turmoil he faced. If he put me down, he could easily rip Belphegor in half and wear him as a hat, but his grip on me only tightened, pulling me closer to him.

"I won't let you go," he whispered, his gaze boring into mine.

"Put her on the cross, Belial," the Lord of Gluttony purred. "There's no escape."

For a moment, I thought Belial would ignore the command and head for the door, but a shifting sound filled the room.

My stomach fell, along with my jaw, as all the cluttered objects surrounding us started to move. Pillows fell from the sofas, trinkets trembling like there was an earthquake.

Belial swore under his breath as ghostly figures began to emerge from the trove of things, oozing out of vases, knick-knacks, and pillows. Holy fuck. Just like in Limbo, souls sought refuge in the objects Belphegor collected, hidden out of sight and out of mind until they were called on.

That time was obviously now.

The ghostly figures crept closer, their vacant eyes locked on Belial, pressing in until we were surrounded. Hands grabbed at me, and Belial managed to dodge the first few, but then, fingers wrapped tightly around my arms and legs. His claws wrapped tighter around me, fighting the mob of souls threatening to take me from him.

They grabbed at Belial, fisting his cloak, pulling at his massive limbs.

"Let her go—unless you want my souls to pull her arms and legs out of their sockets," I heard Belphegor hiss in that cruel, feline purr of his. "You have my word she won't be harmed, so long as you get back into my bed and show me just how appreciative you are for saving your little pet from Mammon's dinner plate."

"Don't let me go," I begged Belial, not giving two shits if they ripped me in half. I didn't want him to get back in that bed.

"Get off us! I'll do it!" Belial bellowed. All the souls went still. "Just let her go. No one touches her but me."

The souls released their grip on us, and Belial gently held me up against the St. Andrew's cross and fastened the manacles to my wrists. Normally, I'd be into this, but knowing he was about to crawl into that bed with Belphegor so he could save me had me shaking as he clicked the locks into place.

"I know I've done little to earn your trust, but trust me on this," Belial said, his voice thick with emotion. He lifted my chin with a finger and pressed the end of his snout to my forehead.

He left it there for a beat, his warm breath rolling over my skin in a comforting wave before backing away and trudging over to the bed.

The demon was right. He'd hurt and manipulated me to the point where I shouldn't ever trust him again, but he'd gone through literal Hell to get me back.

Now that I'd seen what true cruelty was at the hands of the other demon lords, I realized just how much I craved his particular brand of pain. The kind that was meant for my pleasure. The kind that made me feel like every bit the dark queen he intended to make me.

So, I held back my tears and trained my glare on Belphegor, who'd led Belial back to the circular bed with an excited little skip. He fell back onto the mattress, his white hair falling artfully around the pillows like a halo.

"Which form do you prefer, My Lord?" The shapeshifter batted his snowy lashes. "Your pet?"

He morphed, once again taking on my form. He gave one of his bronze piercings a flick, and his nipple—*my* nipple—pebbled with the attention.

Belial snarled in displeasure despite the hard-on in his pants; then again, that always seemed to be there while I was in the room.

The shapeshifter's brows arched toward his hairline in surprise, and he flirtatiously twirled a lock of my jet-black hair around his finger. "No? What about this one?"

Another female form took shape, the perfect feminine mirror of his true form.

Belial growled again, and Belphegor laughed, clearly entertained by this fucked up exchange. "No, you're right. That shape was Mammon's favorite."

He shifted again, this time taking Belial's form again. "What about this? Who doesn't want to fuck themselves at least once?"

Belial arched over him, the terrifying, skull-faced monster that was the Lord of Bones looming over his smaller, human form I'd come to crave in the Labyrinth. "Shift back to your true form, brother. I want to see your real face when I tear you apart."

The words were menacing, but they didn't sound like the threat I knew they were. His voice was hard silver wrapped up in silk and dripping with honey.

He was so seductive, a rush of heat stirred between my spread thighs.

"Really?" Belphegor blinked up at him. "You want my true self?"

If I hadn't grown to hate the Lord of Gluttony so much, I'd almost pity him. His eyes glittered and perked up, almost beaming with excitement.

He seemed so thrilled with the idea that Belial wanted him just as he was. It made me wonder if Asmodeus and Mammon had always wanted him to be someone he wasn't.

He shifted into his own form and rose up on his elbows, grinning like a madman. His coal-black eyes flicked to me, and his smile turned smug. His whole look screamed, *"I'm about to fuck your mate, and there is nothing you can do about it."*

Licking his lips, he ran his hands down his naked body. His skin had a subtle tan, his muscles perfectly toned. His cock was on the slender side but long, accentuated with dozens of bronze piercings, so many that it looked painful. The epitome of gluttony, all in a cock.

"Take your clothes off." Belphegor's demand was met with a mocking laugh.

The Lord of Bones shook his horned skull slowly from side to side. "That's not how this is going to work. You want to bed me? Then you're my bitch, Lord of Gluttony. You do what I say. Do you understand?"

I expected Belphegor to see right through Belial's ploy. I wasn't sure what exactly he was planning, but I trusted him not to fuck the shapeshifter. Belphegor was all too eager to please the Lord of Limbo and agreed with a frantic bob of his head. "Yes."

Belial quirked his head, his great set of horns tilting. "Yes, *what?*"

"Yes, My Lord."

Belial turned, peering back at me, his flaming blue eyes turning a hot white as he focused on me. My heart went still, and while my body was tighter than ever, the twisting pain in my chest eased.

He turned around and kneed up onto the bed, straddling Belphegor's torso. His skull-headed form was so massive, the V of his spread legs didn't touch the shapeshifter below him.

"Very good. Now, be a good demon and touch yourself, Belphegor."

The shapeshifter eagerly reached between the V of Belial's legs, his attention riveted to the still-clothed bulge hovering in front of his face as he fisted his cock.

My breath caught in my chest as Belial reached down, wrapping his hands around Belphegor's throat.

Slowly, he increased pressure. The shapeshifter's chest heaved with labored breaths as his hand stroked his dick faster, urged on by Belial's grip.

Belphegor came with an explosive growl, copious amounts of seed spurting from his tip. His muscles rippled and tensed as the orgasm wracked his body, and he fell limp beneath Belial with a strangled groan.

Belphegor had finished, but Belial didn't stop choking him. The white-haired demon seemed to process what was happening and thrashed. His cock was still hard, his slit weeping cum as he fought for his life.

The Lord of Bones' maw opened, his black tongue slithering out to tongue his deadly teeth as a dark laugh shook from his chest. "What's the matter, *Belly?*" he mocked, using Mammon's pet name for him. "Isn't this what you wanted from me? To abuse you? To punish you? Well, that's exactly what I'm going to do. I'm going to fucking rip your head off for what you did to souls *I* own."

Belphegor choked for air, his eyes bulging as Belial increased the pressure around his throat.

He was going to crush his windpipe. The shapeshifter's skin started to morph, turning different colors and taking on fur and scales but failing to settle into any permanent shape as the life was slowly squeezed from him.

I watched in glee as Belphegor clung to his final seconds in this pathetic show he was putting on beneath Belial, bucking his body and clawing at the great paws encircling his neck.

Belial turned to look at me, and even though he didn't have lips in this form, I could picture his other self, his scared lips pressed into that half-cocked smirk. "This will be the last head I gift to you, my queen. A complete collection. Does this please you?"

I sucked in a breath and gave a little nod as I tried to hold back bittersweet tears. I could barely breathe from the brunt of emotions constricting my lungs, but it was over. It was finally over. "Yes. It pleases me."

"Do you forgive me now?"

I managed a tearful smile and opened my mouth to tell him I'd forgive him. The words crystallized in my throat as my attention fell to Belphegor, whose grasping hands had managed to locate Catherine's dagger, which had gotten lost among the sheets.

His fingers closed around the hilt, and he flung it in my direction. It moved fast, and even if I had reflexes to dodge it, I was stretched out on the St. Andrew's cross, bound and cuffed. There was nothing for me to do but close my eyes and wait for impact.

The blade slammed into my chest, directly over my heart. I'd expected it to hurt more. There was a brief pinch, followed by a dull sting. Everything felt so warm, like I was being drenched in warm honey.

My eyes drifted open, and I looked down to see a wave of red cascading down my front. Blood.

In my last moments, all I could think was how Belial loved me in this color, and I couldn't help but smile.

CHAPTER THIRTY-EIGHT

BELIAL

THE ANIMALISTIC SOUND THAT tore from my maw was foreign to my ears. It was a culmination of all the rage and despair pumping through me, raw and ragged as it tore my throat to shreds.

Everything stood still.

Time, my heart, Hell itself.

I had a decision to make: take the few extra seconds needed to smother Belphegor to death, or go to Rayven. The choice was life or death.

Through this entire nightmare, I'd chosen revenge. Death first, then once I had their heads, only then would I delve deeper through the Hells after her. I'd made excuses, convincing myself it was all for her, but inherently, it was selfish. I'd put my anger first.

Yet another way I'd failed her.

The room faded to nothing as I raced to where Rayven was strapped to the cross. She went slack in her cuffs, and I grabbed the chains and wrenched the bolts from the wood with a snarl. I lowered her to the floor and drew her into my lap. Her tear-filled eyes were wide with shock as she stared up at me.

With shaky fingers, I brushed her dark hair away from her face, my eyes slowly falling to the dagger protruding from her chest.

It had struck just to the left, a hair's breadth from the center of her chest. An inch or so of the silver blade protruded out from her pale flesh, the wound weeping tears of crimson around the metal.

He struck her in the heart. Fucking Hells!

"Rayven," I gasped, her name lodging in my throat as emotion consumed me.

A pang of guilt shot through me as I drew her close, and she attempted to speak, but her voice came out a ragged whisper.

"I forgive you..." she said in a voice so weak, I could barely hear it.

"Fuck, I'm so sorry," I said, lowering my face to graze my maw gently over her forehead.

I'd been so close—so fucking close—to saving her.

The urge to transform into my lesser form, to pull her against my chest and kiss away her tears, was overwhelming, but I couldn't. Not yet. Not until she was safe.

Safe. The word mocked me even as it came to mind.

I'd fought tooth and claw, torn apart Hell itself, killed six of the demon lords, and it hadn't been enough. All that, and she was still going to die in my arms. All I'd wanted was to keep her mortal heart beating, to revel in its rhythmic song forever, and I was going to have to listen to its chorus slow until it beat no more.

Only then could I revive her.

She first had to experience the pain of death, and when it claimed her, only then could I intervene.

"Belial…" Her voice was ghostly faint, and her eyelids started to drift.

I pulled back to take her in. "My grave treasure. All I wanted was to keep you safe, to make you mine."

"I'm cold," she whispered, and the sound nearly broke me.

I could set Belphegor's realm on fire using his broken body as tinder, and it still wouldn't be enough to keep her warm. Not now.

"It's okay," I assured her, my stomach dropping as her heartbeat began to slow. "You're going to be fine, my treasure."

"I'm scared," she said, a tear sliding down her face and landing in her dark locks. "Please, don't let me go. I don't want to leave you. I—I want to be with you."

She was struggling to get the words out as her heart rate began to slow.

"I'm not going anywhere," I promised. "'I'll be right here."

It was coming; her death. There was no way to stop it now. Soon, her heart would give out, and her organs would shut down as blood stopped flowing through her veins.

Her fear was palpable, bleeding into the air. She didn't have much longer, minutes at most.

"You're going to be fine, Rayven. Just go to sleep."

The heart I'd forgotten I had was breaking. It didn't seem to matter that I had the power to bring her back to life once she took her final breath. It was fucking agony, seeing her in pain. I was so jaded to death, but with her, it felt terrifying and new.

"And then you'll revive me." Her paper-thin words wavered and split with fear. "R–right?"

"That's right, treasure," I assured her with a soothing purr, my hand rubbing one cheek while keeping her other pressed to my chest. "I told you I'm never letting you go. Not even in death. *Especially* not in death."

I knew she was terrified—death was new for her—but she'd learn not to fear it. I would teach her how to be its master.

I plucked the dagger out of her chest as gently as I could. The flames in my eye sockets all but sputtered out when a cry of pain left her lips.

This human had completely fucked me, because how could a god of death need anything so terribly that he couldn't live without? I fucking needed her more than I needed anything.

As evil a monster as it made me, I'd snuff out every life on Earth if that was what it took to breathe life back into my human.

Through the thin puncture in her chest cavity, I could see straight down to the pulsing muscle keeping her alive for the moment. The blade had pierced its strong wall, and it was gradually beating slower as a stream of blood poured from the wound.

Every pump had more crimson lifeblood trickling down her chest.

Gathering her in my arms, I pulled her higher to cradle her against my chest, rocking her like she was a child. All the while, I whispered that I would never leave her, that she'd never be free of me. That once I brought her heart back to life, everything would be fine.

"I'll be the last thing you see when you close your eyes and the first thing when you open them again," I assured her, the promise carrying all the weight of a demonic oath.

"You're mine, Rayven. Never forget that."

A lazy smile curved her lips. "You won't let me go?"

"Never. Not so long as the River Styx flows and the Hells run deep."

Normally, I didn't have a kind bone in my body, but I tried my best to comfort her in her final moments.

I knew I was going to be completely fucked for this human the moment I'd dragged her into Limbo, and I couldn't bring myself to regret it.

I'd likely be forever cold and cruel to the rest of the world. To hell with humans. But this one? This one, I'd worship with every breath I'd take from here until the world fell down.

"Close your eyes, Rayven," I said, talking her through the slow crawl of her last moments.

"You're being so...sweet to me. I didn't know the Lord of Bones could do that." She breathed in, then out, the smallest little sigh that let me know she was finally comfortable in my arms.

There was that twist of guilt jabbing at my ribs again. I'd let her down. I'd tortured her. I'd terrorized her. I'd taken pleasure in watching her fight me, no matter how high the odds stacked against her.

Her spirit was indomitable, and fuck me, if I hadn't fallen horns over heels in love with that part of her, with all of her.

Even in death, she was brave.

Her fingers trailed to the gaping wound that exposed her still palpitating heart, its thrum growing weaker as more blood streamed from the hole. "Do you see it?"

Her words were barely intelligible, and I had to lower my skull to her mouth. "Do you see my heart?"

I swallowed and nodded, even though she couldn't see me with her eyes now shut. "I see it, Rayven, and it's fucking beautiful. Worth every second I've obsessed over its beat, teased it just to hear its flutter."

"Belial. Don't leave me."

"I'll never leave you again, grave treasure. This I swear."

Her chest rose and fell one last time, her head going limp in the crook of my arm as her heart ceased to beat. I watched the throbbing muscle go still in her chest.

The agonizing silence that followed tore an anguished roar from my throat.

This wasn't how things were supposed to be. She wasn't supposed to get hurt, not like this.

She was never supposed to die.

Every second that Rayven's heart was still, mine broke a little more. I couldn't stand it, staring down at her lifeless body, feeling the warmth seep from her skin. I could feel the life bleed from her. Her skin grew colder, and her lips were already turning a shade of pale blue—nearly identical to the color of my own flesh. Death came fast in the Nine Hells.

I summoned the magic that would revive her. The power danced over my fingertips, and I placed my palm gently against her chest. It was complicated arcana, a spell I hadn't performed since Catherine's string of suicides, but the magic stirred up, like it had been dwelling just beneath my skin this entire time, and vibrated through my being.

Her skin shimmered for a moment, a silver glow cast over her form before her soul slipped out of its mortal vessel. It swirled and materialized into a visage of her, standing over us with horror-filled eyes, her mouth hanging open.

"Well, this is fucking terrifying." The voice wavered, and I met her worried gaze. It almost broke me to look away, my eyes falling back to her lifeless body in my arms.

"I'm going to fix everything," I assured her. "I promise. A few minutes, and you'll be fine."

I knew things would be fine. I'd brought Catherine back from the dead so many times; this should have been a simple fix. However, the thought of her staying this way forever—still, cold, and lifeless—had my confidence unraveling at the seams.

What would happen if my magic didn't work this time?

Sure, I'd have her soul forever, but it wouldn't be the forever I'd imagined since I dragged her to Limbo. She wouldn't be my living slave queen. I wouldn't get to revel in the way her heart raced when I did filthy, depraved things to her. The way it fluttered when my lips brushed hers. The way it skipped a beat when I ordered her to her knees.

With a growl, I focused on my magic again, letting it pour out of the deepest pits of my being.

It wouldn't have been nearly as complicated if it was just a matter of putting her soul back into the human body, but it was more than that. I had to fix her wound, reconnect the muscle, and revive her before her flesh began to waste away.

"Belial..." The voice of Rayven's soul resounded through my skull, but I was too immersed in the task at hand to pay attention.

I could feel it working, the sinews of muscle stitching themselves back together, the hole in her chest slowly closing to conceal the precious organ it guarded.

"I'm going to fix this," I said, barely aware I'd spoken. "You'll be fine."

I was reassuring myself more than her at this point, clinging to the thin veneer of calm that masked my panic.

Rayven's soul softly replied, "I trust you."

Trust. As though I deserved it after all this mess.

I was so lost in trying to heal Raven, I almost missed the rustle behind me. I craned my head around in time to see Belphegor rushing toward me.

In my panic to save Rayven, I'd forgotten all about the Lord of Gluttony.

"You deserve to fucking die with her, Belial!" he cried as his nails shifted into six-inch knives aimed straight for my chest.

I tensed, gently lowering Rayven's corpse off my lap, preparing to rip Belphegor limb from limb for killing the only woman I'd ever loved. Rage burned through me, the flames in my eye sockets leaping high, and I braced myself.

When he was a few feet from me, nearly close enough to sink my claws into, Belphegor let out a pained wail, faltering and stumbling to the ground. He writhed, frantically reaching for his back until his movements slowed.

"You...bitch..."

When he slumped forward, I saw it: Catherine's dagger buried hilt deep between Belphegor's shoulders, just missing his spine.

Rayven's soul stood behind him, her mouth hardened into a line, her eyes full of hatred.

"That's what you get, you slimy fuck," she gritted out.

I stared up at her in reverence as Belphegor twitched. He was a demon, so he wouldn't die from a simple dagger strike to the back. Rayven seemed to understand this almost immediately and wrenched the blade from him, only to bury it in him again. And again. And again.

He collapsed to the ground, and she kept stabbing him. She moved to his head, burying the knife in his face until it was nothing but a shapeless, torn-up pile of gore. In my periphery, I could vaguely make out Catherine.

She'd woken and was sitting up, the smallest of smiles perched on her mouth as she watched Rayven brutalize the shapeshifter's corpse.

The other souls stood by, watching their master bleed out on the ground. Not a single one seemed to be broken up over the fact that he was gone.

I was completely in awe of my queen.

"Weeping Hells, you're perfection."

"And I'm ready to get back in my body," she said, her eyes falling to her corpse before me. "This is some freaky twilight zone fuckery."

If I could have smirked in this form, I would have. Even in death, Rayven had a delicious, bratty mouth.

"As my queen commands."

I finished the spell as quickly as I could, eager to hear the steady thrum of my grave treasure's heartbeat. I sighed with relief when the delicate muscle started throbbing again, the air catching in my lungs when she opened her eyes and looked up at me.

"As long as I'm the Lord of Death, your heart will never cease to beat again."

CHAPTER THIRTY-NINE

RAYVEN

Nothing will give you a bone-deep appreciation for life quite like dying.

Even after being surrounded by so much death in the cemeteries I robbed and admiring the beautiful souls and bones in Limbo, I'd never been more grateful to be alive.

Relief hit me in waves of exhaustion and tears, images of my ordeal haunting my thoughts as I faded in and out of sleep. Sailing the Styx in Belial's gondola was peaceful, a glaring difference from my first trip down the river. He even let Cecil take up rowing so he could hold me while I slept, whispering delicious little promises in my ear of what he planned to do to me once back in Limbo while I danced with unconsciousness.

This time, Belial didn't use the plum magic to enter my sleep, but I dreamt of him anyway.

All my enemies had been destroyed, their heads skewered onto Belial's oar as a reminder of their betrayal. None of them could ever hurt me again. There was nothing left for me to fear in the entirety of Hell, save for the demon lord who owned my soul.

And as terrifying as he was, I wasn't afraid, not when I knew the lengths he was willing to go to in order to keep me safe. He'd do anything I asked, including destroying the nine layers and adding his head to my collection if it pleased me. That kind of utter devotion was intoxicating, and it did deliciously dark things to me, knowing I belonged to such a beast.

Something told me his obsession with me would be kicked into hyperdrive when we returned to his realm. I'd be lucky if I ever escaped his watchful eye again.

A week ago, the threat of never escaping the monstrous Lord of Bones had been the biggest problem in my life. Now, it was my biggest comfort.

When I stepped off the ferry in Limbo, I wanted to fall to my knees and kiss the ground, but Belial dragged me into him and kept me upright.

"Welcome home," he muttered into my hair.

Home.

I would have killed—again—to sleep for a week straight and binge-eat whatever snacks could be found in Hell, but Belial had other plans. He wanted to crown me immediately as a way of showing his kingdom exactly who I was. He wanted to condemn the actions of his brothers in front of all his subjects, to warn them what painful suffering awaited anyone who crossed his queen.

And who said romance was dead?

The thought of wearing a crown made of bones weighed on me, sparking a wave of unsettling feelings, but beneath them all was fear.

Not because the crown was made of my ex's spine—Mark was hardly more than an insignificant memory in the back of my mind now—but because how in the hell was I supposed to be the queen of...well, Hell?

There was also the matter of dealing with Catherine's soul. After Belial saved me from Belphegor's realm, I refused to leave her behind. Her soul very well could have wandered off and hid in another object, and we could have left her there to rot for all eternity, but the thought didn't sit right with me.

The poor woman didn't deserve to suffer any longer. As long as I was queen, she—along with every other deserving soul in Hell—would never have to suffer again.

It had been easier than I thought to convince Belial to give Catherine a place in the Library of Souls, and as soon as I'd bathed and eaten, he started teaching me the magic of sorting souls into blank soul books.

"You'll get it, my treasure," he said every time I got frustrated. Demon magic wasn't easily wielded by humans, but he promised me that if Cecil could do it, I could.

The day of my coronation, Holga dressed me in a stunning crimson ball gown dripping with blood-red jewels. She did my hair and makeup the way she had for the masquerade ball, and I swallowed down any hint of PTSD.

I didn't have to be afraid.

All of Belial's subjects were coming to see me be crowned. There were no demon lords left to disrupt the procession.

Everything would go according to plan.

Belial took me to the library first to deal with Catherine's soul. Holga and Cecil met us there, the five of us standing in front of the secretary's desk. Catherine was no longer naked, instead dressed in a pale gown that made her look more like a ghost than anything.

She was solemn, her eyes downcast, hands folded in front of her. Belial didn't address her, instead nudging me forward, encouraging me to do what I'd intended to do since we returned to Limbo.

The time had finally come.

"We are here to discuss what should become of your soul," I said to her gently. Her eyes slowly lifted to meet mine when she realized I was addressing her. "I have a proposal for you, if you would accept it."

Her head canted to the side at my words, curiosity lighting up her features. "What kind of...proposal?"

"Paradise," I said, holding up an empty soul book for her to see. "A place offered to the most deserving souls. You would spend eternity reliving your most precious memories."

A tiny gasp escaped her, her eyes bouncing between me and the soul book in my hands. "And if I refuse?"

To be honest, I hadn't considered what would happen if Catherine didn't want to live out the rest of eternity in paradise. I guessed we could shove her into the book. As I understood it, she wouldn't remember any of this anyway, so if we had to force her into her happiest memories, I wasn't opposed.

"You will be sent to a lower layer of Hell," Belial interjected sternly. "You will be under Rayven's rule, for she is the queen of the other eight realms now."

Catherine quickly shook her head. "No, I...I don't want to go back there. Please, I—"

"It's okay," I assured her, smiling for her benefit. I could tell she was terrified, the dark memories of what had happened to her below playing over her features. Aside from what I'd witnessed, I had no idea what had happened to her, and I didn't want to know. "Souls don't typically get to decide what happens to them, but these aren't typical circumstances. If it was me, I'd choose paradise too."

Catherine's gaze nervously flashed in Belial's direction, a mix of heavy feelings banked behind her eyes. There was still a lot of resentment there, and I couldn't blame her, but after a long moment, the dark-haired woman slowly nodded to show her respect. Then, she looked at me and the blank soul book I held in my hands.

"Thank you," she said, her voice cracking with emotion.

She wasn't thanking Belial. I doubted she'd ever forgive him enough for that. She was thanking *me*. After all, I'd been adamant since we escaped the eighth layer of Hell that her soul should finally be put to rest. Before any other business was handled, before any other souls were dealt with, hers would be first.

She'd waited long enough.

"You don't have to thank me." I shook my head. After everything she'd endured—being robbed of her mortal life, dragged to Hell, forced to suffer and be tortured by Belphegor—living out the rest of her existence in her own personal paradise was the least she deserved. "It's my honor."

Catherine sank to one knee, kneeling before me, and a fist clenched my heart. As much as I admired the loyalty I'd been shown by the souls in Hell, I didn't think I'd ever deserve it. I didn't think I'd ever get used to it. She bowed her head, waiting, and I glanced at Belial.

He'd removed his mask for the occasion—he rarely wore it anymore. He looked stunningly handsome in his black formal attire, tailored to fit the lithe body of his lesser form to mouth-watering perfection. He nodded slightly, and I opened the book in my hands, staring down at the blank pages, pages that would soon be imprinted with Catherine's most cherished memories.

Whatever they were, I hoped they were beautiful.

In a swirl of blue magic, Catherine's soul disappeared, pulled into the book's contents. Traces of the glow lingered around the book for a breath before fading completely.

I closed the book, running my fingers gingerly over the leather-bound cover before turning to hand it to Cecil, who'd been standing idly by, waiting for instructions.

"Thank you, Cecil," I told the librarian with a smile.

"Of course, Your Majesty," he said before turning to hobble down the aisle to return the book to its new home.

"I'm not the queen yet," I whispered to Belial. The corner of his mouth lifted in a devilish smirk.

"Almost." He pulled me into him and pressed his lips to my temple. "In fact, everyone should be gathering in the throne room now. We should get a move on."

My insides pretzeled. It was coronation day. In a very short amount of time, I would be crowned Queen of Limbo or Souls or Bones...whatever my title would officially be. I'd wear the spine of my ex-boyfriend on my head and sit upon the Lord of Bones' throne.

"Belial," I said, my feet rooting to the spot.

I knew the time had come, but still, I wasn't ready. I didn't know if I would ever be ready.

"Don't be nervous," he urged me. "You were made for this. You were made for *me*. Come. I have a surprise for you."

"A surprise?" I cocked an eyebrow at him, and his smirk broke into a grin.

"Yes."

He offered me his arm, and I took it, letting him guide me toward the corridor. "Such a gentleman," I mused. "What, no collar? No leash to lead your slave queen to her coronation?"

I was joking, but my smile slipped, and a blush flamed my cheeks at the wolfish look he shot me. "Those things aren't required anymore, not now that I don't have to worry about you wandering into danger again. Though, we can still bring them out for playtime later..."

The mention of playtime, paired with his honied baritone, had the spot between my thighs heating and arousal soaking my panties.

He gave a sinister smile, knowing exactly what he was doing to me.

Holga moved silently to fall in line behind us. As my official handmaid, she spent most of her time making sure I was taken care of—but Belial shook his head.

"Holga, would you meet us in the throne room?"

Her fleshless face was emotionless, but I could have sworn I noticed a shift in her energy. Was I finally figuring out how to read the skeletal witch? Or was the sleep deprivation finally catching up to me?

"Of course, My Lord." She nodded her head and swept past us, disappearing down the long corridor alone. My guess was that Cecil would catch up with her after he finished his duties in the library.

Since we'd gotten back from the lower layers, those two were inseparable. They'd hated each other at the start, just like Belial and me. Turns out, the only reason they didn't get along was because Holga didn't like the Lord while Cecil had an undying loyalty for him. Now that her opinion of him had changed, they saw eye to eye. Well, as well as people without eyes could see.

"What's the surprise?" I asked as we took off in the opposite direction. My crimson gown swayed with my steps, the jewels glinting in the torchlight.

"It wouldn't be a surprise if I told you now, would it?" A sly smirk curled his lips. "Besides, it would be much easier to show you."

We walked through the halls, and a hint of familiarity tugged at my chest. This castle had gone from feeling like a prison when I first arrived to a place I belonged, a place that felt more like home than anywhere I'd ever lived.

I could spend a hundred lifetimes in this stunning castle and never get bored. I might get lost a time or ten, but I wouldn't trade it, especially after seeing what the rest of Hell had to offer.

My Hell, I reminded myself.

Belial was adamant about me taking over the other eight realms, though I'd hardly decided how to handle them or what to do. It was all so much, too much for me to process or think about. All I wanted right now was to get through my coronation. I'd never liked crowds and would be eager for the guests to leave the moment that crown hit my head.

We rounded a corner, and Belial stopped abruptly. I followed suit, eyeing him until he gestured to a giant empty patch of wall.

"Here you go," he said, a proud gleam in his eye.

There was nothing special about the wall at first glance, just a boring stretch of wallpaper that had seen better days. I stared at it for a moment, like a hidden message would pop out at any second. I finally noticed where the wallpaper changed color in a perfect square, fading to an even more unexciting shade of gray. There was a small table topped with a frog-shaped teapot and a candlestick.

My heart skipped a nervous beat.

"I had the painting of Catherine removed," he said, gesturing to the empty space. "And I've commissioned another to be made in its place."

"Belial, I—"

"You don't have to say anything. You can even scold me for not getting rid of it sooner," he assured me. "I don't want you thinking another woman—alive or dead—could ever hold a candle to you. No level of intense infatuation could ever rival the obsession, the love I have for you, little treasure. Do you understand?"

I was speechless. The Lord of Limbo was obsessed with me, there was no denying that, but the way he spoke made the words sink down to my marrow.

"Whatever you want, name it, and it will be yours," he said. There was that panty-obliterating smirk grin again. "I'll fulfill every fantasy, every desire, every dark wish your mind can conjure. You know I'll go to the ends of the Nine Hells to grant it."

My answer came without hesitation. "I want you. That's all I need."

He dragged me into his arms swiftly, his lips crashing against mine and his tongue sweeping eagerly into my mouth. I sighed against his scarred flesh, savoring his scent—strawberries, with that slight hint of pine, like a freshly cut casket. "Keep it up, and we'll be late for the coronation," I hummed between kisses.

He growled against my lips. "I'm the King. I do as I please. The coronation will begin when we decide it begins."

I pressed a hand against his chest, leaning back to meet his stormy gray eyes, and cocked a brow at him.

"Fine," he conceded with a sigh. Blue magic crackled around him as he transformed into the Lord of Bones. The blue fire in his eye sockets flickered in the dim light, and his cloak fluttered before draping around his brawny frame.

"This was *your* idea," I reminded him as one of his giant hands came around my waist to tug me close.

"I know, but after you're crowned, that dress is coming off," he said, a growl rumbling in his throat.

CHAPTER FORTY

RAYVEN

We came to a stop in front of a set of imposing doors, guarded on either side by a suit of armor. I recognized them immediately. It was the entrance to the throne room. These doors had been branded onto the backs of my eyelids since the masquerade ball.

The last time I'd been in that hall, I'd learned the truth about Belial being the Lord of Bones and the manipulative game he'd played. After getting my heart cleaved in two, I'd been chained to his throne and dragged across the hall in front of a crowd of masked spectators. Then, I'd met Belial's brothers.

My heart rate lurched as the memories came flooding back, and I struggled to force air into my lungs. This wasn't remotely the same thing. So much had changed since the ball, but it didn't stop the panic sparking through my system.

"Breathe, my treasure," the Lord of Bones rumbled beside me. "You don't have anything to be afraid of."

"My Lord," squeaked one of the suits of armor before bowing with a rusty groan. The other suit of armor followed suit before they sprang to life and reached for the doorknobs.

I held my breath, feeling lightheaded as the doors slowly opened before me.

After everything I'd been through, it was amazing that I still feared anything at all. I'd seen the worst of what the nine realms had to offer, been tortured and even died, and I'd overcome it all.

Being crowned queen should have been a walk in the park.

Then why did my stomach still knot with anxiety the way it did, icy dread clinging to my spine?

The throne room beyond the doorway was more packed than it had been for the masquerade ball, hundreds of souls crammed into the space, shoulder to shoulder. This time, none of them wore masks, but they were still all elegantly dressed. A wide aisle carved a path down the middle of the room, leading straight to where the throne awaited.

No. Where *two* thrones waited.

A tiny gasp shoved a breath of relief into my lungs.

To the right of the Lord of Bones' throne was a second made of bones: *my* throne. The back of it stretched up and fanned out toward the ceiling, with nine severed heads speared on evenly spaced spikes.

Asmodeus—the rapist, Lord of flesh and suffering.

Vine—the demon who hadn't lifted so much as a pinky to help me when I'd passed through his realm.

Leviathan—the envious snake demon who locked me in a cage and forced me to dance.

Mammon—the fire demon who tried to make me into his *royal meat.*

Baal and Paimon—the spider demon and the eyeball monster who showed up in full support of Mammon's feast.

And Belphegor, the shapeshifter who'd topped all of them in cruelty.

Even from a distance, I knew Belial had repurposed the heads from the oar and placed them on my throne.

A smile tugged at my lips until I dragged my gaze away and scanned the crowded room. Every eye present was zeroed in on me, waiting expectantly.

As Belial's enormous hand pressed against my lower back, urging me into the throne room, I steeled my nerves.

Maybe it wasn't the notion of being queen that filled me with anxiety, but the idea of letting down everyone in this room, everyone who would be counting on me to do whatever a queen of Hell did. I thought of all the poor souls trapped in the lower layers of Hell, forced to live out the rest of their existence there. What would become of them? What would become of the souls languishing around Belial's castle?

I entered the throne room with my heart in my throat, every step closer to the throne making my pulse race faster. The weight of hundreds of eager eyes on me made my skin crawl, but Belial was there, urging me on.

What a great way for my new subjects to see me: my human nerves acting up.

I lifted my chin, donned a confident smile, and marched down the aisle, my eyes locked straight ahead. I shoved all the doubt from my mind.

When I reached the end of the aisle, I paused in front of the River Styx, staring down at the bloody current for a long moment before turning to face the court. Everyone was staring, watching silently, picking me apart with their curious gazes, their attention making my skin itch.

Belial stepped into the river and offered me his hand. He helped me across the current and pulled me out on the other side, a splash of crimson coating the stone beneath my feet as it poured off my dress.

"Your throne," he said, gesturing with his free hand to the enormous seat before me.

I looked up, my gaze lingering on each of the demon lord heads decorating the top of it. Brutal, bloody, and macabre as fuck, it was dark perfection.

A twist of rage and satisfaction swirled through me upon seeing them, each speared on a bone pike forevermore. I took comfort in knowing they would forever pay for their transgressions. Even in death, they would serve me as adornments on my throne.

Served them fucking right.

Fingers tingling and heart fluttering, I cautiously took a seat on the new throne. It was so silent in the hall that I could hear the blood pounding in my ears, anxiety burning its way through me.

The Lord of Bones tore his attention from me to look over his subjects, his burning glare dragging slowly through the room.

"You've been summoned to witness the crowning of Limbo's very first—and last—queen," his growly voice thundered through the hall.

He continued with his speech, his address to our subjects firm and absolute.

With a wave of his hand, he produced the crown of bones he'd fashioned from Mark's spine. The image haunted my thoughts—not to mention, it looked uncomfortable as fuck. But since the last time I'd seen it, it seemed Belial had set some gems into it that glimmered a deep, bloody red in the light.

It was a gothic queen's wet dream.

I met the Lord of Bones' gaze, sitting up straighter on my throne as he moved to place the crown on my head. It fit perfectly, feeling much heavier than it actually was.

"She is your queen. Any act against her is an act against me and will be handled accordingly," the Lord of Bones growled, a warning to anyone foolish enough to try anything stupid like his brothers had.

I blinked out over the crowd, the breath hitching in my chest when they began to kneel. I picked out Cecil and Holga standing in the back, and the sight of them had the tension in my chest ebbing some.

Starting with the front row, they dropped to their knees and bowed their heads in fealty, and the rest of the room soon followed. An invisible hand tugged at my heartstrings again, the same way it had in Asmodeus' throne room when the souls bowed to me.

Every being in the hall knelt to honor their new queen, and I flashed a nervous glance in Belial's direction. He tipped his head slowly, staying there for a beat before taking a seat on his own throne.

His enormous hands clutched the armrests, the blue flames roaring in his eye sockets as a twisted crown of bones appeared on his head. He was a vision of darkness and power, a cruel king who'd also shown more compassion than I thought him capable of.

Fuck, he was so goddamn sexy.

So sexy, and all fucking mine.

"Long live the Lord of Bones," the crowd chanted together. "Long live the Queen of Carrion."

We sat there for a moment that seemed to drag on forever. I had no idea what to do next, what was expected of me. Was I supposed to make a speech? Did they expect me to put on a show? Entertain them? Behead someone?

Skeptically, I cast another glance in Belial's direction, and I heated when I found him looking back at me.

"What is your first decree?" he asked, stirring something primal in me. I wanted him to order away all these souls and have his way with me right here and now.

"Send them away."

A dark chuckle escaped his maw, his black, forked tongue slipping out to paint a lick over his lipless mouth.

"Leave. All of you. Now," he said abruptly, his voice booming in the silent room. It was so abrupt, so informal, but this was the Lord of Death we were talking about here. He was right. He could do whatever he damn well pleased.

Waiting for them all to file out of the throne room was agonizing, but I sat perfectly still, chin raised regally like I imagined a queen would. Truthfully, I had no idea what the fuck I was doing. Belial ruled so effortlessly, comfortable in his role and the power he held.

For me, not so much. It was like I was trying to ride a motorcycle when I'd never even been on a bike.

I swallowed hard, watching his—our—subjects trickle out of the throne room. When they were all gone, Belial ordered the doors to be closed.

Finally, we were completely alone. My skin burned hot, and the apex of my thighs tingled with the sensation sinking through my core.

I knew what came next.

"Come here," he demanded, and I rose from my throne at the order. He ushered me over to stand before him as his head canted to one side, his great set of horns tipping with his skull.

"You are stunning," he said, his gaze falling down my body before creeping its way back up. "A vision in red. Royalty fits you, my queen."

I couldn't fight the smile winding its way across my face.

"I told you I'd get you out of that dress." He leaned forward on his throne. "I'd carry you up to our bedroom, but your Lord can't be made to wait."

"Here?" I flashed a nervous glance around the empty hall.

A dark chuckle escaped his maw. "Of course. I told you I would fuck you on my throne before everything was said and done. But first, I want to see you in nothing but your crown."

I followed his instructions, turning around so he could unlace the corset of my gown, and I let the fabric fall to the floor at my feet. Nude aside from my bone crown, I gave him a twirl, reveling in the feral noise that clawed up his throat.

He stood, towering over me, and guided me to sit on his throne.

Then, in a twist I didn't see coming, he knelt before me.

"As the queen of Limbo, your enemies will kneel before you in terror. Your loyal subjects will kneel in fealty, and your king will kneel before you in unholy reverence."

His tongue slithered over his teeth, wriggling in a way that let me know he was giving me a preview of what was to come.

"Now, spread your legs for your king and let me worship you."

CHAPTER FORTY-ONE

RAYVEN

BEFORE I COULD OBEY Belial's order, his large hands wrapped around my calves, completely engulfing them. With an eager growl, he pried them open.

"That's right, my treasure," he said in an eager growl. "Show your Lord all he owns."

I licked my lips, allowing him to spread me as wide as my thighs would go.

It didn't feel wrong, being this exposed to him anymore. Sure, he was a monster in every sense. He was going to eat me, but I was going to thoroughly enjoy being devoured.

I held my breath as I watched his terrifying maw part. His teeth dripped with thick beads of saliva, covering my thighs and pelvis, dripping into the thatch of hair between my legs.

"Remember when you hated me so fucking much, you could barely stand to look at me?" His voice vibrated over my skin, making my flesh pebble with goosebumps.

How could I forget? It hadn't happened all that long ago. It was funny, how quickly everything could get flipped on its head.

I nodded, and an evil chuckle rolled from the depths of his monstrous body. "I think it had less to do with kidnapping you and more to do with you refusing to admit how much you wanted me to own your heart, your soul..." He painted a long lick over my slit. "And your sweet cunt. Even after I ripped out your pathetic mate's spine."

Another lick. A delicious shiver shot down my back, and he laughed again, the rumbling sensation vibrating through me and making my nerves light up like a circuit board. "Hells, especially after I ripped out his spine and fashioned you a crown from it. You look so fucking sexy draped in the bones of unworthy men."

If that line hadn't robbed me of all my breath, his tongue thrusting into my pussy did.

The wet muscle slipped inside, filling me. I could feel every twitch as he flexed it, the new feeling sending ripples of pleasure skittering down my limbs. When he curled it inside me, searching for my G-spot, I twitched so hard, I nearly slid out of the throne.

With a dark chuckle, the tongue slid out of me, and I repositioned myself, panting and eager for more.

"Grip my horns if you need to, little human."

I reached for the tines of his antlers, the girth so huge, it was hard to get a handle on them. They weren't like the smaller set of charm-covered antlers of his other form.

The tip of his black tongue lapped and circled my clit for a few teasing licks before plunging back inside, deeper than before. It thrust in and out a few times, copious amounts of saliva and arousal dripping down my ass to coat the seat of his throne.

Then, a new sensation had my back arching, a scream of pleasure lodged in my throat.

His split tongue. It parted inside me, rubbing me at different angles I didn't even think were possible to reach.

I came with a strangled moan, the brutal orgasm sending me flying back to the surface for some of the most intense seconds of my life.

It was mind-obliterating bliss.

As my breath turned short and frantic, his claws gripped me tighter, biting into the soft flesh of my thighs.

He held me tight enough to leave bruises, and I found myself hoping they wouldn't fade any time soon. I loved the idea of being covered in his marks.

The heat from his monstrous appendage probing around inside me consumed me. I dropped my head back onto the backrest of his throne and moaned as he thrust into me at a diabolical pace.

"Fuck!"

My cunt clenched around his tongue, and he released a low and throaty groan directly into me.

His tongue was unrelenting, twisting and twirling and splitting inside me, seeing how much I could stretch for him. I knew he was training me to take his monster cock, and I was eating up every depraved second of it.

My monster feasted on me like I was his last meal, his hands spreading my legs wider while pulling me up so my ass barely touched his throne.

My entire body turned to putty in his hands, and my eyes crossed with the overload of pleasure.

"Fuck, fuck. Oh, sweet Jesus, *fuck.*"

At that, he pulled out of me, snickering as he slathered one last lick up my center. "Jesus? There's no earthly savior here, Rayven. Just the demon who owns your soul. Forever and always, your prayers will be made out to me. Isn't that right?"

I gave him a sloppy nod, and he purred with approval. "That's right. Now, tell me who owns this pussy?"

"The Lord of Bones."

"Good girl," he praised in his gravelly cadence. "And who does your soul belong to?"

"The Lord of Bones."

"That's right, my grave treasure."

He ran his tongue between my breasts, teasing the fresh scar on my chest. "And who does this heart beat for?"

"The Lord of Bones."

Suddenly, he released me. I fell back into his throne, a tiny "omph" knocked from me. Before I could adjust, his arm banded around my waist and plucked me into the air.

He held me against his side, tucked up under one arm like I weighed nothing as his free hand worked to loosen his pants. Sounds of tearing fabric filled the air as his patience ran thin.

He sat down on his throne and pulled me into his lap, guiding my knees so they clamped around his hips.

I stared down at his erection, seeing his monster form's cock in real life for the first time.

Fuck. This motherfucker really was hung like a horse. I found myself transfixed by the ribcage-like ridging on the underside of his shaft.

Recalling what the texture felt like in my dream and imagining what it would feel like in reality just about broke my brain.

I had sex with his monster form in the plum dream and, as real as that felt, it had been less daunting fitting that thing inside me.

"I... I'm not sure that thing is gonna fit."

"You've done it before."

"Yeah," I snorted "In my wildest dreams. Literally. There's no weird sex magic to make you fit, is there?"

He gave a chuckle of his own. "No, but it will fit. And if it doesn't, I'll enjoy training your sweet little mortal holes to be better about taking your Lord's cock in all his forms." He patted his thigh. "Now, settle down on your throne, my queen."

Tamping down on my nerves, I reached down to fist him. My thumb ran up and down his shaft, feeling the texture of his ridges.

Oh, fuck me. I was not built for taking a dick like this. RIP to my vagina. Worst case scenario, I'd die from too much monster dick. *What a way to go*. Though Belial would probably just revive me so he could do it all over again.

"You can do it," my monster encouraged. "Your body is so needy and desperate for me, you're sopping wet."

His clawed hands gripped my hips, but he didn't force me to take him, instead allowing me complete control. I lined him up with my center and slowly speared myself on his cock. He sat back, his horns tipping back as a lusty moan rolled from his throat, spurring me on.

I went at my own pace, sliding him inside me inch by inch.

My hips lowered, writhing to work him inside me. The entire time, he talked me through it, purring and murmuring his dark little praises. "Fuck... Look at you. You take your Lord and Master so well."

My thighs trembled as I sank the last inch of him inside me. My eyes rolled back into my head as the texture of his demonic cock rubbed against my walls. I fluttered and twitched around him as I settled, and he growled his delight at the way I sheathed all of him.

He reached up, his large hand wrapping around my throat with just enough pressure to have me moaning. "You look so damn beautiful impaled on your king's cock, my treasure."

I panted, his cock stretching me to my limit, but, fuck me, was the pain delicious.

To my disappointment, his hand dropped from my throat, but I noticed a blue chain forged from magic now wrapped around his fingers. The rest of the chain formed, attached to a magical collar around my neck.

My eyes widened, and he laughed, a wolfish, sadistic laugh that had me wet and burning, ready for friction.

"You will no longer wear a collar, not like the one I made for you before. As there is no more danger to you in the Hells, I don't need to track your every step. But, while you'll wear a crown before our subjects, you'll still wear a collar for me when it pleases me. Do you understand?"

I nodded, and he licked my lips with that monstrous appendage, the split sections dancing over my flesh. "Good. Now be a good slave queen and ride your demon lord."

Grabbing his shoulders to steady me, I slowly moved my hips up and down. The pain quickly dissolved into delicious heat as I stretched around him, molding to his massive girth. A moan fell from my lips as Belial's massive hands gripped my hips. He helped me ride him until I was a trembling mess on top of him.

"What a good little cock sleeve you make." He chuckled, the booming sound filling my head and sinking straight to the place where we were connected. He gripped my hips harder, the magic chain digging into my flesh as he dragged me down onto his cock.

"I'm going to fuck you so deep, you'll taste me." He leaned over me, the fire in his eyes consuming my vision and making little beads of sweat pebble my skin.

Here I was, wearing the crown made from the bones of my ex, riding the cock of Death himself, all while souls from the River Styx drifted by as our audience.

It was so fucked, and it was perfect.

Belial rocked his hips up to meet me, increasing his pace until I shattered. I cried out, my voice echoing off every polished surface in the throne room and shaking the bone chandeliers.

Belial's pace became frantic as he fucked me through my orgasm, and a second later, he came with a roar, filling me to the brim with thick jets of hot cum. I quivered on his cock as he held me down, keeping me impaled on him as he emptied every drop of monster seed he had to give.

So full.

So complete.

The spell he'd used to create the chain and collar faded.

We stayed like that for several peaceful beats, the only sound in the throne room our heavy breaths and the sounds of rushing water from the river.

He began to shift beneath me, his broad form shrinking as he took on his human form with his cock still sheathed inside me. The silver charms on his antlers clinked together as he canted his head to meet my gaze.

"I'd move the stars for you if you asked it of me, Rayven."

Gods, I loved this monster. I loved him to the point of pain. He was darkness, he was death, and he was mine.

He gripped my chin, searching my eyes with a flicker of concern in his own. "After everything that's happened...I want to know if you're okay."

I considered his question for a moment before answering. "If I wasn't fine, what would you do about it?"

"Hmm. Everything I'm capable of, and I'm capable of a great deal. Teach you magic. You can peruse the Soul Library as much as you'd like. You can visit your father's book or any others you wish to see. I'll show you every inch of your new realms, allow you to do whatever you wish with them. Build your perfect sanctuary or burn them to the ground for all I care. Whatever your heart desires."

"What else?" I tipped my face to his, a seductive smile cresting my lips. "If none of that works?"

"I'll fuck every torment from your mind and fill you so full of me that there won't be anything else. I'll fuck you so thoroughly, all that will be left is you and me, Rayven."

You and me.

A grave robber and the lord of death and bones. Who would have thought?

"I guess that doesn't sound too bad," I mused with a grin, nuzzling into the crook of his neck. "I can spend an eternity or so as your queen."

He laced his fingers with mine, bringing them up to brush his lips across the backs of my knuckles.

"And somehow, an eternity doesn't feel long enough. No matter how much time passes, you'll always be my little thief, my human, my Queen of Carrion."

The End